After You
WERE GONE

After You
WERE GONE

———————•———————

Alexis Harrington

Montlake
Romance

Published by Montlake Romance, Seattle

www.apub.com

Amazon, the Amazon logo, and Montlake Romance are trademarks of Amazon.com, Inc., or its affiliates.

ISBN-13: 9781503941755
ISBN-10: 1503941752

Cover design by Laura Klynstra

Printed in the United States of America

Writing is a solitary job, but I have a support crew, each of whom helps me in countless ways they might not even be aware of.

Thanks, in no particular order, for the love, the cheering, and the laughs, to Margaret Vajdos, Lisa Jackson, Penny Lainus, Jim Midzalkowski, Ali Bosco, and Jean Nielsen. To Charlotte Herscher, my fabulous developmental editor, I'm grateful for your laser eyes, patience, and inspiration.

PROLOGUE

Violence begets violence.

It was an old saying—maybe it was from the Bible. Maybe not. Julianne Emerson couldn't remember. But she knew what it meant. More than that, she knew how it felt, because it was in her now. That hot, insistent desire for revenge.

She sat in the front row of the witness chairs, the ones right behind the railing, sensing the eyes of the other spectators ping-ponging between her, the judge, and *him*. Tension and anticipation filled the courtroom like a sickening green vapor.

Up front at a table off to her left sat the man who had been found guilty of killing her husband, Wes. The days of testimony, of watching the prosecution re-create the horrible event in excruciating detail, of sitting on the witness stand and facing *him*—she could barely think his name, much less say it to herself—had all come down to this moment. Julianne's heart beat nearly as fast as the child's she carried in her womb.

The indecent irony of wanting to see a life ended while carrying another was not lost on her.

But she maintained her gaze on the partial profile of the man whose punishment was about to be announced. She wished she were sitting up there on the bench, instead of the Honorable Carlos Schmidt. She would sentence that guilty man to old-fashioned Texas justice. She'd do the same thing to him that he had done to Wes. She'd shut him in a tinder-dry barn, set it on fire, and watch the flames engulf him. The only mercy she would show him would be to make sure he was dead, and to not let him linger for two days of hell in an ICU, as charred as a hickory log in a barbecue pit.

The judge shuffled some papers, then looked over his black-rimmed reading glasses at the condemned man.

"The defendant will rise."

The defendant pushed back his chair and stood there in his cheap, go-to-trial suit, probably the only one he'd ever worn in his life. His court-appointed lawyer rose with him. Deputies stood close by, as if expecting an eruption of chaos. They'd probably watched too many judicial dramas on *Law & Order*.

"In accordance with the laws of the State of Texas, you have asked that the court rather than the jury impose your sentence. You committed a grievous act, Mitchell Brett Tucker. You took a life. You might not have meant to, but you did. You deprived a woman of her husband, their unborn child of its daddy, and the town of Gila Rock of an upstanding citizen." He paused and glanced at the rest of the Tucker clan across the aisle from Julianne. Everyone in Presidio County knew the Tuckers could be called a lot of things. *Upstanding* wasn't one of them. "We just don't tolerate that kind of business here." Judge Schmidt tapped the edges of his papers on the desk. "But I am also taking into consideration the circumstances of your crime and your youth, although I'd expect a nineteen-year-old to know better. During testimony, you repeatedly stated that you had no idea Mr. Emerson was in the barn when you started that fire, and I believe you."

The silence in the courtroom was a palpable thing, as if the world itself held its breath.

"In light of that, I'm sentencing you to seven years in the state prison in Amarillo. That should give you some time to think about how you want to lead the rest of your life. For your sake, and society's, I hope you come to the right decision."

Julianne let out an involuntary cry, and for a moment her vision seemed to narrow and darken like the picture tube in an old TV set. She felt as if she'd been punched in the head. Seven years? *Seven?* For killing a man? For burning down the barn? Drug dealers got worse for selling cocaine from the trunks of their cars.

The rest of the Tucker men lurched out of their chairs, voicing loud complaints. A buzz erupted among the onlookers and continued until the judge banged his gavel on its sound block, demanding order and threatening to clear the courtroom.

Only Mitchell was quiet. His jaw was clenched, and he said nothing.

She had seen that stony look just one other time: the day she'd told him she was marrying Wes.

CHAPTER ONE

BIG BEND COUNTRY
GILA ROCK, TEXAS
EIGHT YEARS LATER

WELCOME TO GILA ROCK. The trucker nodded at a tourist-grabbing sign. "Looks like this is the place."

"Thanks, man, I appreciate it." Yeah, this was the place. Mitchell Tucker jumped down from the air-conditioned, long-nose Peterbilt that had brought him to the outskirts of a town he'd once known as well as he knew his own name. Dragging his duffel bag after him, he slammed the cranberry-red cab door, gave it a slap with his hand, and waved to the driver hauling a load of cattle feed. The man had picked him up about forty miles south of here, and not a moment too soon—he'd been walking and trying to hitch a ride since morning.

The driver gave a short blast of his horn and pulled out. The sound of crunching gravel and shifting gears faded slowly as the truck left Mitchell in a hot cloud of dust and diesel exhaust. When the air cleared, he looked around, through shimmering heat waves across the two-lane asphalt and to the emptiness beyond.

West Texas. Mitchell had once heard an old fart at Lupe's Roadhouse say that it was so flat out here, a body could stand on a case of beer and see all the way to the next county. To prove his point, the guy had even gotten Lupe Mendoza herself to give him a case of Lone Star empties, which he lugged out to the bare dirt parking lot. With a group of the tavern's noontime regulars tagging after him to watch, he climbed onto the cardboard and glass. Yup, he claimed, there was Jeff Davis County up there to the north. He added that he'd probably have been able to see past it to Culberson County if the bottles had been full. Mitchell almost believed it.

This was still the real West, a wild place where scrubs of creosote, sage, cactus, and an occasional patch of fading bluebonnets were all that relieved the endless vista of Big Bend Country. The far-off hills seemed so remote they might as well have been on the moon. Between here and those hills, it was flat, hot, and desolate, the kind of place that was only right for him to have come from. Given the events of his life, it was also the kind of place he had to come back to.

In the near distance, Gila Rock waited for him under a chrome-blue sky. Except for a few old brick buildings like the high school and the library that stood out, the main structures looked as bleached and weather-beaten as their surroundings. He could still picture most of them. After all, there wasn't much more than a couple of silos, some taverns, and two churches, bracketed by sorghum fields, a hog farm or two, and miles of cattle range. This was the vast area where the movie *Giant* had been filmed back in the fifties, and rain was damn near a miracle. There was no Walmart here, no Kmart, no Valero gas station or H-E-B grocery store—none of the big chain businesses that Mitchell had seen in the past year, knocking around the state. Gila Rock probably hadn't changed at all.

But Mitchell Tucker had.

Seven years in prison could do that to a man. It changed the way he walked and talked, how he looked at other people and the world in general. He had a whole new vocabulary that he'd acquired over time, one that most people on the outside heard as a foreign language. And he was about as different as he could be from the scared, angry . . . kid who'd been sent off to the state penitentiary eight years before.

Originally, he'd planned never to come back—there was nothing for him here but that crappy single-wide he'd shared with his brothers and his old man down by the slow, muddy creek. At least that's what he'd thought.

There was more, though, something he needed to take care of. Some unfinished business that had nagged at him for more than two thousand days and nights.

He could still see *her* sitting in the Presidio County Courthouse during his trial, flinging daggers at him with her ice-cold stares. He could hear her voice as she'd testified against him on the witness stand, tear-choked and accusing. It still made his gut twist to think about it, even after all these years. Mitchell had taken his chances by letting the judge decide his sentence, and he'd lost.

Seven years.

Under the glare of the afternoon sun, sweat popped out on his forehead, and he rubbed at it with the sleeve of his T-shirt. Then he picked up his duffel bag and started walking toward town. His boot heels made a dull, rhythmic thud on the hot asphalt.

Julianne.

Julianne.

Julianne.

Oh yeah, he had business here, all right. He would finish that business, then move on again.

"I'll be goddamn-go-to-hell! Mitch? Is that really you?" Mitchell's younger brother, Darcy Tucker, stared at him from the doorway of the mobile home they'd grown up in. It stood beside an arroyo that saw water about two months out of the year. The screen door was just a useless aluminum frame with shreds of old netting hanging from it.

"Yeah. It's me."

Darcy turned and called over his shoulder, "Hey, old man, look who's here! The prodigal has come home."

Mitchell winced at the announcement, and at the smells of stale beer, dirty ashtrays, and cooking grease that wafted over him from the dark interior of the mobile home. Within, he heard the clattering of a window air conditioner that sounded as if it were trying to breathe its last, and the low drone of a television.

Darcy pushed open the screenless screen door. "Well, come on in, come on in. You know we don't stand on no ceremony around here."

Mitchell stepped inside, dropped his duffel bag, and waited for his eyes to adjust to the gloom. Darcy slapped him on the back in welcome. "By God, we've been wondering if we'd ever see you again."

From down the narrow hall came the gurgle of a flushing toilet; then his father shuffled into the living room, zipping his fly.

"Mitchell? By God, Mitchell! You back?" His old Dickies pants, shapeless blue twills, were held up with suspenders, under which he wore a dingy gray tank top.

"Yeah, Earl. For a while, anyway." Earl Tucker shook Mitchell's hand and squeezed his arm. He saw a brief glimmer of emotion replace the usual anger in his father's faded eyes. God, the old man looked as if he'd aged thirty years. He was nearly bald, shriveled, and shorter, and his grin revealed a few missing teeth, too. Even Darcy was skinny, leathery, and hard-looking, especially around the mouth, where deep lines had begun to form. Up the length of one arm ran an old-style tattoo that rivaled those Mitchell had seen in prison. It was an image of a snake wound around a sword. In its fangs, the viper held a banner with the inscription BORN TO RAISE HELL. His other arm featured an equally sinuous naked woman that strongly resembled Marilyn Monroe's famous calendar photo.

"Sorry we didn't get up to see you in Amarillo very often," his father said.

"You came twice in seven years." It was a sore point with Mitchell. He'd taken all the blame for the crime—the least his family could have done was visit now and then.

"Twice—naw, that can't be right." For a moment, Earl Tucker couldn't meet Mitchell's gaze.

"It is."

"Huh, I'll be. It seems like the time just flew by," Darcy commented.

Mitchell supposed that depended upon which side of the razor wire a person lived on.

"When did you get out?" his father asked.

"About a year ago."

"That long? Where have you been?"

Mitchell shrugged, noncommittal. "I bounced around the state, doing jobs here and there."

"Legal ones?" his brother asked with a smoker's harsh chuckle that dissolved into a cough. Darcy had always been full of jittery, restless energy that he'd never managed to channel into something productive.

"Don't devil him, Darcy. We all know that Mitchell got a poor man's justice, what with that lousy court-appointed lawyer. He never shoulda been found guilty."

"That's a true fact," his brother put in. "It's a damned shame, a pure damned, dirt-eatin' shame you got that rotten sentence. I thought they'd at least parole you."

Almost unconsciously, Mitchell rubbed at one of the burn scars on his arms. "It came up a couple of years ago. I didn't want to be paroled."

"Why not? Jesus, I'd have flown that coop as soon as I could." Darcy put one foot on a plastic milk crate that stood next to the TV.

Mitchell hedged. "I just wanted to do the time and not have to report to someone. On parole, you've got someone expecting to hear about everything you do, and you have to tell them."

His father nodded, then flopped into a rocker-recliner with an audible grunt. "Then why didn't you come home when you were released?"

"Hell, Earl, after everything that happened . . ."

The old man leaned forward suddenly, jabbing a rough finger in Mitchell's direction, his face red and animated with the quick anger that Mitchell remembered so well. "Those damned Boyces made plenty of trouble for us over the years, and don't you forget it. They got their pound of flesh from us on this one. You're a Tucker, by God, and you belong with your kin, right here in Gila Rock."

You're-a-Tucker-by-God. How many times had Mitchell heard that in his life? As if the Tuckers were blue-blooded royalty.

"Anyway, you're home now, aintcha, son?" Darcy chimed in, slapping him on the back again. "Boy howdy, we've got some lost time to make up for! James will get the surprise of his young life when he comes home from work and sees you. Have a seat." He went to the kitchen and opened the refrigerator to pull out three beers.

The same shabby furniture that had stood in this room when Mitchell had left was still here, now in worse shape. Yellowed foam padding erupted through the torn upholstery, and every surface was covered with clothes, newspapers, nudie magazines, empty beer bottles, and cans of engine spray paint and primer.

He had forgotten how much he detested this place. And now it was worse than ever. From the fly-specked side window he saw six cars in various stages of decay parked next to the mobile home. A dead refrigerator stood among them, its door hanging open like an old hag's toothless mouth. A skinny mutt wandered over to it and stuck its head inside, as if trying to decide on a snack. Mitchell pushed aside a heap of dirty clothes and sat on the sofa.

"I guess the tables got turned on that Boyce bitch," Darcy said. He whacked the beer bottles on the chipped edge of the kitchen counter with an expertise that suggested lots of practice. The caps somersaulted around the kitchen and stayed where they fell.

At the mention of Julianne, Mitchell froze, then gave his brother a sharp look. "Why? What happened?"

"That hog farm of hers is for sale. She couldn't make it." Darcy gave his father a beer, then handed one to Mitchell and sat next to him.

"She'd be near broke if Joe Bickham hadn't left her his dime store." There was a note of disgusted disappointment in his father's voice. "Damn it all, somebody is always helping that family. Over to Lupe's, they say she's gonna move into town and take over that store."

"Is there a husband?"

Darcy downed half the beer in one gulp and let out a belch that might have registered on the Richter scale. "Nope, she never remarried. She won't let no man even get close enough to ask the time of day, except for that hired hand she's got. Cal, Carl—something or other."

"It would be just Julianne and her kid, who would be what, seven? Eight?" Mitchell asked.

"I don't remember any kid," Earl said, squinting at the label on his beer bottle.

Darcy stretched his spine, which produced a series of cracking sounds. "Oh yeah. I think someone or other said she lost a baby after the trial. Anyway, she doesn't have one now." He shrugged. "Just one less of the Boyce family to worry about."

Mitchell stared at his brother. Even for Darcy this attitude seemed pretty callous. "It sounds like there really isn't much *family* anymore."

"There's enough." Darcy's hand clenched into a fist on his knee, and the viper tattooed on his arm flexed. "She always thought she was better than everyone else, anyway."

Mitchell remembered that once, a long time ago and after downing most of a six-pack, Darcy had admitted to wanting to "get into that snippy blonde's jeans." If he'd ever approached Julianne, Mitchell didn't know about it. In any case, the Boyce-Tucker feud was apparently still alive and well. The entire topic ate at him, so he changed the subject. "What about you, Darce? What have you been up to?"

"No good, mostly," his brother replied, laughing and making the hard lines around his eyes and mouth all the more prominent.

"I thought you'd be married by now. You're what, twenty-two?"

"Twenty-three, but who's counting? Anyway, I don't want no ball and chain telling me what to do. I got a little gal over in Marfa I see sometimes and it works out fine." He looked around the tiny living room. "Although it wouldn't be bad to have some female spruce up this place a little."

A little. The mobile home needed a twister to land on it and carry it off to perdition. Mitchell took a long swallow of beer. It was cold and smooth going down his throat. "Where do you work?"

"I have a few business concerns." Darcy lit a cigarette with the same old Zippo he'd had since he was a kid. He exhaled a chain of impressive smoke rings with as much flair and importance as a man sucking on a twenty-dollar cigar.

Earl Tucker snorted. "'Business concerns' my rosy rump, Mr. Big Shot. You parked those raggedy-ass lemons outside with grand plans to fix them up and sell them. Every one of those things sounds like an old tractor and farts like the judges at a chili cook-off. The cars and that truck have been sitting there for six months, waiting for you to work on them."

"I sold one!" Darcy shot back.

"One."

"What about James?" Mitchell interrupted, hoping to head off one of the Tuckers' frequent arguments.

"James—now that boy has a real job." His father said this while glaring at Darcy. "He loads rock down at the gravel pit for road crews. Makes pretty good money at it, too."

"He's not married, either?" James was the youngest, so Mitchell figured him to be twenty-one by now.

"*Hell* no. I'm telling you, women are just a shitload of trouble, and not much good for anything except getting laid and cleaning up." Darcy drained his beer. "Didn't we learn that from Mom?"

An awkward, silent moment fell over them, and Earl sped up his rocking chair.

Cindy Tucker had taken off when Mitchell was fifteen years old. She'd begged the boys to go with her, and Mitchell had wanted to. But he'd also been brainwashed to believe that loyalty to his father was more important. He was a *Tucker*, by God. When Mitch wouldn't leave, neither would James or Darcy. So Cindy had gone off on her own. She'd left her husband, left her sons—she'd even left her wedding rings on the kitchen table. The rings had belonged to Mitchell's grandmother. Beside them was a brief note that said she couldn't take this life anymore with their part-time sometimes-cowboying, sometimes-wildcatting father. He'd be away for weeks, even months at a time, in the oil fields up in the Panhandle, or off at some ranch, doing God knew what. He had rarely sent home any part of his pay, that much was certain. Money, and life in general, had been unreliable, and they'd seen their share of welfare and food stamps.

The Tucker males never heard from Cindy again, and like it or not, Mitchell knew it affected the way all of them had turned out. Baseball had kept him grounded for a while—his high school coach had told him he had the serious makings of at least a minor league player, especially after a scout had come down to have a look at him. Mitch had sensed his natural affinity for the game. The feel of the 108 double stitches under his fingertips, the smell of the leather ball cover, the solid, certain grip of his hands around the bat. When he'd played baseball, everything had seemed to make sense in his mind. But after a while even that hadn't been enough to keep things from falling apart. He didn't suppose Darcy or James recognized that. But he'd had a lot of time to think about it, and he guessed he'd made the wrong decision when he'd chosen to stay. He'd had two prime chances to get out of here, and he'd thrown both of them away for a trip to the penitentiary.

Still, growing up without a mother wasn't a good excuse for a couple of grown men to be living in this pigsty with their embittered, grudge-bearing father. Even prison had been cleaner than this. The Texas Department of Criminal Justice did not tolerate dirt or disorder. Or much else, for that matter.

His father interrupted his thoughts. "Your room is still at the end of the hall, Mitch. You'll probably have to dig yourself a tunnel to get in there, but you might as well stow your gear."

"Okay." Who was he to judge? He swallowed the rest of his beer. He'd come back to live in this pigsty, too.

But only for a while. Only until he caught up with Julianne again.

"'As is'—does this thing work or don't it?" Old Alvie Bennett pointed to the handwritten sign taped to the top of an avocado-green dryer.

Julianne Emerson waved a hand in the general direction of her laundry flapping on the clothesline next to her house. "It shuts off too soon, Alvie, but I'm sure it just needs a new timer or something."

He'd been eyeing the appliance for an hour, returning to it now and then to open and slam the door a couple of times, like someone checking out a used car. This time he twisted the control knob two full turns, as if he could discover the answer to his question, even though the machine was unplugged and sitting on the front lawn.

Whatever the dryer needed, she couldn't afford it right now.

He rubbed his silver-bristled chin, making a scraping noise. "Twenny dollars . . . seems like a lot of money for something that don't work." His frayed, blue biballs looked as if he'd worn them night and day for months, long enough to allow them to stand up on their own. What he'd want with a dryer was a mystery.

"I'll let you decide."

"I guess I'll give you ten for it."

She curbed a sigh. "All right," she agreed, just to be rid of the dryer and Alvie, too. "Cash, though, no checks." It was a phrase she'd repeated many times throughout the day.

The old man reached into his pocket and produced a worn leather snapper purse. From it, he extracted an equally worn ten-dollar bill.

Julianne had been out here in the front yard for the better part of the day, watching as what seemed like half of Presidio County pawed over her belongings and poked through things that were part of her earliest memories. But they were also buying them, which was why she was holding this yard sale—to raise money. Her late mother's china cabinet, a wringer washer that her grandmother had used, a deck of playing cards depicting San Antonio's Tower of the Americas from the 1968 Hemisfair, a paint-by-the-numbers portrait of Davy Crockett (his eyes looked like two fried eggs), a gaudy bronzed statuette of a nymph with a clock mounted in its stomach, farm equipment, feeders, livestock chutes, stock tanks—the assorted flotsam that got collected by several people's lifetimes.

Of course, there was the biggest item of all—the farm itself. It had been in her family for four generations. It had to go, too.

As Alvie handed her the money, he gazed around at the old house and the seven-year-old barn. "So, you're really going to do it? Take over your uncle Joe's dime store?"

Gila Rock's older locals still referred to the place as the dime store, a quaint, dust-covered term that Julianne wasn't really familiar with. She couldn't think of anything that sold for a dime now. "Yes, as soon as I can."

"I don't s'pose your daddy would be too happy about this, you sellin' this place and all."

Julianne tightened her spine. "I think he'd understand," she lied. She already knew that Paul Boyce must be rolling in his grave. She'd considered all her options—renting out the store her mother's uncle had left her, selling it, just sitting on it. She always came back to the same answer—to get out of farming. It would be hard for her to leave the only home she'd ever known. But she was desperate. This was her chance to escape, to start over, to gain some independence and build something that wasn't affected by weather, disease, and daily price fluctuations.

It had been a hot day for late April, but with only a hint of the summer heat to come. She looked across the still-green lawn and saw Cade Lindgren, her hired hand, in deep discussion with a man over a galvanized tub full of old tools. As if feeling her eyes upon him, he glanced up and gave her a nod of acknowledgment. Cade had been a big help to her, but it wasn't enough. There were just the two of them, trying to do the work of six or seven, and it was impossible. She had no money to hire anyone else—the vet bills for the hogs alone would have paid half a crew for a year.

"Julianne," a woman called from the porch, "how much for this old vacuum cleaner?"

"Three dollars."

The woman nodded and rooted around in her purse for three ones. Julianne climbed the steps to take the money and stashed it in the canvas carpenter's apron she wore. It had lots of pockets, and she could make change easily. She felt like a ticket seller at the county fair.

The Boyce farm had hardly been a booming success, but her father had never told her that. They'd scraped by like every other small farmer in the country. He'd placed great value on family tradition, and she knew that he'd counted on her and her husband to carry on. They might have been able to turn it around, she and Wes; things had begun to look promising. But there hadn't been enough time. After Wes died, Julianne couldn't make a go of it.

The town support generated by his death seemed to dry up after the trial was over. She'd faced the daunting job of carrying on alone. It wasn't as if she hadn't tried. She had worked hard, and she'd lived on this hog farm long enough to understand what it needed to succeed.

But for every forward step she took, she slipped back three. Fate resisted her efforts to bend it to her will. It had come back at her with a hard, uncaring fist to visit a string of calamities upon her. A scour epidemic, brought in on a crewman's work boots, had wiped out three-quarters of the stock. The price of feed had spiked at a time when she could least afford it. And one by one, she'd been forced to let her workers go. The last of them, Ángel and Guillermo, had been with the farm for so long they were like family. In fact, they had called her *niña* till the day they left, even though she was an adult and a widow. Now, years after she'd inherited this land, she had to admit defeat. She'd sold off most of the surviving hogs and was ready to move on.

As the last shoppers left and the shadows grew long, Julianne watched dispassionately as Cade and Alvie lifted the dryer onto the bed of his pickup. Then she walked to the end of the long gravel drive to take down the SALE TODAY sign she'd posted on her mailbox. She waved at Alvie as he pulled out onto the road.

"Cade," she called, "when you go back through town, will you get the signs we put up on the telephone poles?"

All lanky limbs and long torso, he jogged up to her, the change in his jeans pocket jingling with his keys. "I thought I'd stick around and help you pick up this stuff." He gestured at the odds and ends that remained unsold. The time-telling nymph still stood on the front porch steps of the house.

She put her hands on her waist and leaned back to stretch her tired muscles. "That's okay. There isn't that much to do. It's Saturday night and you ought to go back to Cuervo Blanco. Get a beer at the Turnbuckle Tavern and ask some girl to dance. I can handle the rest of the chores till Monday. We have just the two sows left."

"Did you make enough money to cover the mortgage payment?"

She pulled open one of the pockets on her apron and glanced down at the jumble of bills. "I don't know yet. I'll have to count it when I get back to Gila Rock. You go on—you haven't seen your family for over a week." He usually lived in the foreman's cabin when he stayed here. Cuervo Blanco, the next town over, was fifteen miles away.

He grinned and kicked at a dirt clod. "Oh hell, the old man will pester me again to work in their feed store, and my mom will just rag on me for not being in church tomorrow. She thinks that's the place to find a wife."

Julianne knew that his parents had never approved of him working for her, but she wasn't sure why. He was in his late twenties, certainly old enough to make his own decisions, and too old to still be living at home. But she didn't say so. "I guess church is better than a tavern for that. You'd make some woman a good husband, Cade." In the three years that he'd worked for her, he'd been a comfortable, familiar presence. Lately, though, she'd begun to sense that he might have a crush on her. At least he'd never crossed the line of friendship, and she was careful to make sure he didn't. She liked things the way they were and had no interest in romance. Not now, anyway, and not with Cade. It was as if her heart had seared itself shut to nurse two wounds that would never heal. She saw something in his brown eyes, a hint that he wanted to say more, and she shook her head to stave off further arguments. "Get going. Thanks for your help, and I'll see you Monday morning. We'll get to work on the store. I need you for that more than I do this."

His shoulders drooped a bit, as if he were disappointed. "Well, if you're sure—"

She waved him off. "I want to go home, too."

He adjusted his low-crowned Stetson, pushing it down more firmly. "All right, Monday. At the store." He headed toward his truck, an old, grumbling blue Dodge that had more lives than a cat.

"You'll get the signs?" she asked.

He gave her a short salute and climbed into the cab. When he was finally gone, Julianne released a tired sigh.

She had a lot of thinking and planning to do.

17

After she cleaned up the front yard, she walked into the nearly empty house. What furniture she hadn't sold or given away—the kitchen table and chairs, her bed—she and Cade had moved to the cluttered, untidy apartment over the store. Her boot heels on the pine flooring echoed through the bare rooms and hallway. She wandered the house her grandfather had built, remembering when both her parents had been alive and she had been a little girl. Standing in the kitchen doorway, she could still see her daddy at the table in the early morning darkness, sipping coffee from a thick, white mug and listening to the farm report on the radio. At the stove, her mother would tend a breakfast of fried eggs and sausage while she hummed to herself.

Julianne walked down the hall to the room she had shared with Wes. The night after he'd died, she'd sat up in the chair by the window, unable to sleep in their bed. She'd never slept in it again. The next night, she'd moved back into the pink-papered bedroom that had been hers in her girlhood. In those easier days of her ripening youth, before Wes, before her father had lost his battle with a wasting cancer, her heart had beat with a desperate, forbidden desire for a man she was not meant to have. A man who had filled her dreams at night and made her believe that her future would be much different than it had turned out to be. In the end, he had betrayed her in a way that she could never have envisioned, not even in a nightmare.

She straightened away from the doorjamb. All the people who had ever lived under this roof were dead now, except her. Their ghosts lingered as painful memories in her heart.

From the living room, the harsh *brrinngg-brrinngg* of the old black Bakelite phone jolted her out of her bittersweet reminiscing. It was a relic, a rotary dialer left over from the days of rural party lines, and it was due to be disconnected early next week. She'd get by with her cell phone for now.

She trotted down the hall and reached for the phone where it sat on the bare pine floor with its old round cord coiled up beside it like a cowboy's lariat.

"Hello?" At first all she heard was a jumble of background noise—a tinny radio, a sound of something like an old refrigerator or a wheezy air conditioner. *"Hello."*

"You thought it was over, Julianne, but it's not. It's not over at all." The voice was no more than a hoarse, rough whisper, unknown yet familiar. She couldn't even tell whether it was a young person or someone much older. "You've had some quiet years, but they're done with now."

Gooseflesh rose on her arms. "What? Who is this?" She heard the single bark of a dog, then a *click*. She pushed the switch hook a few times, but the connection was broken. A recording came on.

"If you'd like to make a call, please hang up and—"

She slammed down the receiver, surprised to find her heart thumping hard in her chest. It was just a crank call, just a dumb crank call. Yet . . . yet it had been made by someone who knew her. He had spoken her name. On this ancient equipment, there were no conveniences such as caller ID.

What wasn't over? *What?* Suddenly, the idea of being here alone with dusk purpling the sky was an uncomfortable prospect. She wanted to get back to town, closer to civilization.

Maybe it was good to be moving away from the farm, she decided. Good to get away from this place. She tightened her long ponytail, then turned and walked outside to her truck, resisting the urge to look back over her shoulder as she went.

Julianne swore Uncle Joe Bickham had never thrown anything away. He'd been a lifelong bachelor, and it showed in the stacks of old newspapers and accumulated junk in the one-bedroom apartment over the store. She'd found jars of rubber bands, bent nails, and long-expired seed packets. He had a pile of *Texas Highways* magazines that went back years, and old drugstore calendars that served no useful purpose. The place needed a good cleaning, as did the business downstairs, and if Julianne was going to live here, she would have to paint and decorate, too. She had spent just two nights in this apartment, and her to-do list, written on a yellow legal tablet, was growing by a page per day. There weren't enough hours for all the work that needed doing.

In the small kitchen, she nudged a box of empty canning jars out of the way and pulled a cold fried drumstick from the refrigerator for her dinner. That appliance was the only thing she'd washed out so far. The first time she'd opened it, the foul gust of spoiled food that poured out had almost pushed her back downstairs.

Holding her chicken with a paper towel, she emptied her apron pockets on the table. It looked like a lot of money—cash always looked impressive. But there were as many ones as there were twenties, and when she counted it, she came up with just under $700 plus change. Added to what she had in the bank, she'd cover the mortgage payment, but there wouldn't be much left. She stared at the neat piles of greenbacks as she nibbled on the chicken leg. She would need money to fix up the store and for inventory. She would rename the business and give it a fresh, new look. That all required working capital.

On Monday morning, she'd go to the bank to make the farm payment and talk to the loan officer about borrowing against this property.

Thank God she had been her uncle's last living relative. He'd owned this building free and clear, and now, so did she. She could mortgage it if she had to. And if there was such a thing as an easy death, Uncle Joe had died one. He'd been a spry, eighty-year-old smart-ass until his final day on earth, when he'd dropped dead from a massive heart attack at Lupe's Roadhouse last winter. One moment, he'd been of this earth; the next, he'd moved on to a place beyond its troubles. That sure beat suffering through a long illness like the one her father had endured.

Or suffering the agonizing torture of third-degree burns . . .

CHAPTER TWO

Darcy Tucker walked into the Captain Gas, his cowboy hat pushed low over his eyes and his T-shirt sleeves rolled up to show off his tattoos to their best advantage. Going to the back cooler, he pulled out a case of Lone Star longnecks. There were a few guys hanging around the counter for no obvious purpose—they weren't gassing up or buying anything. Then he saw the reason. Cherry Claxton was running the cash register. Her loud, smoky laugh wasn't exactly easy on the ears, but at least you knew she meant it.

She was a pistol-hot firecracker, with that waist-length, flame-red hair and nails to match. She drove a shiny black Camaro with rumbling dual exhaust that always drew men's looks when she drove by. Some divorcing people fought over custody of the kids, or even the dog. She'd gone to the mat to get that car away from one or another husband. Her long legs gave the impression that she was a much taller woman, and she had a high-riding ass that begged a man to plant his hands on it. She liked tequila shooters and a good time, and although she could beat most of them at the pool table, she softened the blow to their egos by wearing tight, low-cut tops. It gave them something interesting to look at while she broke their balls, both with the cue stick and her sharp tongue. Nobody got anything from Cherry that she didn't want to give, and she could switch moods as fast as a drop of water bounced across a hot skillet. Luckily, that good-time streak of hers often won out, and Darcy had been on the receiving end of it a few times.

He toted his case to the counter. Behind it was a wall secured with locked plastic doors that guarded cigarettes and other forms of tobacco, a variety of condoms—some in party colors, whatever the hell that meant—and assorted merchandise that was attractive to kids and sticky-fingered customers. "Hey, there, sweet thing."

Cherry considered the brand of beer. "Special occasion, Darce? You usually look for the bargains."

"We've been doing a little celebrating back at the old homestead."

"Yeah? Did you find a job?" The other men standing around laughed.

Dull heat filled his face. Darcy Tucker never liked being the butt of anyone's joke, and his expression apparently reminded them of that fact. "My used-car business is doing just fine, thanks."

Cherry turned seductive, half-closed eyes on him. "Oh hell, Darcy, don't get your whities all tighty. We're just teasing you. What's the good news?"

Appeased, he gave her a sly smile. "I've got a little surprise for you. If you meet me after your shift ends, I'll tell you all about it."

She somehow managed to punch the cash register keys with her red eagle's claws. "Brother, at one time or another every joker around these parts has promised to show me a 'little surprise' after my shift ends." She let her gaze drift over the idlers hanging around. "Well, they got the *little* part right." She uttered that throaty laugh, and the guys leaning on the end of the counter chuckled again with less enthusiasm but couldn't meet each other's eyes.

Darcy dug into his back pocket for the wallet that had taken on the shape of his skinny butt. He threw a twenty on the counter. "Naw, I'm talking about something else." He lowered his voice. "But when you hear about it, you might be so happy you'll want to reconsider *this* old boy's equipment."

Obviously intrigued, she stared at him as if trying to decide whether he was telling the truth, and whether the truth was worth her time.

"Okay," she agreed. "After 1 a.m."

Darcy picked up his change and the case of beer, and gave the other guys a smug look. "Right. See you then, sweet thing."

"My family has done business with this bank for forty years, Charlie. We've had hard times, but we've always paid." Julianne sat across a desk from Charlie Sommers, the loan officer at Presidio Farmers Bank. "I'm not asking for more time or more money on the farm loan. Look"—she pushed a check across the surface to his blotter—"here's the current payment. All I want to do is borrow on that property my uncle Joe left me."

Yesterday she'd spent hours filling out the voluminous loan application that she'd picked up from the bank last week. She'd thought of little else but this Monday-morning appointment. She had dressed carefully in a slim denim skirt and a white knit top, and had curled her hair instead of letting it hang in its usual ponytail. She'd even shaved her legs, a task she sometimes let slide these days because she so often wore jeans. While a tiny voice in the back of her mind had whispered that she could be denied the loan, she really hadn't expected that. The Boyces had a long relationship with Presidio Farmers, as their thick file implied. While Charlie shuffled papers and punched keys on his computer keyboard, Julianne was thinking ahead about paint, shelving, updated inventory, ordering a new sign for the front of the store. In her imagination, she had that money spent and was already ringing up sales.

Finally, he sat back and looked at her. "That's a lot of money you're asking for," he said. "If it was just up to me, I'd say yes without thinking twice. But you know this bank was bought out by a bunch of big

Eastern investors a couple of years ago. They're calling the shots now and they have strict rules. The economy is circling the drain."

She felt as if her stomach had fallen to the insoles of her shoes. "Do I qualify for anything?" she asked quietly, wishing for more privacy than that provided by the ratty philodendron next to her.

"A bit less than half."

She sighed. Less than half. Chances were good that she'd have to make the next farm payment out of that money. That place just had to sell soon so she could be rid of the debt. And there were so many things she wanted to do with the dime store. Some of them would simply have to wait. She straightened her back and lifted her chin. "All right. Like my mother used to say, half a loaf is better than none. Where do I sign?"

Charlie reached into a side drawer and drew out a set of new, blank loan application forms. "You'll have to start again."

"What? Can't I just cross out the old figure and write in the new one?" Though she tried, she couldn't keep the note of harried exasperation out of her voice.

He pushed the papers across the desk and put a leaky bank pen on top of them. "Sorry, Julianne. The rules have changed."

Mitchell Tucker walked some of the familiar streets of Gila Rock, looking at what had changed, and there wasn't much. Norby's Shoes had painted their storefront, but he couldn't remember what color it had been before. The doughnut shop had a new awning and a list in the window that featured all sorts of coffee drinks, including something called a chipotle latte, which sounded like it would eat through a radiator.

Some people did double takes when they saw him and stared until he passed. He'd expected it, but it still bugged him. He moved on and found himself at Gila Rock High School, where he slowed to a stop. He realized that this was where he'd been headed when he'd left the single-wide. Beyond the chain-link fence enclosing the property, the baseball diamond stood glaring in the sun, the baselines permanently etched by the bright caliche that kept grass from growing on it. He hooked his fingers in the fence and watched the kids playing there. The one at bat was struggling with a looping swing that was about to make him strike out. Mitchell glanced at the coach, someone he didn't recognize, but the man wasn't paying attention to his batter. By the time the guy looked up, the kid had hit a pop fly. He dropped the bat to run, but the second baseman caught the ball, and the boy trudged back to the bench. It wasn't an unusual batting problem with younger players. He'd had trouble with his swing himself until his coach had solved it with some fence drills. It worked, if this coach knew what *he* was doing.

He thought back to a time so long ago, it could have happened in a dream. But the details were too sharp to be anything but real—the sun pounding down on him on the pitcher's mound, the signals from the catcher, his left hand one with the glove, the ball an extension of his right . . .

Everything had changed. Leaning against the chain-link made Mitch feel like he was always on the wrong side of a fence, trapped inside, stuck outside. He should be used to it, but he hated it.

Behind him, he heard a car pull up. It was so close he could feel the heat from the engine. He turned and saw Sheriff Dale Gunter at the wheel of his cruiser. Shit.

"Reliving your glory days? I heard you were in town, Tucker. I'm surprised you came back. Gila Rock doesn't need your kind. Or want it."

"It's still a free country, isn't it? Texas didn't secede while I was gone. Besides, I've got family here." He wasn't about to volunteer his true reason for coming home.

"Yeah, well, you're on my radar—you and the rest of your clan," he replied. "A wrong step or even a ticket for jaywalking could get your parole revoked. And don't think I wouldn't make sure to help that along."

Mitchell worked to keep a lid on his anger. Dale Gunter was a typical small-town lawman with big-city fantasies. "Your *radar* must need an adjustment, Gunter. I'm not on parole. I served my whole sentence."

He gave Mitch a sly look. "So, parole denied. I should have known."

Mitch breathed an irritated sigh. There was no point in getting into a tangle with this man. It would just make life harder than it was already. "Anything else?" he asked, as if closing an interview.

"Not right now. Later, who knows?" The cruiser pulled away.

"Son of a bitch," he muttered, and turned to head back up the street.

Four long and frustrating hours after she first met with Charlie Sommers, Julianne emerged from Presidio Farmers Bank with a receipt for the loan money that had been deposited in her checking account. At least she hadn't had to wait days, which Charlie had originally thought she might. He'd pushed everything through as top priority. She knew she should feel some sense of triumph and gratitude, but mostly, she felt whipped. She had to make it this time—she just had to. If she didn't, the bank would take the farm and the store for sure.

But even more than that, she had to prove to herself that she could stand on her own two feet and succeed. For as long as she could remember, someone had been arranging her life and trying to shelter her from a world that she knew she was smart enough to live in. Even after Wes had died, she'd been held prisoner by the precarious business of the hog farm. The store was her chance.

Standing there on the pavement, readjusting her purse strap on her shoulder, she spotted a figure coming toward her along the edge of the sidewalk. He seemed familiar to her. It was probably James Tucker, the least evil of the Tuckers, and that wasn't much of a compliment. He looked so much like a younger version of—

Then she realized who it really was. For a horrible, stunned moment her heart froze in her chest; then it took off at a furious rate, pounding so hard she swore she could feel it trying to knock through her breastbone. Her mouth and throat turned as dry as sand.

Mitchell Tucker. Oh dear God in heaven, Mitchell was in Gila Rock. It couldn't be—he'd come back from prison. Feeling dizzy and breathless, she doubled her pace, meaning to keep her eyes fixed on a spot down the street. But at the last moment, she glanced up, and their gazes locked. She felt those green eyes on hers, searching for something, but she couldn't imagine what. Just when it seemed that he might actually stop and speak to her, she hurried past him. Practically running, she headed for Diller's Pharmacy on Alamo Drive, three blocks over. Fragmented memories, like single frames of different movies, washed over her in waves. At last she reached the drugstore and ducked into its coolness. She took a seat at the fountain, out of breath and shaken. There were a few people sitting on the red vinyl stools, having a late lunch.

"Hey, Julianne." Mary Diller greeted her from behind the counter. Against the quilted stainless steel back wall, there stood a green milk shake mixer, glass jars, and all the other trappings of an old-fashioned soda fountain, just as they always had. The comforting aromas of ice cream, coffee, and grilling burgers surrounded her. Overhead, ancient ceiling fans turned slowly.

"A Diet Big Red, Mary—please." She slipped her purse off her shoulder and let it drop to the floor beside her. A couple of stools down, Victor Cabrera, the new foreman at Benavente Hog Farm and a newcomer to Gila Rock, sat wolfing down a hotdog and cheese fries. He nodded at Julianne, and she nodded back. She had talked to him a couple of weeks earlier about buying her last two sows.

The pharmacist's wife studied her for a moment. "Sure, honey." She filled a soda glass with the crimson soft drink and set it in front of her. "Julianne, are you all right? You look like someone who's seen the bottom of her own grave."

She took a straw from the dispenser on the counter and discovered that her icy hands were trembling. "Worse than that. I just saw Mitchell Tucker."

The woman poured more lemonade for the man eating his cheese fries. "Uh-oh. He's been back for a few days now. I figured you'd have heard about that already. He's living with his brothers and his father down there by the arroyo."

She stared at Mary, that light-headed, breathless feeling coming over her again. She had been so caught up with her own concerns and worries, she'd paid little attention to anything going on around town. "N-no, I didn't hear."

"I gave him a job yesterday," Victor Cabrera announced between bites of hotdog. "He told me he spent time in prison, you know, but he seems polite and able enough."

"Oh God . . ."

The other customers looked down the counter at Julianne, then at Cabrera.

The man shrugged. "What? He paid his debt to society and I figure a man deserves a second chance."

Mary gave the foreman a sharp look that told him to hush. "We don't see it that way around here."

"Excuse me." Julianne snatched up her purse and dug out some money, leaving her drink unfinished. She had to get out of here, she had to get away from the curious stares.

"Julianne, honey, wait . . . ," she heard Mary call as she hurried to the door. Then in a lower voice, Mary asked Cabrera, "Did Mitch tell you he went to prison for killing Wes Emerson? Wes was that girl's hus—"

The door slammed behind her, and she fled to the refuge of her rundown store, two blocks over. Cade's truck was parked out front. Oh, damn it, she'd forgotten that he was coming in. She didn't feel like talking to anyone right now. The insides of the windows were hazed over with an opaque coating of Glass Wax from an old can she'd found in the storeroom. Maybe she could sneak in unseen. Hurrying around to the back, she unlocked the door quietly and slipped into the storeroom, hoping he wouldn't hear her.

She sank down to a folding chair hidden amid stacks of boxed merchandise, most of which she hadn't yet had time to investigate. Her breath was short, and sweat had begun to pop out on her scalp. How was she going to stay in Gila Rock with Mitchell Tucker on the streets? How could she bear to see him and be forced to remember . . . *everything*?

When he'd left the courthouse in handcuffs and was put into a sheriff's car, headed for the state prison in Amarillo, she'd hoped to never lay eyes on him again. Now that he was back, she was bound to run into him over and over. Gila Rock was a small town. There were few secrets here, and fewer places to hide. At least the farm had given her some distance and privacy. Then she remembered that creepy phone call she'd gotten over the weekend.

Now the farm seemed isolated and more vulnerable to intruders. Living in town, though . . . her plans for a new start did not include the Tuckers, or the pointless, disastrous feud that had lain mostly dormant all these years and could very well spring back to life with Mitchell's return. Darcy Tucker, that mean-boned do-nothing, had thrown a few rude remarks at her after his brother went off to begin his sentence, but otherwise, she'd had peace for years. She wanted no part of that dumb feud, and never had. But it seemed to have acquired a life of its own many years earlier.

Some mornings she or Wes would open the front door to find that the porch had been drenched with rotten eggs. There were no shells— that would have made a noise and woke them as the eggs pelted the floorboards and walls. No, someone had gone to the trouble of cracking the whole stinking mess into a container, maybe a bucket, and hurled it at the house. Other times, the shed or barn got spray-painted with profanity that the vandal probably considered to be quite clever: **Fu-Q**

EMERSONS. On another occasion, the hogs were let loose to roam. It had taken three full days to round them up.

Julianne never had a doubt as to who was behind the pranks, and neither had Sheriff Gunter. But without an eyewitness, he'd said he couldn't do much about it. He couldn't arrest a man on a flimsy suspicion. She hadn't been alone back then, though.

The ugly brown curtains that separated the back room from the main store parted, and Cade poked his head in. "I thought I heard you back here. I expected to see you earlier." He stared at her bare legs and strappy white sandals. "Wow, I don't think I've ever seen you in a skirt. You look great."

She breathed a weary sigh. "Thanks."

"Hey, are you all right?"

"It's been a tough day. A very tough day."

"Huh, we could all use a few less of those. I had a couple myself over the weekend with my folks yammering at—"

"Mitchell Tucker is back in town." She hadn't meant to blurt it out, but her problem seemed far more critical than Cade's ongoing family squabbles.

"Oh man." Cade didn't know him. He hadn't come to Gila Rock until long after the trial. But he knew the part Mitch had played in Julianne's past. Well, he knew some of it. He pushed through the curtains and sat on a case of canned peaches opposite her. "How did you find out?"

She told him the story of her day, leaving out the details about her finances. Giving him a shaky, humorless laugh, she said, "I was standing outside the bank. I looked up and there he was, coming down the sidewalk. For a second, I thought I was wrong, that maybe it was his brother James, or that I was hallucinating. I wish I had been. But it was him."

"Did he say anything?"

"I thought he was going to, but I just looked past him and hurried over to Diller's."

Cade leaned against the wall behind him and fiddled with a pencil attached to a string that hung next to the old wall phone. Apparently Uncle Joe had never seen the need for note paper—faded names, phone numbers, and notes were written on the unpainted sheet rock in his scribbled printing.

"Does he look like a mangy ex-con?"

She shifted on the chair and shook her head. Mitch looked none the worse for the years he'd spent in prison. Older, of course—different, especially around the eyes. But none the worse. He was still tall and lean, still attractive, damn him, but he seemed to have lost the swagger he'd had as a teenager.

"Is he here to stay or just passing through?"

"Mary Diller said he's living with his dad and brothers again. And the foreman at Benavente's gave him a job. It sounds permanent to me." She wound a long strand of blonde hair around her finger. It was a habit that came out when she was worried or nervous, one she'd had since childhood. Sighing, she told him about the phone call she'd gotten. "Maybe Mitchell was the one behind it—the timing certainly works. I never thought he'd come back. I don't know why, but I figured he was gone for good. And he should have been for what he did."

Cade studied the teeth marks on the pencil. "Well, maybe I can do your errands and running around for you. That way, there'll be less chance that you'll run into him."

She suppressed a sigh. "Thanks for the thought, really, but it's too much to ask. Besides—"

"I'd do anything for you, Julianne," he said, dropping the pencil and leaning forward. "If I could, I'd change everything . . . I mean, well . . ." Color rose in his face, and he dropped his gaze to the floor. "I can't change the past, but maybe I can do something about your future."

Cade Lindgren had been a good friend to her, and looking at him now, with his mild expression, and his brown eyes and hair, she couldn't help but think of a childhood friend or a distant cousin. He came whenever she needed him, was always willing to pitch in, always going the extra mile. No hired hand on the farm had ever been more helpful.

She released her hold on the strand of hair and dropped her hands to her lap. "Cade, I appreciate it, but I have to live my life. I can't let the Tuckers keep me from doing that." Looking around the storeroom, she added, "Anyway, I have plenty of work to keep you busy right *here*. That's what I need from you—help getting this place up and running again. Oh, and tomorrow, I need you to deliver those last two hogs to Benavente's for me. That will help. What with Mitchell working there— well, I'll just have to hope that he'll leave me alone now."

"Julianne, I wish . . ."

She waited. "Wish what?"

He paused as if trying to get his words out, then simply said, "I hope he leaves you alone, too." He stood. "If I'm going to help, I guess I'd better get back to it."

Dumb jackass.

Cade berated himself as he tossed packages of expired aspirin and allergy pills into a galvanized garbage can. Most of the over-the-counter remedies in the store were sun-faded and dusty with age. Joe Bickham seemed to have done his briskest business in tobacco, magazines, and sundries. Diller's had the market cornered on nonprescription medicines.

The world's dumbest damned jackass.

He continued to chew himself out as he worked. Every time an opportunity came up to talk to Julianne on a personal level, to maybe even tell her how he felt, he either stuck his foot in his mouth or waved bye-bye to the chance like a kid watching a train pass. Of course, this time the sight of her had sucked all the plans out of his head as neatly as a shop vac. She was dressed up, her long blonde hair loose and curled, her face all pretty with makeup. Not that she wore much besides mascara and a little lipstick. She didn't need to.

There she was right now, alone in the back, trying to shoulder the burden of this new enterprise and the bad news about Mitchell Tucker. It was a prime moment to offer his support and begin to, well, *court* her. The term was old-fashioned, but Cade had grown up in an old-fashioned home.

He'd been a late child and probably something of a surprise to his parents. After all, they were as old as some of his friends' grandparents. They'd drummed into him a sense of rigid responsibility, didn't take much guff, and they wanted him to get married and settle down. But not with Julianne Emerson. They didn't like the fact that he worked for her; they'd never even met her, and they seemed to resent her. Whenever he said he was going to Gila Rock, he faced the tight line of his mother's mouth and the lowered, barn-owl brows of his dad. Just escaping their suffocating disapproval gave him a sense of freedom. He had one sister he'd never met. She had taken off when he was little, and he thought he understood why if they'd kept the same tight rein on her as they did on him and the rest of his siblings. He should have moved out on his own a long time ago, but they managed to keep him around with excuses that they needed him close by. Oh man, if they knew how he felt about Julianne—

If only *she* knew how he felt about her, and had since the first day he'd met her.

He'd dropped some pretty broad hints to her. That comment he'd made about wanting to do something for her future was as bold as he'd ever gotten. But plainly, she didn't see him as more than an employee.

He wanted to change that in the worst way.

He wanted her to see him as a man. As her man.

His mom and dad were always after him about working in their feed store. But his older brother and his whole family—wife and kids—were running the place, and they liked it. There wasn't even enough room for all of them in the store at the same time. Cade loved the land and would rather live on some acreage than be stuck behind a counter.

He'd do it here for Julianne, though, and maybe someday, if everything went right for them, they'd have their own land again. He could marry her, give her the children he suspected she longed for. If . . .

As he tossed a dusty box of old laxative into the garbage can, a thought occurred to him. He didn't know Mitchell Tucker, but he knew what he'd done to her. He'd made a young woman a widow. Even though she'd put on a brave face in the back room, Cade had seen how upset she was. She needed someone to turn to. Someone to look after her and defend her.

Because Mitchell Tucker was back.

Smoke.

She smelled smoke.

And out back, the night was lit as bright as noon. Fire—dear God, the barn was on fire.

Wes was in the barn.

Julianne tried to reach the back door, to run to him, but her legs felt as if she were wading hip-deep through molasses. She saw the flames through the kitchen window, white-hot, searing, blinding.

Suddenly, the back door flew open by itself. A tall, muscular man stood there, holding Wes in his arms. Her husband's face was burned as black as charcoal. She recognized the scorched remains of his clothes, but not his features.

Whose fault? Her fault, Mitchell's fault, hers . . .

Julianne wrenched herself from the nightmare and found herself half out of bed in her apartment bedroom, trying to run. Her heart thudded like a hammer on a rock, almost painfully, and sweat glued her nightshirt to her skin. She sat down on the mattress with her head in her hands and stared at the slice of moonlight on the floor, waiting for her pulse to slow to normal.

She used to have this nightmare three or four times a week. Sometimes more than once a night. The details never varied. It had been torture, but after enough years passed, the bad dreams had finally left her. Now, apparently, they had returned with Mitchell Tucker.

She massaged her damp temples. That horrible night Mitchell had carried Wes into the house, smelling of gasoline and whiskey, a scared, blank expression on his face. His own hair and skin had been singed from the flames, and Julianne had believed him to be a hero who'd rescued her husband. At least until she'd found out he'd started the fire.

Whose fault? Her fault, Mitchell's fault, hers . . .

She folded her legs up under her, as if trying to shrink away from the very real fact that she had once loved Mitchell Tucker with all her youthful, emotional heart. And he had loved her—he'd told her he had. It had been an exciting, forbidden, despairing, nerve-racking affair, filled with all the angst two lovers from enemy families could have imagined. His hands on her body had made her feel as if her insides had turned to hot honey drizzling through her, warming her heart and every nerve till she'd thought she might die of the love and passion he'd roused in her. It was a feeling she'd never known before or since. Had they been caught, the consequences would have been dire.

She lifted her head from her hands. They had never been found out, because she had become Wes's wife. Hah, if only she had known what catastrophe really meant back then. She'd learned soon enough, though.

Mitchell had never understood or even believed her reasons for breaking off their relationship to marry Wes. He'd barely listened to her, and they'd parted in fury and tears.

Seven months after she and Wes had married, Mitchell had set the barn on fire.

Wes had lived for two agonizing days in the ICU in Alpine. The doctors had hoped to stabilize him, then airlift him to a burn unit in Dallas. He'd died before that could happen.

At the trial, Mitchell had claimed with all sincerity that he hadn't known Wes was in the barn and in fact had meant only to set fire to the nearby shed. She had wanted to see him convicted for murder, but manslaughter and arson had been the worst the criminal justice system would mete out.

Just then, she heard a noise at the back door downstairs that broke in on her thoughts. She straightened, listening, gripping the sheet in her fist. The door—had she locked it? Yes, yes, she was sure she had, even though no one around here usually bothered. She always had. There it was again, a hard thump this time, followed by a grunt, and her throat seemed to close.

She glanced at the green display on her clock radio. It was almost two in the morning. Wes's shotgun was downstairs, and the shells for it were somewhere amid the hodgepodge of unopened moving boxes. Trying to decide what to do, she stood and tiptoed to the window that overlooked the back of the store and the empty lot behind it. The moon provided faint light, but there was no other illumination back there. She saw nothing. She worked her way to the stairs and crept down them on rubber legs, one step at a time, gripping the railing as she went. She felt a little like the typical dumb heroine in a horror movie who insisted on going to the basement of a haunted house, while the audience groaned, *Don't go down there, you idiot!*

But Julianne refused to live in fear, even though adrenaline made her armpits prickle and her palms sweat.

She reached the back door and pushed aside the faded gingham curtain to look out the window. Still nothing. Her lungs paralyzed, she flipped open the dead bolt, then closed her hand around the knob to turn it. Opening the door no more than a crack, she was hit at once by the odor. It was the smell of enamel paint.

36

She flung open the door to read the warning painted on it in clumsy, dripping block letters.

IT'S NOT FINISHED

Below this was a crude but effective grinning skull.

She slammed the door again, locked it, and leaned against it, the smell of paint lingering in her nose and at the back of her throat.

Oh God, it had begun again already. Was Mitchell so bent on revenge that he'd taken up his old ways? A hundred thoughts collided in her head at once.

She should call the sheriff.

She should get a sturdier door and new locks.

She must have a floodlight installed on the back of the building.

That Remington shotgun—

Which was worse—or better—living in town or on the farm?

A dog, she ought to have a big dog.

At last, she corralled her galloping thoughts and forced herself to take several deep breaths.

When the strength returned to her legs, she went upstairs to the small bathroom to splash cold water on her face. She switched on the light, which sputtered to life on either side of the old medicine cabinet above the sink. The fluorescent tube fixture was ancient and ugly, giving her an unflattering, pasty-green tint. At least she thought it was the light. Maybe the memories of days past, now unearthed from the back of her mind and laid bare, contributed to the appearance of the haggard, weary-eyed woman who stared back at her in the mirror.

After Wes had died, Julianne's world began to crumble. And no matter what happened or how long she lived, she knew she would never be the same again.

Mitchell had seen to that.

CHAPTER THREE

Mitchell lay awake in his stifling bedroom in the single-wide that he shared with the slat-sided mutt named Knucklehead he'd seen hanging around outside. He noticed that whenever Darcy was around, the dog made himself scarce, which led Mitch to suspect his brother had given the dog more than a kick or two. Despite being too thin the dog was big—maybe a little bit yellow Lab and some kind of shepherd—and before Mitch had come back, this old double bed had been Knucklehead's alone. The dog seemed very happy with the new arrangement, although the two of them on the small mattress were a tight fit. Earl said that James had picked up the stray somewhere and given him that name, but he'd latched onto Mitchell with a desperate devotion that had him underfoot most of the time. Mitch didn't really mind— the dog seemed starved, not only for a decent meal but also for the attention. At least Knucklehead didn't care about his past or offer an opinion about everything from politics to the weather, like Earl did. Neither did the dog constantly remind Mitch about what a lousy deal he'd gotten from The System.

Mitchell knew better. He'd deserved worse.

He'd done a terrible thing, setting fire to that shed, and fate or God or man usually exacted some kind of punishment for terrible deeds. The fact that he'd been too drunk to remember actually pouring the gasoline or lighting the match to burn the barn didn't change matters—he'd gone to the Boyce farm with that intention. Wes Emerson had been in that barn, and even though Mitchell had been eaten through with jealousy every time he thought of the man, he'd never wanted to kill him. He hadn't known that Wes wasn't safe in the house with the woman who should have been Mitchell's wife.

Julianne had looked different when he'd seen her today, but just as pretty as he remembered. She'd also looked startled upon seeing him, and he'd been almost as surprised, although he'd been on the lookout for her. He'd wanted to say something to her, but his throat had closed up, and she'd raced by him, a deep frown creasing her forehead, before he could get out a single word. He hadn't supposed it would be so difficult.

Outside in the darkness, the brush rustled with the passing of some nocturnal animal. Knucklehead lifted his chin from Mitchell's chest, gave a halfhearted *woof*, and settled down again with a loud, contented sigh. There was just enough moonlight in the room to reveal the stained acoustic tile overhead, and Mitchell stared at it as if it were a movie screen, while the events of that other, long-gone night replayed in his mind.

James and Darcy had been with him at the Boyce place. They'd all been drinking, passing around a bottle of their daddy's bargain-label whiskey, but Mitchell had swallowed the most. After only a few months, he'd still been bitter about losing Julianne. He couldn't even bitch about the situation to anyone, because their love affair had been a horrific secret. But what had pushed him over the top and led him to hatch his plan was what had happened earlier that day. Julianne had come to town, and he'd seen her going into Dot's Fashion Corral. She'd been wearing a dark-blue T-shirt with the words UNDER CONSTRUCTION emblazoned across the front. Below that was an arrow pointing down toward her slightly rounded belly. Julianne had been pregnant already with Wes Emerson's baby. The baby that should have been his.

He'd meant only to set fire to the shed—not an admirable prank under any circumstances—but somehow things had gone so wrong. His brothers had been young and still had futures back then. At least that had been one of the few coherent thoughts that had passed through his booze-soaked brain. So he'd told them to run—after all, they'd just been kids—and he stayed behind to save Wes.

The case had seemed so hopeless to him that he would have pleaded guilty right up front if his court-appointed attorney hadn't talked him out of it. Despite what his father said, Mitchell believed the lawyer had done his best given the circumstances. Much later, after most of the truth had come out and the guilty verdict had been rendered, he'd chosen to let the judge impose his sentence. A man had to face his responsibilities. That judge, he'd given him seven years. Even now, he sometimes wondered whether it had been a kindness or a curse—guilt still burrowed into his soul like a cancer, comfortable with the residence it had taken up inside him. Seven years in prison hadn't killed it. A year of freedom hadn't budged it.

So it had occurred to him that perhaps the only way he might be rid of it at last would be to receive absolution from the person he had wronged. Not Wes. Wes Emerson couldn't forgive anyone now, at least not on this earth.

But he'd do whatever it took to get what he wanted. Only then would he be shut of the past. Why Julianne's absolution was the key to his true freedom, he wasn't sure. But it mattered, a lot.

And that was why Mitchell had returned to Gila Rock. No one living in this tin can of a mobile home knew that, and he figured it was none of their business. He breathed a deep sigh and smelled the scent of dog, the fumes of engine paint, and the stink of stale bacon grease left over from dinner. The dog he could handle, but the reek of time and apathy that hung over this place was more than enough to drive him away. He'd leave as soon as he could, after he closed the door on Julianne.

Permanently.

Julianne stood on her back porch in the harsh morning sun, brush in hand, trying to paint over the ugly warning Mitchell had left for her. She'd tucked her ponytail down the back of her polo shirt to keep it out of the way, and it itched. She'd found the shotgun and loaded it. It now leaned against the wall beside her like a sentinel.

Uncle Joe had stocked quarts of paint, so she'd had several colors to choose from. But they were all as ugly as the bottom of a birdcage. Sunburst Lemon was the least unattractive option, and that wasn't much comfort. It was so bright, it made her eyes ache. At any rate, it would do until she could have the door replaced. Her fear from last night had simmered away to anger, and that fury put a lot of energy into her work. She needed it. It took some doing to cover the black spray paint, and the old, dry wood sucked up the yellow latex like a sponge. As she swept the brush over the graffiti in long, firm strokes, she heard the sound of footsteps crunching on the gravel on the side of the building.

Instantly, she dropped the brush and grabbed Wes's Remington. Pointing it toward the source of the noise, she said, "Unless you want to get your head blown off, you'd better stop right there and tell me who you are." Thank God, neither her voice nor her hands trembled.

"Julianne?"

She sighed and lowered the weapon. "Come on, Cade."

Cade sidled around the corner of the building. "Damn, girl, what's this all about?"

"I had a visitor here last night." Then she noticed his right arm, encased in a blue cast and suspended in a sling. "Cade! Good Lord, what happened to you?"

He walked toward her and climbed the porch steps, looking both sheepish and disheartened. "Oh hell, it was my fault. I was trying to saw a low branch off the tree in my folks' front yard. I thought the ladder was steady."

"It wasn't?"

"Nope." He nodded at the cast. "Broke both forearm bones clean through, just like snapping two sticks. I spent most of last night in the emergency room at St. Luke's." It showed in the dark smudges under his eyes.

"Are you able to drive?"

He shook his head. "I can't shift gears—the truck doesn't have an automatic. I tried, but I was so bad at it I figured I'd probably put the truck in a ditch and do even more damage. My brother was coming to Gila Rock to send off an express mail package at the post office so I hitched a ride with him. It took me more than a half hour just to dress myself."

"Oh, that's awful!" In this part of the country, a man's truck and his ability to drive it were equal to a cowboy's relationship with his horse two generations back. A man never walked when he could ride, or in this case, drive. She knew it was a blow to Cade's male ego. It created a big problem for her, too. She'd been counting on him to deliver her hogs to Benavente's to avoid any possibility of running into Mitchell. Now it looked like she'd have to do it, and probably have to hire someone to take Cade's place. "But you didn't have to come all the way over here. You could have just called. I'll bet that arm hurts something fierce."

"Yeah, well . . ." Men never liked to admit that anything hurt. "They gave me pain pills to chew on for the next few days. Anyway, I decided to get out instead of just lying around with the TV on while my mother's cats climb all over me."

"I guess you'll be laid up for a while, at least till your arm mends." She returned the shotgun to its place against the wall and picked up the paintbrush.

A shadow of what looked like panic crossed his mild features. "The docs said that would take a couple of months. But once I get the hang of using my left hand and arm, I can still work around here."

She glanced at the back of the building. The paint was peeling, and really, more than the door needed a good going-over. "But there's a lot of heavy lifting and moving to be done. Cade, I might have to hire someone else to do that until you're healed. I signed loan papers yesterday that pretty much put my back against the wall. I've got to get this business up and going. You can understand that."

He sighed and nodded. "Yeah, I do." He tapped the toe of his boot against the can of paint sitting on the concrete step next to her. "What are you doing, anyway?" Though the black paint still showed through the yellow, it was now a dull charcoal-gray shadow. At least the message was no longer legible.

She told him what had happened the night before. "I called Sheriff Gunter earlier this morning, but you know, it's the same old story. He said it would help if I'd actually seen the 'suspect.' But he promised to check into it."

"You think it was Mitchell Tucker?"

"Of course. Who else would leave me a message saying it's not finished? If you were Mitchell, wouldn't you want revenge on the person who sent you to jail?" Even as she said it, though, she knew that really didn't match the man she'd once known. Mitchell hadn't been as vindictive as the rest of his clan. But he'd been furious when she'd split up with him, and after seven years in prison he probably would have learned what hate really meant. Now, she felt like his next target.

"That's not the way I heard it happened. You didn't *send* him. The law caught up with him."

She shrugged. The history she shared with Mitchell included so much more than that one horrible night, but she couldn't tell Cade about that. The secret of her relationship with Mitchell Tucker lived on, despite the passage of years and events, and in that way she was still tied to him by a strange, indefinable bond. "The outcome was the same. Anyway, this kind of stuff used to happen at the farm, too, before Wes died."

"Yeah, I know, and that's got me worried." He touched her forearm with his good hand. "Julianne, if he's going to harass you, I don't like the idea of you being here alone."

Neither did she, but she lifted her chin, unwilling to admit it. "I refuse to live in fear." It was the same thing she'd told herself last night. Saying it out loud reinforced her determination. "Besides, this is my home now and I'm not going to let anybody chase me out of it."

"You need someone around here—a man—to protect you."

She looked at him and saw the spark in his eyes that she'd noticed a lot lately. An awkward tension sprang up between them. Maybe that crush she suspected was a reality. That was all she needed right now, on top of everything else. "Why, sir, what a quaint notion," she drawled in her best Texas accent, trying to keep the moment light. "And a noble one, too, y'all wanting to save a damsel in distress. But I do believe I'll manage just fine." She tipped her head toward the weapon. "I know how to use that thing, and I'm even a decent shot. I'm thinking I'll get a dog, too."

He wasn't smiling. "I'm serious."

"So am I."

"Well, I'll tell you what. Maybe I can't do much lifting and hauling, but I know how to run a retail store—I've been doing it for years. You have a computer, right?"

"Yes, I brought it over here from the farm." She'd used it to keep track of the farming operations, although toward the end, there hadn't been much that needed tracking.

"I could work on the computer for you."

"Do you have experience with it?"

"Um, yeah, some. How hard can it be?"

She gave him a skeptical look. "I don't have the money to pay you for that. I'm still going to have to hire someone to do the other work."

"Look, just give me a cot in the back room and a meal, and I'll do it for nothing."

She put her fists on her hips, still clutching the brush. "You can't live here with me under the same roof. And no one can afford to work for free. What is this really about, Cade?" If there was something going on, she wanted to know.

He glanced away for a moment, then looked at her dead on. "I care about you, Julianne. I want to be more to you than a hired hand. I feel like we have a shot at something good. We have more things in common than not. I admit I don't have a lot to offer in the way of money or possessions . . . not now anyway." He turned and gazed across the gravel parking area behind the store, and the words tumbled out, as if this were his one opportunity to speak his mind—and heart. "I-I know you said there haven't been any other men in your life since your husband. Maybe you've been waiting for the right one to come along." He looked at her again and took her paint-speckled hand. Blotchy color filled his face from throat to hairline, and his obvious discomfort radiated to her. "Maybe you've been waiting for *me*. I'd like the chance to prove to you that I'm the right one. I want to be that man."

Before she realized his intent, he moved closer and pressed a soft kiss on her lips. He smelled of soap and a faint whiff of aftershave.

Julianne pulled back and stared at him with raised brows. This was a lot more serious than infatuation, and the suddenness of his confession and the kiss astounded her. She'd never thought of Cade Lindgren in a romantic light and didn't really want to. For her, he was a friend, a buddy. He said he "cared" about her, but instinct told her his feelings ran deeper than that. She *cared* about a lot of things and people—she had cared about Wes, and she cared about Cade—but she had loved only a few, and she knew the difference. It had taken a lot of courage for him to reveal his feelings. But this changed everything, and at the moment, she wished he'd kept his mouth shut.

Feeling panicky, she took her hand from his. "Cade, I can't . . . this isn't the time . . . we don't . . ." She couldn't seem to wrap her mouth around a single complete sentence. At last, she thrust the paintbrush into his hand and jammed her straw cowboy hat down on her head. "Is your brother coming back to pick you up?"

"Yeah." He looked a little downcast. Plainly, this wasn't the response he'd been hoping for.

"All right, then." She opened the door, grabbed her wallet and keys from the stool just inside, and slammed it again. Then she picked up the shotgun. "I'm going out to the farm to pick up those hogs and drive them to Benavente's." Right now it seemed the least fearsome of the two problems. "We'll have to talk about—everything—later."

He grabbed her arm again. "Julianne? Will you think about it, anyway?"

She opened her mouth, but again, no words came out. Bounding down the stairs, practically running toward her truck, she left him standing there with his blue cast and her yellow paintbrush.

Damn, damn, damn it all to hell, Julianne fumed, as she turned her truck down the rutted dirt road that led to Benavente's. As she bumped along, the two sows in the back grunted and squealed their complaints loudly, but she barely heard them. With everything else she had to worry about right now, Cade had decided to goop up the works and turn into a romantic. He'd actually kissed her. At best, it put her in an awkward position. Worse was the confusion he'd stirred up in her by upsetting their nice, well, *buddyship*. It was good, comfortable, to have a male friend who didn't hit on her.

During the first years after Wes died, she had fended off a number of tacky, bad-mannered passes. One of them had even come from, of all people, Darcy Tucker. It had been years ago and happened outside of the Shoppeteria. He was coming out of the place as she was going in to buy groceries. *Hey, how 'bout if we go out for a beer sometime and get better acquainted, now that you're a widow and all?* God! His crude come-on had shocked her even more than Cade's admission of his feelings. She hadn't bothered to answer and had breezed past him. She'd encountered him a couple of times after that, and that had been when his evil temper had shown in the rude comments he'd thrown at her.

Cade's kiss hadn't been all that bad, she supposed. It even felt kind of nice, maybe because no one had kissed her or really even touched her in the past eight years. Of course, that had been the way she'd wanted it.

But sometimes it got lonely. There were times, deep in the night, when the bed seemed as vast as the Big Bend itself, and Julianne craved the joy and mystery of intimacy. Not just sex—she could get that anywhere. Anyone could. What she yearned for was that feeling of her soul mingling with another's. She'd known that once. Not for long, and it now seemed like a lifetime ago. She hadn't forgotten how it felt, though—the tenderness, the sweetness of it.

That craving could make her heart ache as little else could, save the memory of one thing.

She steered her mind away from that memory, the most painful one of all, worse than Mitchell's treachery, worse than Wes's death. It was locked up tight in the core of her being, and though she would never forget, she didn't want to remember, either.

But even these thoughts couldn't distract her from the very strong, distinct odor of hogs. The ripe smell hung over the farm, despite the fact that Rafael Benavente ran a very tidy and well-tended operation. There was no way to describe the odor, and no way around it, especially with a place this size. Although she was long accustomed to it, she wouldn't miss it.

She pulled the truck into the yard and honked, two long, sharp blasts to bring someone out who could tell her where they wanted her to park to off-load the sows. After a moment, Rafael himself appeared and waved to her. He walked around to her side of the truck and pushed back the brim of his straw cowboy hat. He was about the age her father would have been, had he lived. In fact, Rafael and her dad had been friends.

"*Hola*, Julianna!" Except it came out *Hoolie-ahna*, and that always made her smile.

"*Hola*, Rafael. I brought the two sows I talked to Victor Cabrera about."

He moved down and put both hands on the side of the truck bed to get a look at them. "They look good," he said, coming back to her window. "Nice young ones."

Yes, and that was a problem for her. Julianne wished she could have kept them a bit longer. The females were small and not worth as much as they would be in a few months. But she didn't have a few months. She had to sell them now.

"I'm sorry to hear of your troubles with the farm. I know it must be hard for you."

She shrugged slightly and looked past his shoulder to the hills on the distant horizon. "I think everything changes eventually. We just have to make the best of what we end up with."

He nodded philosophically, and patted her hand where it gripped the steering wheel. "You have a plan?"

She told him about the store, and they chatted for a few moments in an *olla podrida* of English and Spanish. After they agreed on the price, she asked, "Where do you want me to park?"

He put up a big, work-rough hand. "No, no, you don't trouble yourself. You wait here. I get your money and send one of the boys to take the sows. They're not so big and there are only two, yes?"

"Yes, thanks, Rafael. Tell Mrs. Benavente hello for me. Oh, and have her drop by the store the next time she's in town. It'll be good to see her again."

"Yes, I will tell her." He walked back to his office and returned quickly with cash, which Julianne appreciated. She put the bills in her wallet and was sitting in the cab of her truck when she heard someone drop the tailgate.

Automatically, she opened the door and jumped down. "You'll want to be careful of the black-spotted one. She can be a little cranky when—" Julianne stopped in her tracks, thunderstruck.

"Hello, Julianne." She recognized the voice before she looked at the face that went with it. It was whiskey-rough and as familiar as an old pair of shoes—shoes that hurt like hell to walk in.

Mitchell Tucker. *Again.* He was holding a ramp to put on the end of her tailgate. More jumbled pictures flashed through her mind as she stared at him, unable to tear her gaze away from those sea-green eyes. It was like looking at a gruesome accident, or something so wicked and profane that it fascinated. He wore a white T-shirt and dusty, boot-cut Wranglers. The afternoon sun picked up the flecks of red in his dark hair.

Then the most recent image flared—one of black spray paint.

Didn't Rafael know that she wouldn't want to have anything to do with him? How could he send Mitchell out here to unload her hogs? Shaking with righteous anger and nerves, she reeled toward the office.

"*Rafael!*"

"Wait, Julianne. I'll get these pigs and—"

Her stomach had tied itself into a knot and climbed to her chest. *"Rafael, get another man out here!"*

The owner appeared in the door of his office, took one look at the situation, and started gabbling in Spanish too fast for her to follow. The one name she did catch was when he yelled for Victor Cabrera. A string of vague profanities followed regarding the species of Cabrera's parents.

Behind her she heard the sound of the plank hitting the bed of her truck. One squealing sow ran down the ramp and scampered off across the dusty yard. The other followed close behind.

She swung on Mitchell and snapped, "I'm surprised you have the energy, what with your night job and all!"

His brows went up. "What are you talking about?"

Her throat was as tight as a clenched fist, and even if she'd wanted to bother with a response, she wouldn't have been able to. She climbed back into the cab. Slamming the door, she cranked the ignition and threw the truck into gear. In a rooster tail of dust and spraying gravel, she spun the tires before they grabbed and cut a sharp U-turn, narrowly missing the other hog as it raced after its litter mate. She had a brief glimpse of Rafael and Victor in a heated conversation, complete with wild gestures and angry faces. As she headed back down the rutted drive, in her rearview mirror she saw the ramp on the ground and a couple of other men chasing after the wayward pigs while the argument continued.

In the midst of the chaos, Mitchell stood and watched her retreating truck, his features flat and speculative.

CHAPTER FOUR

Under a pulsing spring sun, Mitchell approached the main entrance to Gila Rock High School with a sense of futility. He knew he was on a fool's errand, but he'd come this far, and he had an appointment, sort of, so he might as well see it through. He'd managed to slip out of the single-wide without being seen: the old man had been asleep, and both James and Darcy had been gone. That was good. He'd worn the best of what he currently owned for this meeting, and that alone would have generated a lot of questions he didn't want to answer.

A few kids charged out the doors as he went in, but none of them gave him a second glance. At least not *everyone* remembered him or had a reason to stare. The smell of the hallways—paper, books, and aged asphalt tile, all so familiar—hit him in the face as he made his way to the office and approached the counter.

Miss Lou Emma Bently, old Bad-Ass Bently, the school's head secretary, still presided at her desk behind the counter. He couldn't believe it. Ancient and yet ageless, she'd always had a face that looked as if it had been rough-chiseled from granite, and a personality to match. The passing of nearly a decade hadn't softened that face. Only her black hair, now the color of a horseshoe, had faded. When she saw him, recognition struck, and her mouth tightened into a hard line.

"Mr. Tucker."

"Yes, ma'am. I have an appointment with Principal Schroder."

Her lips nearly disappeared. "I have no information about an appointment. It's not on my calendar."

He wanted to sass her. That urge hadn't died, but it wouldn't do him any good, either. "At four o' clock."

A younger woman at the next desk piped up. "I took that call, Miss Lou Em. I put it on Ray's schedule."

Obviously stuck, Miss Bently turned and went to the closed, glass-panel door that read **RAY SCHRODER, PRIN.** in block letters. After tapping on the glass with the end of her pen, she stepped inside, and he heard a murmured conversation that he couldn't quite catch. But when she came back she wore an expression of profound displeasure. She looked at the clock over her shoulder. It read 3:50. "You're early." It sounded like an accusation.

He didn't reply but just gazed at her.

"I suppose you might as well come on back, then." She buzzed him through a gate in the counter. "In here," she added, indicating the office door, then watched him until he got there, as if expecting him to steal something.

He nodded his thanks, and with a lead sinker in his stomach, he walked past her to face the man who had promised him he'd fail in life if he didn't get his act together. Now here he was again, and by his own request, having fulfilled the man's dire prediction. Ray Schroder waved him in.

The office looked like a museum exhibit, frozen in time. Same furniture, same American and Texan flags. The wall calendar was current, but the birdcage he'd always kept on a stand in the corner was still there. Right now it housed a chirping blue parakeet. The last one Mitchell had seen had been yellow. Why he remembered that escaped him.

The administrator had aged no more gracefully than his secretary. His round, creased face resembled a shar-pei's. His brow drooped in deep furrows, nearly obscuring his eyes, and his hairline had crept back a couple more inches.

He looked Mitchell up and down. "Well, now, Tucker. I heard you were in town, but this is a surprise." He gestured at the chair Mitchell had occupied many times before. "I admit I agreed to meet with you because my curiosity got the better of me. Did I understand this correctly—you're interested in a job here at the school? The janitorial staff is pretty much fixed until Pedro Ramirez retires or dies, whichever comes first, and I don't see that happening anytime soon."

Of course, why would the man who'd known him all those years before expect him to want something more than a custodial job? The lead sinker gained weight. "Actually, I was thinking of something else. You could use a baseball coach."

"We have a baseball coach."

"Not really."

Schroder's brows flew up, temporarily lifting that sagging brow, and he sat a bit straighter in his chair. "Do you actually—are you talking about yourself?"

"Yep."

"Tucker, you can't be serious. Aside from the obvious problem, what in hell makes you qualified to coach baseball?"

"I took us to state two years in a row. Scouts even came down here to have a look at me."

"That they did. And I remember that you were so cocky and sure of yourself, the night before you were supposed to meet them you got good and drunk with your JD friends." His expression soured briefly. "Oh—we're supposed to call them 'justice-involved youths' now. Your performance that next day was not exactly what they were looking for, as I recall."

Mitchell suppressed the long sigh he almost let out. He'd hoped he was the only one who remembered the details of that episode. He hadn't felt cocky at all. He'd been so wringing-wet terrified, he'd let some of those troublemakers he hung out with convince him that a little party was in order. "I remember it, too."

The principal sat back again and drummed his fingers on his desk. It was a familiar gesture of frustration and impatience that still made Mitchell want to fidget in his chair. "People don't get chances like that very often, especially around here. You had a gift—we really thought you'd found a good way to get out of Gila Rock. A few of us were pretty disappointed in you."

Big news flash there. He'd told Mitchell the same thing eight years earlier. It had only made him sullen and angry then. Now he understood it a lot better. He hadn't come here to get chewed out again, but he supposed it wasn't realistic to hope for something else. "Yeah, I realize that. But I'm looking for a new start now."

"First of all, Jimmy Thornton does a good, solid job coaching the team for us."

"No offense, Mr. Schroder, but I've seen him with those kids out on the diamond a few times, and Jimmy Thornton is doing a pretty *lousy* job. He might be solid, but he doesn't have a passion for the game. He doesn't know much beyond the basics, as far as I can tell. He's not giving the players the extra edge they need."

"I have no reason to consider replacing him, or his assistant." *Especially with you*—his obvious, unspoken comment hung between them.

Mitchell didn't expect his jaw to drop, but it did. "A coaching assistant at a tiny school like Gila Rock?"

"Jimmy's daddy was on the school board for thirty-five years. That gives him certain benefits." Schroder's glance flicked away to the parakeet for an instant.

So Thornton had the same kind of tenure that Pedro Ramirez did, but at a higher salary and with more perks. It was who you knew, not what you knew. "Uh-huh."

Schroder pushed away a coffee cup on the desk. "Tucker, I can't say I was expecting this when you asked to see me. How did you think this would play out? You probably have the skills and the ability, the 'passion for the game,' as you put it. Whether I thought you deserved a spot like that—and I'm sorry, but I don't—what are your credentials? And with your record, you know you wouldn't get past writing your name on an application. This is a small town. Everyone knows what happened to Wesley Emerson, and who did it to him. Convicted murderers just don't get jobs in schools, not even janitorial jobs."

Mitchell winced. Now he did sigh, and said, "I figured I was chasing a pipe dream." He stood and put out his hand to his old principal. "I had to try, though."

Schroder gave him a straight look with those shar-pei eyes and shook hands with him. "Mitch, I knew you'd had a hard time of things before the night of that fire. That's why I was pulling for you when the chance for the minors tryouts came along. If you didn't have that past hanging over you, I'd see what I could do to find a place for you. I'm sure you wish you had that night to do over."

"Every damned day of my life, Mr. Schroder. Every damned day." He straightened and walked out.

The next afternoon, Julianne stood with the phone cradled against her shoulder while she peered at the dirty, blue-backed ledger Joe Bickham had used for his accounts. Cade's call had come at the moment her head had begun to ache at the base of her skull. Clearly, Uncle Joe's accounting system had been one of his own invention, and he'd left no translation.

"Hey, Julianne, did you get those pigs to Benavente's?"

"Yes. He gave me a fair price." She decided not to tell him about Mitchell. She just didn't want to go into it.

"I'm sorry I couldn't drive them over there for you."

"I know. I understand. How's your arm?" She asked the question but was more focused on a cramped column entry than she was on his answer. Why would her uncle have ordered $500 worth of *birdseed*? She peered around the shelves, looking for some evidence of the stock, but she didn't see it.

"Well—still broken."

"Uh-huh." Distracted, she squinted at another notation, something about thirty cubic yards of potting soil. Oh yes, now she remembered. The bags were stacked in a corner up near the front window.

"How's it going over there?"

She sighed. "Cade, I've been staring at Joe's ledger for an hour, and I still can't make heads or tails of it. He ordered goofy inventory like a mountain of birdseed and a gross of novelty key chains. It looks like he gave credit to people all over town. As far as I can tell, they still owe this place money, and the business still owes vendors. If I could collect these outstanding debts, I'd be way ahead of the game. But first I have to figure out what on earth he was talking about in these entries. For the life of me, I can't understand what he did."

In the background, she heard the squeal of childish voices and knew he was calling from his parents' store. "Okay, I tell you what—I know I can't build shelves or do some other stuff that takes two arms. But I can probably help you untangle that bookkeeping mess your uncle left you. Like I said, I know about the business side of running a retail store. You don't have to pay me." He had a confident, positive tone, which gave her some comfort. But there was an edge of eagerness in his voice, too.

Julianne twiddled with the curly cord that connected the receiver to the phone. "No, no, *not* for free. It's good of you to offer . . ."

"But?"

"Cade, we talked about this. If you can help me collect these outstanding debts, I'll be able to give you the same wages as before. But I can't—I won't promise more than a job. You know . . ." She wanted to nip in the bud any romantic notions he might be harboring. Regardless of her private yearnings, Cade didn't fit into that picture.

There was an awkward pause. "Yeah, Julianne, I know. You have your priorities." It wasn't bitterness she heard. Was it longing? Hope? "Have you had any more trouble since the other night?"

"No, it's been quiet. Maybe the Tuckers have had their fun and won't bother me again." Privately, though, she didn't believe it. She looked over her shoulder every time she went out and carried the shotgun upstairs at night. But she tried to sound convincing.

"That's good—those lousy bastards have given you enough grief." Another shriek sounded in the background, followed by a youngster's great, gulping howl that pierced Julianne's head through the earpiece. "So, I'll start tomorrow, okay?"

She smiled. "Anxious to get away, huh?"

"Well, yeah," he admitted. "It's a little crowded around here."

"But you still can't drive your truck. What are you going to do for transportation?"

"I think I can borrow a rig with an automatic. My sister used to drive it back and forth to school."

"Okay, great. I can use your help. This old place might get a second life yet."

He would not, though, stay on a cot in the back room, as he'd suggested before. It would be convenient, it would even give her a sense of safety, having him there at night. Safety from outsiders, at least. But the idea of Cade sleeping one flight of stairs away from her gave her other worries. Not that she believed he'd ever overstep his bounds, but she didn't want to give him false encouragement, either. And she didn't need the town making assumptions and gossiping about such an arrangement. It had been different out on the farm. There had been a foreman's cabin, separate from the house.

"You can't stay here, you know," she said, just in case he wasn't clear about that.

"Okay, I understand," he agreed.

With a feeling of some accomplishment, she hung up the receiver and went to the front window, still fogged over with Glass Wax. Using an old towel, she cleaned off a square spot on the pane to put up a red-and-black **HELP WANTED** sign.

After that, she grabbed her purse and headed out the door with a handful of bright-pink signs she'd run off on the printer. She'd post one on the bulletin board at the Shoppeteria, on the wall at Lupe's, and at any other good spot she saw.

"Mitch, it's for you."

James called to him through the screen door frame and gestured with the cordless phone he held.

Mitchell was outside in the late spring afternoon, tossing a tennis ball around with Knucklehead. He'd just finished installing a rebuilt carburetor in a sickly Buick Skylark, and by God, the thing had even turned over when he cranked the ignition. Of course, it put out more exhaust than an old man gumming a diet of beans and cabbage, but it would run. Where Darcy found these beaters he couldn't begin to imagine. They weren't worth stealing—they were barely worth parting out. Still, Darcy's inventory changed occasionally, so he must be finding buyers somewhere. At least it gave Mitchell something constructive to do while he was out of a job. It kept him busy enough to divert his thoughts from Julianne. Not for long, though, and that was good. He didn't want anything to distract him from his purpose.

Knucklehead jumped forward and back, the tennis ball clamped in his teeth. He loved to catch it, but he wouldn't give it back. He turned it into a game of keep-away, and Mitchell had to chase him around the cars.

"Have it your way," he said to the dog, turning back toward the trailer. Knucklehead immediately dropped the dirty yellow ball, a look of doggy disappointment on his canine face.

Who the hell would be calling him? Mitchell wondered, taking the phone from James, who hitched his eyebrows slyly a couple of times. Probably not Rafael Benavente to give him back his job. The scene that had followed Julianne's visit to the farm had been a bitch—both he and Victor Cabrera had received their final pay envelopes. Oddly, Rafael had seemed even more angry at Cabrera than at Mitchell. And after that crappy meeting with Schroder, he had no prospects for work anytime soon. He had some money socked away, but he couldn't just hang out here while he tried to catch up with Julianne. He'd go crazy.

"Yeah, this is Mitchell." He sat down on the narrow wooden steps that served as the front porch with the phone tucked between his chin and shoulder. Knucklehead picked up the ball again and carried it to his feet.

"Hey, baby, remember me?"

Mitchell paused. That teasing, smoky voice—it didn't purr, exactly, but it was familiar. Unforgettable, in fact. In moments of sweating, screaming sex, that voice could screech like a cougar's and practically strip the shingles off a roof. "Cherry?"

"I hoped you hadn't forgotten. I sure haven't forgotten *you*. I heard you were back in town. I've been wondering when you're going to come by and see me—we've got some lost time to make up for."

Making up lost time with Cherry Claxton was not on Mitchell's to-do list. He'd dated her in high school, and after Julianne had told him to get lost, he'd caught her between boyfriends for a while. In fact, she was the last woman he'd had sex with before he'd gone to prison.

The realization was vaguely depressing. "Yeah, well, I just got back into town. Besides, I thought you married Steve Brea."

"Oh, you *are* behind the times, aren't you, honey? Steve was two divorces ago. I'm a free girl now, in every way you'd want. Didn't you get my letters while you were in prison?"

"I got a couple of them, saying you were getting married."

"A couple—well, I wrote a lot more. The damned post office must have lost them."

Oh sure. Mitchell knew it wasn't the post office. With Cherry, if a man was out of sight, he was out of mind, and she moved on. "Two divorces, huh? Sounds like you've been busy."

"I was just trying to get over you, Mitch. You know it broke my heart when you went off to Amarillo. I cried every night for a month."

It was such blatant bullshit, and said with wry humor, he had to laugh. Cherry was always good for a laugh, as long as a man didn't set fire to that temper of hers. "Yeah, I'll bet."

"It's true!"

"Uh-huh. That's why you never came to visit."

"Well, those husbands did keep me hopping." He could hear the grin in her voice. "For a while, anyway."

"Any kids?"

Her own laugh was rough. "Me? Kids? No, no, that would be such a bad combination. The little monsters always want something, need something—always crying, always hanging on like possum babies. They're okay as long as they belong to someone else. They'd just cramp my style."

Yeah, that was Cherry, too. Always interested in Number One. "At least you knew it before you had them. Some people don't figure that out until it's too late." His own mother's image flitted across the back of his memory.

"Motherhood is one thing I don't miss. But I sure miss you, lover."

"Right."

"I'll prove it!" she challenged. "You come by the Captain Gas. My shift ends at eight tonight; then we can get a few drinks and talk about the good old days."

Did he really want to start this again? he asked himself. There hadn't been many "good old days" in Mitchell Tucker's life. And the few he'd known had not involved Cherry. Then he heard his father inside, coughing his phlegmy smoker's cough and swearing at the TV news anchor reporting a story about government spending. Maybe it would be good to get away from here for a while, after all.

"I guess I could meet you at Lupe's," he said, not wanting to be pinned down to anything more. It wasn't a date, at least not in his mind. And he wanted his own car in case he wanted to make a quick exit.

"Ooooh, brrr! That's not too friendly—what's the matter?"

"Nothing, I've just got some things to do. I'll meet you at Lupe's at nine." He'd take the junker Skylark. It was the only car in the yard that would actually start.

"All right, then," she said, apparently satisfied. "I'll see you there. I can't wait to get a look at you again."

Mitch chuckled and clicked off, then looked at his hands. They were covered with grease. He'd need a shower and probably a shave, too. He stood and went inside.

"Got a date, huh?" James said, grinning. "I knew the females would be jumping your bones once they found out you were in town."

"It's not a date," Mitchell said, thrusting the cordless phone into James's hand on his way to the bathroom. "I'm just going to have a beer or two with Cherry."

James wiped the greasy receiver on the leg of his jeans. "Cherry Claxton? We've all been out with her one time or another."

Mitchell stopped. "Yeah?"

"Sure. Cherry doesn't much like being tied to one guy. We gave her a spin while you were gone."

A funny quiver went through Mitchell's gut, but he ignored it and shrugged. "Well, that's her problem."

"So I told that son of a bitch if he thought he was going to rob the place while *I* was there, he was in for a world of hurt. Nobody cheats Cherry Claxton." She downed her shot of tequila and slammed the glass on the laminate table. "Nobody."

Mitchell raised his brows and sat back. "It's pretty hard to argue with someone pointing a gun in your face."

Cherry dismissed the comment with a careless wave. "Oh hell, I figured it wasn't real. Anyway, some guys came in just then and saw what was happening. They jumped that little shit and held him till Gunter showed up in his squad car." She flipped a long red curl over her shoulder. "A few months later, some meth head and his dumb girlfriend came in and tried to hold up the place with a pair of pliers. *Pliers!* Can you believe it? By then, I'd talked Ernie, the owner, into getting me a shotgun. So this time *I* had the gun, and those scabby tweakers ran like their butts had been dipped in Lupe's hot sauce." She laughed and cuddled up to him on the seat of the red vinyl booth. "But enough about my glamour job at the Captain Gas. Let's talk about you."

They had been sitting here for about an hour, and Cherry had done most of the talking. It was a slow night at Lupe's, but it looked and smelled the same as Mitchell remembered it. A blue haze of cigarette smoke hung over the place, and Vince Gill wailed from the jukebox about being a victim of life's circumstances. God, if that didn't fit. Mitchell had caught a few curious glances, and some people leaned their heads together to mutter about him. For the most part, though, he was invisible. It was like that everywhere he went. People didn't harass him, but they weren't likely to forget the most sensational bad guy in Gila Rock's recent history.

He took a long sip from his beer and shrugged, inhaling Cherry's heavy cloud of perfume. "There isn't much to tell. You know where I've been the last few years."

"Did you ever think about me?"

He gave her a dry look. "As often as you thought about me."

She smiled. "You might not realize how often that was. We go back a long way, you and me." Her freckled face lit up, and she barked out another laugh. "Remember that summer night before our junior year when a bunch of us got together with a pony keg out on the flats? Billy Jamison decided we should play another game of mailbox baseball, so down the road we went in his beat-up Eldorado, the radio blaring. You had that great swing! Old man Bennett's mailbox went flying. I think it bounced off his roof and landed in the yard. I was hanging onto the back of your belt to keep you from falling out the car window. We were all laughing our heads off."

Mitch chuckled. Everything had been different then. "Yeah, I remember. I damn near dislocated my shoulder hitting that post. And then Alvie was so mad he built a brick monument around the next one. I suppose after losing a couple, he decided to put an end to it. A smashed mailbox is just one of the joys of living in the sticks."

"At least we never got caught." She arched a brow and gave him a better view of her cleavage. He felt her bare foot creep up the inside of his thigh beneath the table and nestle against his crotch. "Not at that, anyway."

Mitchell grabbed her foot and put it on his knee. "Keep that up and we'll get caught now."

"*Pffft*, no one is paying any attention to us. But if you're feeling shy, we could go back to my place," she said, with her boobs pressed against the tabletop.

That thready streak of hesitation went through him again, especially when he thought about all the other men who'd probably gotten the same invitation from her. Then he shrugged. He didn't want to start up something with Cherry, but he didn't have anything else to do. Beer had put a slight but pleasant blur on everything, and he sure as hell didn't want to go back to the mobile home. "Okay, why not?"

She straightened up and gave him a come-hither look. "Great! We'll have a little party of our own. You can follow me over."

He drank the rest of his beer in one gulp and edged out of the booth. "I'm just going to stop at the head first. My back teeth are starting to float." He threw a couple of bills on the table. "I'll meet you outside."

She slithered across the vinyl seat after him and put her sharp-heeled shoe back on. "Okay, honey." When she walked toward the door, her hips swayed, and she looked back. "Don't be long."

He made his way toward the restrooms, past the neon beer signs and crummy, wood-paneled walls. In the john, which still smelled like farts overlaid with deodorizer, he saw that the old condom vending machine was there. The price had gone up, though—three bucks. Someone had written on it with a permanent marker, *This gum tastes like rubber.* Yeah, everyone was a comedian. He shuffled through the remaining cash in his money clip and fed the machine.

On the way out of the bar, he glanced at the bulletin board that had hung there next to the doors as long as he could remember. All sorts of notices and ads got posted on it: church pancake breakfasts, livestock for sale, babysitting services, real estate—even Benavente's had a help-wanted flyer stuck in the cork, looking to fill two recent openings, his and Cabrera's, no doubt.

But one in particular, copied on neon-pink paper, stopped him dead.

HANDYMAN NEEDED
FOR ODD JOBS AND REPAIRS
APPLY AT BICKHAM'S ON ROSALITA ST.

Bickham's. This was perfect, too good to pass up. Like an open invitation right into Julianne's living room. The other chances he'd had to confront her had failed, but this time he wouldn't let her blow him off. He pulled the sign off the cork board.

He remembered that Cherry was waiting outside for him, but suddenly his halfhearted interest in spending the night with her fizzled completely. He turned and headed for the parking lot, dreading her reaction. She'd be typically pissed off, but he was going to send her on her way for now. Alone.

He had some planning to do.

"Look at this, Dale! This is the worst yet. You know who's responsible for this—are you going to tell me there's nothing you can do?" Julianne stood in her oldest jeans and a blue tank top under early morning sun, with the shotgun cradled in one arm. Her clothes didn't look much better than the charred remains of flaming dog-shit bags—nine in all—that sat side by side on each tread down the center of the back steps of the dime store. They were like disgusting luminaires from a bad home-and-garden magazine. Martha Stewart would never envision this. Fat, lazy blowflies buzzed around them, landing occasionally in the mess, grooming their iridescent bodies and wings with their legs.

At least the concrete steps couldn't burn, too, or the whole building might have caught. She could see Sheriff Dale Gunter making a mighty effort to keep a straight face, which only made her angrier. Considering everything, how could he possibly think this was funny?

They stood at the bottom of the steps behind her building. His squad car was parked next to the side, a gleaming black-and-white Crown Vic with a light bar that was probably never used except in speed traps on the highway into town. Not that Julianne expected sirens and flashing lights, but nothing around here seemed to qualify as urgent to Dale Gunter.

"Nope, I'm watching the Tuckers. But this feud between your families has been going on longer than even I can remember," he said.

She stiffened, and the shotgun slid down to her palm. "I never had anything to do with that! That was between Earl and my father, and I never knew what it was about." Even Mitchell hadn't known. They'd talked about it during those stolen, desperate moments and nights they'd spent together so long ago.

Gunter gestured at the Remington. "I'd feel a lot better if you put that down for now, Julianne."

She nodded and propped the weapon against the building, but not without reluctance. This ongoing problem was making her jumpy.

The sheriff offered, "I can lean on Mitchell Tucker and push pretty hard. Do you have anything solid I can use? Did you see him out here?"

She crossed her arms and couldn't smooth the sullen, frustrated tone off her answer. "No." She'd just seen the light of the flames reflected on the apartment ceiling. She wasn't afraid of fire in general, but that displaced glow had jolted her out of bed and summoned the memories of the barn fire that haunted her sleep, even now. "By the time I got downstairs and saw what was going on, he—or they—were long gone. And there are the midnight phone calls . . . some voice I don't know . . ."

"Julianne, if I'm going to make this stick, it would help to have something to go on. It doesn't matter if I know the perp who did this."

She straightened her arms to hang stiffly at her sides, her hands clenched into fists. "Perp—*perp*! This isn't *CSI Miami* with a big city full of possible suspects. It's just Gila Rock. Mitchell Tucker comes back to town and all this starts up again. That seems pretty cut and dried. *He's* your perp."

The sheriff shook his balding ginger head. "Yeah—or maybe some high school kids could be behind this. It's a pretty juvenile prank, not the sort of thing grown men would do."

She tightened her lips into a thin line. "Should I look for an accomplice—like the dog?"

He pulled off his mirrored sunglasses before he stuck one temple in his shirtfront and leveled his pale-eyed gaze on her. "I want to help you—I'm not your enemy, y'know."

Right now he wasn't much of a friend, either.

He gestured at the scorched remains. "Uh, you didn't step on these, did you?"

She heaved a deep sigh. "Of course not. I came around from the front door. But how bad does this harassment have to get before I *can* get something done about it? You can't have forgotten how Wes died, and—and everything else that happened. That was supposedly a juvenile prank, too. I hope it won't take a repeat of that horrible, *horrible* night to get something done."

That got him—he couldn't just brush it off. He straightened and shifted the weight of all the equipment strapped to the paunch of his middle-aged waist. "Okay, I'll send a car around at night to step up patrols here."

Under the circumstances, Julianne knew that was the best she could hope for. Her shoulders sagged. "All right, Dale, thank you. I appreciate it."

He nodded and put his sunglasses back on, then headed for the patrol car. "You call if you see anyone out here, day or night."

It took considerable willpower to keep from reminding him that she was doing just that. At least he was trying.

She watched the cruiser pull out, its tires crunching the gravel. Turning to look at the mess on her stairs, she sighed. She could easily imagine those idiot Tucker brothers sneaking over here last night with no witnesses except katydids and crickets to see them leave this calling card. The sun climbed higher, and so did the stench. There was no help for it—she had to clean it up, and it would take more than a hose. Cade had already called to say he couldn't borrow his sister's truck for a few days, because she was using it to help haul stuff to the church for a rummage sale. But with that broken arm he wouldn't be able to push a shovel or a rake anyway. There was so much to be done inside, but here she was, fooling around with this nonsense. Except this was worse than nonsense. It was an insult, juvenile or not, and it her made her feel more vulnerable, and Julianne hated that.

She marched to the small shed and grabbed a few tools, plus rubber boots, a gallon bottle of bleach, a bucket, and the garden hose. Then she sat on an upended old Nehi soda crate, pulled on the boots, and took up her weapons. Shoveling and scraping the steps, trying to hold her breath and wave off the flies, she could easily imagine how those bastards would laugh if they could see her now. The image infuriated her. Suddenly she glanced around, wondering if that had been their plan all along—to complete her humiliation by watching her clean this up. But the back of the building didn't provide many hiding places. The higher vantage spots looking down on Gila Rock were too far away to provide as much satisfaction as front-row seats. Just a lot of craggy boulders sticking out of the earth at sharp angles, streaked here and there with various minerals. Still . . .

No, she thought, those people were *not* going to run her out of town. Not now. And she refused to give into the galloping paranoia she'd lived with for so long. But that damned feud—she considered the trouble and grief it had brought about, the lives affected. And even now, after all these years, she still didn't know what had triggered it. The long-simmering grudge had survived the years and those originally involved. Her own father's death hadn't ended it, and neither had Wes's.

Marrying Wes had been such a horrible mistake. She should never have let herself get talked into that.

She had never dated another boy except Mitchell, and Paul Boyce had assumed that his daughter had never gone out with anyone except friends. So when he was diagnosed with inoperable cancer, he'd worried about what would happen to his girl with no one to help her after he was gone. He'd always been convinced that women needed protectors, not partners.

He'd had an old friend with a nice son named Wesley, and they'd arranged an introduction of the two young people. Julianne had been just seventeen. She'd wanted to argue and scream to her father that he was blackmailing her with his illness, and that it was unfair of him to put this burden on her shoulders. She'd wanted to tell him she loved Mitchell. That this arranged marriage was an old-fashioned relic of a plan that wasn't necessary. But she couldn't do it to him. He'd been only a pale, fragile shell.

In a panic, she had told Mitchell what was happening. If they didn't do something—run away, elope, *something*—she might very well end up married to Wesley Emerson. But Mitchell had fiddle-farted away his time, playing baseball, unwilling to commit, and was busy running around with his friends. He'd asked her to wait a little longer, to stall on the wedding and not lose faith in him. He'd said that baseball scouts were considering him for the pros, and he couldn't make any moves until he'd heard what they'd decided. He hadn't seemed to grasp that the clock was ticking, and the crushing weight of familial duty was pushing her inexorably toward that arranged marriage to Wes. She'd felt abandoned and used by Mitchell. But when she'd told him about the wedding, his expression had turned to stone, and he'd accused her of having no faith in him, of being fickle.

After she'd married Wesley, then . . . oh, then, the problems had begun, dished up by the Tucker brothers in great, heaping portions. The harassment, the pranks. And then the ultimate calamity that had turned Julianne into a widow. Mitchell had claimed he hadn't known Wes was in the barn when the fire had started. Maybe he hadn't, but the result had been the same. Wesley had been a good man, earnest and sincere. In fact, Cade possessed a lot of the same qualities that Wes had had. Wes's attraction to her had been immediate and shyly intense. Five years older than she, he'd grown up on a ranch on the other side of the county, and he'd known what it took to keep a family operation afloat in this economy. Wes had loved her with his whole, simple, honest soul, and he'd been thrilled when she'd told him she was pregnant.

But Julianne had not loved him. In their short life together, he'd never guessed that another man still owned her heart, and for that she was grateful. He hadn't realized that when they made love, only her body had been present, nor had he known that his touch had never quickened her or reached the empty, longing part of her. She had cheated him of everything he'd thought he'd won when he'd married her.

But it *still* wasn't over.

The more her mind churned through the memories, the harder she worked, and the hotter she became. Her tank top stuck to her back, and her hair was soaked with sweat. They were well into May, and that meant summer was already underway here in the Big Bend, with scorching heat that bleached most vegetation and tanned or burned nearly everything else. She'd supposed that running a store would be cleaner, cooler work than pig farming, but—

"Julianne—"

Between the scraping, disinfecting, and hosing, she hadn't heard anyone approach, despite the gravel. She jumped and saw Mitchell standing not more than fifteen feet away, holding her neon-pink advertisement. What he'd said hadn't really registered. She knew only that he was her worst enemy.

She dropped the hose and grabbed the shotgun from where she'd left it leaning against the back wall. A cyclone of thoughts spun through her mind, but she marshaled her courage and fury. "You get the hell out of here, Mitchell Tucker, or I'll shoot your head off and work my way down from there!"

She saw the alarm on his face. Standing on the working end of a weapon had that effect. She felt a surge of grim satisfaction pump through her, sharpening her adrenaline edge. He held up his hands in a gesture of surrender, the paper still clutched in his grip, and backed up a few paces.

"Careful with that thing. Someone could get hurt."

"Yes, *you* this time." How dare he stand here on her property with his world-weary eyes and tell her to be careful? "It's not fun to be threatened, is it? You've got five seconds to turn around and leave before I start shooting."

"Julianne, listen—"

She tightened her grip on the stock. "Tick-tock, Mitchell. Tick-tock. One, two—"

"Put that shotgun down!" he ordered, in a voice so commanding, so unlike anything she remembered, her aim wavered. He must have noticed. "Put it down, *now*! I just want to talk to you for a minute."

Uncertain, she lowered her aim a bit but didn't take her hands off her weapon. It gave her an unquestionable advantage. "What are you doing here, Mitchell? Had to return to the scene of the crime?"

He frowned slightly. "I've been out of jail for a year. I came back to settle something between you and me."

"Really? By doing this?" She gestured at the steps. "And all those other insulting, lame-brained stunts you've been pulling?"

He shook his head, obviously feigning bafflement, and she wasn't buying it. "I don't know what you're talking about. The last time I had anything to do with you was at Benavente's. I guess you'll be happy to hear I got fired after that. So did Cabrera."

"I'll cry about it all night," she said. "You haven't answered my question. What do you want?"

"I came to talk to you about this job advertisement." He waggled the paper in his still upheld hands.

Finally, she recognized it and felt her jaw drop. "You can't be serious! What . . . why . . . are you *crazy*? What would make you think I'd hire you to do anything? You killed my husband!"

He flinched as if she'd pulled the trigger on the shotgun. "I don't expect you to pay me. I know you need the help and that money's tight for you."

"What makes you think that?"

Slowly, he lowered his hands. "This is a small town. You know no one can have secrets here. I heard about the farm and your plans for this place. I'll work for nothing just till you get back on your feet."

That now made two men who'd volunteered free labor, and she didn't trust either offer. "So you can burn down this place, too?"

He dropped his gaze to a clump of tenacious bunch grass growing up through a crack in the hardpan. "I can understand that you wouldn't trust me."

What an understatement. "No, I don't. I don't think much of any of you Tuckers."

"They don't know I'm here. And they won't know."

"Because it won't happen. You can clean up this mess you left on my stairs and leave." She gestured at the unfinished job.

He shook his head. "What are you talking about? I didn't do this!"

"Mitchell, come *on*! Who else would have left burning bags of dog crap here? Who else would be harassing me with odd phone calls and vandalism? It started up again when you came to town. I'm not stupid, you know."

"I'm sure as hell no choirboy," he said, his features fixed and angry-looking. "But no matter what happened in the past, I never lied. Not to you, not to anyone else. I'm telling you I haven't done anything to bother you and I don't know who's responsible for that stuff."

She cut a wide path around him and headed for the front door. "Clean it up, or I'll call Sheriff Gunter back here and he can haul you in for trespassing. I already showed this to him, so he's keeping an eye on you."

CHAPTER FIVE

Seeing Julianne again, talking to her, gave Mitchell dreams of the past. He'd been fueled by his own rage over Julianne's easy abandonment of their relationship, and by a slashing pain so deep it felt like a knife twisting in his chest. One night he woke up with a sweaty lurch, nearly tumbling Knucklehead off the mattress. He wasn't that kid anymore, but in the twilight world of sleep he was still nineteen, full of fragile confidence, running wild in the few streets and the low, craggy hills of Gila Rock, angry, careless, and secretly scared of what his future held.

His encounter with Julianne had not gone the way he'd hoped. Man, she *hated* him. He'd never before seen her with a gun in her hands, but her steady grip had given him no doubt that she could and would fire it if she decided to. He sat up on the edge of the mattress, wondering whether his return to this flea-bitten town might have been another of his life mistakes.

After all, this was no step up from Mitchell's most recent life, he thought with more than a touch of irony. He was sleeping on what amounted to a dog bed in this old tin can of a hovel, and the mutt was overtaking Mitchell's meager real estate. As if to reiterate his satisfaction with the situation, Knucklehead burrowed into the space Mitchell had abandoned when he'd sat up, and pushed his big paws against his back with a contented sigh.

He just wanted to accomplish one thing—to cut out the cancer that still gnawed at his soul. Confronting Julianne again was his only hope for that, so he'd try again. And again, until he'd found that cure.

Darcy Tucker bounced into the Captain Gas with keys jingling at his waist and a cigarette clamped between his teeth. He was happy to find Cherry Claxton working the counter, and even more pleased to see that she was alone for the moment. He had chugged up to the gas pumps in his latest acquisition, a 1987 Ford Escort with four different-color quarter panels and a dribbling crankcase. The passenger door was strapped shut with lashings of duct tape. "Hey, sweet thing. Ring me up for fifteen bucks of regular."

She scowled at him, punching the keys on the cash register while he rummaged through a bin of marked-down packaged snacks and squashed candy bars. "Don't 'sweet thing' me." She lifted her chin and looked out at the Ford. "I see you still have a good eye for death-trap cars."

"Hey, you know me. Just like the Petty-man says, one foot in the grave, and the other on the gas."

"Tom Petty wouldn't be caught dead *or* alive in a piece of shit like that."

Darcy straightened and gave her a hard look. "Someone got up on the bitchy side of the bed this morning."

"So what?"

"I thought you'd be in a better mood. I heard you got cozy with my big brother the other night."

"Well, I saw him. We had a few at Lupe's; then he left me standing in the parking lot, claiming something important had come up. I guess that something wasn't a party with me."

"He left?"

"Hell yes, he left. I don't like being stood up."

"He didn't exactly stand you up—"

"And I don't play second string for any man."

Darcy fiddled with a display of e-cigarettes that stood on the counter, trying to figure out how they worked, and how something that looked like a kid's toy could possibly compare to an honest-to-God, burning, paper-and-tobacco smoke. "He's a different man than he was before he went to jail. I s'pose that's to be expected. But don't give up on him. I know he's got a hot thing for you. It never went away, no matter that it's been seven, eight years since he last nailed you." He didn't know anything of the kind, but if Cherry believed it, that was good enough. "I'll elbow him along if you play nice."

She frowned again and swatted his hand off the display. "Either buy that damn thing or leave it. Don't just stand there fingering the merchandise like a ten-year-old sneaking looks at a *Playboy*."

"I'm not buying a candy-ass gadget like that."

Flipping her long red hair back behind her shoulders, she said, "What's your interest in this thing between me and your brother, anyway, Darce? You get a little nibble from me, but you're pushing me toward Mitch. That doesn't make much sense."

"We're just having some fun, you and me—it's fun, ain't it? Our little games? That low sound you make in your throat, I never heard anything like it."

Finally, she grinned. "Yeah, it is. It's fun."

"I know he's the one you really want. You just help butter my toast now and then, so to speak, and I'll see to it that you get to work your magic on Mitch. What say, pretty lady?"

She gave him an arch look. "Sixteen-twenty, Toast Boy."

He threw down some rumpled bills next to a big jar of beef jerky, then withdrew a piece of the dried meat. "See you later, Deep Throat." He winked at her and walked out. He heard her smoky laugh before the door closed behind him.

Two days after the dog-crap caper, Julianne pulled up to the back of Bickham's with eight gallons of paint in the bed of her pickup, plus all the paraphernalia she'd need to roll it onto the walls and ceiling. Cade had called every day, but he was still a no-show. Without his help to unsnarl the bookkeeping, she had to move on with those things she could manage by herself.

After her unnerving, surprise visit from Mitchell, she'd been equally surprised to discover that he'd cleaned up the steps. She'd told him to do it but hadn't expected anything. He'd even washed all the tools and coiled the hose. Was he actually innocent of this, as he'd claimed? No, this was his way of trying to lure her in, to make her believe in his sincerity. But why? She pulled the key out of the ignition and envisioned his attractive face, made flinty by time and circumstance. What did he expect from her, anyway?

Under a scorching midday sun, she got out and went around to drop the tailgate and haul out the paint. *Damn it.* She'd asked Mike Carver at Carver Hardware to give her single-gallon cans. Now she discovered that he'd sold her only three. The rest of the paint was in a five-gallon bucket that weighed close to fifty pounds. He'd had someone load it all up while she was still in the store, and she hadn't realized what she'd brought back until now. It was dead weight, in an inconvenient place and at an awkward height. Even with a hand truck, getting it down was going to be monumental task because she didn't really have what she needed to manage it. Julianne wasn't afraid of hard work—she was used to it after years of running that accursed pig farm with very little help. Sighing, she went to the shed to get the hand truck and a couple of two-by-sixes she'd seen in there to use for a ramp. It would be tricky, but it was the best she could do for now. After positioning the boards, she climbed up and shimmied the nose plate of the hand truck under the bucket, then rolled it to the end of the tailgate. "Careful, *careful . . . ,*" she said to herself. With a nudge, she started it down the ramp.

One plank slipped. "No, no, no!" she said, as if that would stop what happened next.

The handle jumped out of her hands as the tool lurched forward, and both bucket and hand truck tumbled off and hit the ground. The bucket lid popped off and rolled across the yard. A geyser of paint splashed back on Julianne, and a flood of pale-taupe latex, so fashionable on the paint chip, now looked like a stale, coffee-flavored milk shake as it gushed out in a thick glop.

Julianne stared at the mess, stupefied, her dry mouth open slightly, before she sank to the splattered tailgate and lay back, her legs dangling at the knees, feeling defeat and the wet heaviness of latex paint soaking into her clothes. She put an arm over her eyes against the bright glare of the sun. Oh dear God . . . What—Why—Why was everything so damned hard? Who had she offended, what evil deeds had she committed, that kept sending bad luck to her by the carload? Tears ran over her temples into her ears. Yes, she had regrets, she wasn't perfect, and she'd made some bad decisions, but how long would she have to pay for the past? Did that past warrant ongoing punishment?

"Julianne?"

Apparently, it did—she knew that voice. She yanked her arm away from her eyes to see Mitchell Tucker looking down at her from the side of the truck. The shotgun was in the rack inside the truck cab, so close, but too far. Hoisting herself to an upright position, she snapped, "Mitchell, what the *hell* do you want? Why is it so hard to understand that I don't want anything to do with you? Just leave me alone!" She could hear the tears squeezing her voice into a quaver, and her frustration increased. She didn't want him to sense her growing desperation.

He gazed at the lake of paint spreading ever wider across the dust and weeds. "You need help around here. You admitted it yourself when you posted that help-wanted notice. I want the job."

"I can't believe this. Are you insane? Did you not hear what I just told you—what I told you the last time you came around here? Besides, I've got help. He just isn't here right now."

He glanced around the yard, then let his eyes settle on her. "So it seems."

She scrambled to her feet on the tailgate and towered over him. "I asked you the other day why you came back. You said you wanted to settle something. What is it?" She reached into her front pocket and jimmied out her cell phone. "If you're going to try to kill me, I'll fight and bite and bash in your head with anything I can get my hands on. If you just want to talk, this is your chance to explain, so you'd better be fast, because I'm calling the police."

"Will you come down from there? It's like trying to talk to Godzilla," he said, squinting up at her.

She scowled and jabbed her passcode into the phone, even more inflamed when she saw the paint prints she left on the screen.

He put up a hand, as if to stop her. "No, Julianne, don't call the cops. I didn't mean it as an insult. It's just hard to see you against that bright sun."

She sat down on the edge of the truck box again and stared at him. "I'm waiting."

He glanced at the ground, then looked into her face. "I think you're in a jam. You need help and I can give you that. And I've had nothing to do with the troubles you've been having. You have to believe that."

"I don't have to believe anything you say, Mitchell. I told you, I have help. I can't pay two people. What do you really want?"

He dodged the blunt questions and shrugged. The midday sun caught a faint reddish glint in his dark hair. "Think of it as community service—after everything that happened. A couple of hours here and there, to help get you on your feet."

"Right. Mitchell, I just don't trust you."

A gulf of silence opened between them, and he jammed his hands into his pockets. In the distance the *teakettle-teakettle* call of a wren sounded. Finally, he said, "Yeah . . . yeah, I know." Then he turned to walk back to the side street where he'd left a clunker of a car, one that had been old when they'd been in high school. "Sorry to bother you—*Mrs. Emerson.*"

The barb, true and sure, found its target, and it stung. She had been the one who'd broken off their relationship, and even now, she could still see his stricken, furious expression when she'd told him she was marrying Wes. Why did she still feel guilty for that after all this time?

She looked at his retreating back, then at the spilled paint that seemed to have left no immediate surface untouched, and sighed heavily. A disgruntled noise escaped her, and she plucked at the clammy fabric of her shirt. It had been days since she'd first posted her ad around town, and not one suitable person had inquired about it. She'd had a twelve-year-old boy come around, and frail, old Grady Dunham, who had turned eighty last month, had expressed interest. Time was flying, but she was at a standstill. So far, Cade was no help, and there was no one else. As much as she might wish for it, she couldn't do this alone. The first bank payment would be due in less than forty-five days, and there was still so much to be accomplished before she could open for business.

Mitchell said this was his community service. For a single irrational moment she wondered what *she* could do to atone for her own guilt in the events that had led to that horrible night eight years earlier.

She stared at his back again. He gripped the door handle and was about to swing onto the ripped upholstery of the driver's seat, and good riddance—

"Mitchell, wait!" she called after him, amazed to hear the words come from her mouth.

He waited. She gestured him toward the yard.

When he walked back, his boot steps kicked up wisps of dust from the hardpan. Julianne couldn't see his eyes behind his sunglasses.

She drew a fortifying breath. "All right. I'll probably hate myself for this, but all right."

"All right, what?"

Briefly, Julianne pursed her lips. Oh, if he made this harder than it was already . . . She plunged on. "Yes, I can use your help."

His brows rose, and he took off the sunglasses. "Okay, then."

"Remember this, though, Mitchell. I swear on every family grave I have in the cemetery, if one thing—*one thing*—goes wrong or makes me uncomfortable, I'll have the county sheriff after you and the entire Tucker tribe."

He nodded. "If one thing goes wrong, I'll call Gunter myself. And I'm not going to tell anyone about this. It's probably best. Word will probably get out, but not from me." He'd never been good at hiding his thoughts from her. She let herself glimpse the sincerity in his eyes and hoped she was right.

She wouldn't be able to relax a minute as long as he was around. But he'd made a spot-on observation—she was in a jam. She looked at the paint, then at him, then at the building. She didn't hide the sigh of grim resignation in her voice. "When do you want to start?"

He gestured at the paint. "This looks like a good time."

Cade turned his sister's truck down the side street that ran next to Bickham's on a cool, gray morning. It looked like it might rain, but he knew better. The overcast would burn off by ten o'clock to reveal the hot blue sky above it. He spotted an old root-beer–brown Skylark parked next to Julianne's pickup. He'd never seen it around here before, and none of the people she'd had dealings with on the farm would drive something like this. He pulled up behind it and reached around the steering wheel to put the shift lever in park. He'd been trapped at home for three days, and life there had ground his nerves down to a pulp. He was a grown man; it was way past time for him to be out on his own. If only his parents didn't cling to him like burrs—

He got out and walked around to the back door, noticing the pale gray-brown splotch of spilled paint Julianne had told him about. She said she'd gotten the hardware store to make it right—huh. He wouldn't have wanted to be Mike Carver when she was finished with him. It made him smile just to imagine it.

Even though he'd checked in with her, she didn't know he would be here today. The idea of seeing her again also made him smile. He'd win her over yet. He just needed to make her realize how great they would be together. There was a powerful connection between them. He felt it as surely as he would feel that sun once the clouds melted away.

When he got to the top of the stairs, he picked up the scent of fresh paint and regretted not being able to help with it because of this stupid cast he was still wearing. But a wrong-armed painter would be as useless as a three-year-old with a brush, and she'd already had enough trouble with this chore. He turned the doorknob and walked through the back stockroom that also served as the office, then into the store. There was Julianne in a pair of white painter's coveralls and a baseball cap, taping off the last unpainted wall. He wouldn't have expected her to look cute dressed like that, but she did.

With all the shelving dismantled and moved out, the place looked and sounded cavernous. Plastic sheeting covered the floors. Then Cade saw a man, dressed the same way as she was, wielding a paint roller on an extension pole.

"Cade," Julianne said, looking up. "I wasn't expecting you today."

He tore his gaze away from the stranger. "Uh, yeah, I managed to get Carol's truck."

She walked over to him where he stood near the back curtains. "Be careful where you step. We've got wet paint in some places and on the drop cloths."

81

"It looks nice," he said, "really good." The man glanced at him but kept on with his job. "Did you hire a painter?"

She put the roll of blue tape on her wrist like a bracelet. "No, but you know I mentioned I'd have to hire someone to help with the heavy lifting since you're still out of commission." She gestured at his cast. "I do need you for that bookkeeping thing. I hope you can make more sense of it than I could."

Cade dropped his voice. "Who is this guy?"

She fidgeted with the tape roll and brushed off her T-shirt sleeves. "He's someone I used to know. He needed the work so . . ."

"Yeah, so?" he prodded.

She smiled. "So far, so good."

"And?"

"And what?"

"What's his name? Maybe I should call him something besides 'hey you.'"

Julianne groaned inside and had to stop herself from wringing her hands. It was silly, but she'd worried about how Cade would take this. The only way to avoid conflict would be to send him home, and that wasn't an option. "It's Mitchell."

His eyes opened so wide she expected them to pop out of his head like cold duck corks. "Mitchell Tucker—the man who made you a widow?"

"Shhhh!" She dragged him into the back room. "Yes!" she whispered.

"Why bother shushing me? He knows what he did. Isn't he the same one who's been giving you trouble since he came back to town? At least that's what you told me. Have you taken leave of your senses, woman?"

She straightened her back, something she tended to do when pushed far enough. Everyone at Carver Hardware had seen her rigid posture when she'd gone in to settle the paint problem. "He said he isn't responsible for the vandalism."

"And you trust him."

"No, I don't." But she'd allowed desperation to draw a filmy veil over every screaming objection her rational mind tossed at her. She knew she might have made an extremely foolish decision. If she was wrong about Mitchell, she'd find out. She'd kept her distance from him as they worked on the painting, and there had been no easy chitchat between them.

Cade gave her a brief look that suggested she might be the dumbest person on the planet. "If he's not behind the harassment, who is it?"

Julianne frowned. She resented his badgering. "I don't know. Cade, this is really more my business than yours. I can understand your curiosity, but I don't owe you a detailed explanation for my actions."

Color filled Cade's face, and he looked at the floor. "I just worry about you is all."

"I appreciate that, but it's not your job. Trust me, I worry enough about me for both of us. And my chief concern is getting this place ready to open for business as fast as possible. It has to look better and completely different than plain old Bickham's did. I need display shelves rebuilt and furniture moved around. And I needed someone who could help with that since you can't. I have loan payments to make." She knew it sounded as if she were blaming Cade for breaking his arm, but he couldn't help with the labor. And she couldn't wait until the cast came off and he shuffled through physical therapy.

At that moment, Mitchell appeared in the doorway. "Sorry to interrupt your whispering about me back here, but, Julianne, I have a question."

She winced before facing him, embarrassed over being caught. "Yes, Mitchell, what is it?"

"The trim around the doors and windows—do you want it painted white or the gray?"

"It's taupe."

"Yeah, okay, taupe. Which do you want?"

Cade looked away, and Julianne felt herself flush. She sidestepped the obvious and said, "Mitchell, this is Cade Lindgren. He used to work for me out at the farm." There were muttered acknowledgments between the two men. Mitchell glanced at Cade's cast and gave him a dismissive once-over. The tension among them felt so tangible, so volatile, that if any of them had lit a match there might have been an explosion. "Let's go with white for the trim," she continued.

He nodded. "I think I can finish up here by tomorrow if you do the taping."

"That would be great. I need to get this business going."

Mitchell ducked out again, and she turned to Cade. "I really could use your help with the accounting. You did offer that."

"Right," he said with an uncomfortable chuckle. "Show me what you're working with."

Julianne got him set up in the back room on her computer, along with Uncle Joe's cryptic record books, and gave him a cream soda from the apartment-size beer refrigerator she'd brought with her from the house. "Are you familiar with this software?" she asked, gesturing at the monitor. "I've used it for a while and I didn't see a reason to buy something else right now. I think it will work for us, if we can just get Joe's stuff unraveled."

He looked at the monitor and moved the mouse to the left side of the keyboard. "Yeah, this looks pretty straightforward. But when you want to make a switch a year or two down the road, I'll be fine with that, too."

Plainly, he was thinking of this as a permanent arrangement. She tapped the stack of ledgers and said, "Let's just get through the next week or two."

"Pull up a chair so we can go over these, then." He pushed aside the soda can and made room for her.

Exasperation threatened to make her snappy. "No, you just do the best you can. I'll be out front taping off the trim if you need anything," she said, relieved to get away from him.

She found Mitchell where he should be, rolling paint on the walls. It helped that he'd convinced her to buy a power-pump system. It attached directly to the paint can, so he was able to get a lot more done without having to refill trays—which always got dumped over, in her experience—or reload the roller.

They were all making real progress, it seemed to her, until Cade started interrupting her for every little dot and dash he came across. Initially, she believed he was having as much trouble as she'd had, which wasn't very comforting. But then she began to suspect he was only looking for reasons to drag her into the office and away from Mitchell. At first he didn't bother to get up—he just called loudly enough for her to hear him. When she began to ignore him, he came out to survey the redecorating process and to ask other questions.

After nearly ten such episodes, she tossed the roll of tape on the floor and went to the back, motioning for him to follow. "What's the problem, Cade?" She had trouble keeping the exasperation out of her voice.

He pointed at an item that straddled both the deposit and deduction columns of a check register he held. "Oh—what do you suppose he meant by this?"

"It looks like a phone number to me. Uncle Joe was kind of bad about making notes on whatever was handy." She pointed to Uncle Joe's doodle-covered wall.

"Right. I see that now."

She heard Mitchell's footsteps. "Julianne, I guess I'll take off for the day. I've gotten as far as I can until you finish your part. I left the overalls hanging on the hook in the bathroom over there again, if that's okay." He'd changed back into his jeans and T-shirt.

"All right, thanks. It'll be done before you get here tomorrow."

"See you later, Lindgren."

Cade turned. "Uh, yeah. Later."

After Mitchell's footsteps died away on the gravel and they heard his car door slam, Cade said, "He's coming back *tomorrow*?"

Julianne heaved a sigh and leaned a hip against a case of paper towels. "I don't like this, Cade. I don't like the way you're acting. If this arrangement is going to be a problem for you, or"—she nodded at the computer—"if you're not comfortable with doing the work you offered to do, you'd better tell me now."

His eyes widened briefly. "No, no, I'm fine with everything." He rubbed his free hand across his hair. "Well, I admit that finding Tucker here was a ripe surprise. After all, you've been pretty outspoken about what you think of him."

"Yes, I know. I never expected this myself. In fact, it's the last thing I would have imagined doing."

"He looks pretty low-end, especially with those scars covering his arms. Who knows what trouble he got into in prison to earn those?"

She stiffened again. "They're burn scars. He got them when he carried Wes out of the barn the night of the fire."

"Oh . . . well . . ." He took her hand in his and interlaced their fingers loosely. "Look, I know you're a little shy about your feelings for me, but I've had a lot of time to think about this. We'd be so great together, you and me."

"No, really, Cade—"

"Just hear me out, Julianne."

She looked at his earnest eyes and waited.

"You've been alone for a long time. I have, too. I haven't come right out and said so, but I've imagined you as my wife so many times, I can even see you waiting at the altar for me with our friends lining both sides of the aisle. I believe you care about me, and I'm crazy about you."

She tried to pull her hand out of his, but he tightened his grip on her fingers. "Cade—"

"Now, now, don't get nervous . . . please, just listen for a minute. You can't make me believe you're happy with your lot, facing the world by yourself, struggling with burdens that would be easier to bear with another set of shoulders. And kids? What about having kids?"

Julianne sighed. Everything Cade said was true. She *was* lonely; she missed knowing that someone would care whether she came home or not, missed the sound of familiar footsteps, of sharing a life. The true intimacy of body and spirit—well, that was something she hadn't known, even with Wes. Maybe it was just a happy fantasy poets and songwriters talked about, moonlight and champagne, the tooth fairy and rose petals. Once, a long time ago, it had seemed real . . .

"Julianne, marry me. I can give you all that."

Startled out of her ruminations, she said, "Marriage! Oh, Cade, no, no. I'm not the woman you want for that."

"Yes, you are. I promise if you're my wife, I'll do my very best to make you happy and give you everything you've been missing. Don't say no. Just think about it. Please?"

He kissed her then, as if to emphasize his promise. It felt weird. He smelled of cream soda and some cologne she didn't recognize. It wasn't the sort of experience that kept a woman awake at night, with her imagination running free and her lips still swollen from kisses that were all the sweeter and more exciting because they were so forbidden. She hadn't liked it much the first time, and this kiss was no different. If anything, it was just strange.

She pulled back. "Cade, I think you're a great guy and we're friends—"

"Being friends is important—of course we're friends."

She couldn't argue with that, exactly. "Don't go around assuming that we're engaged, because we are *not*."

He grinned. "Right."

Yanking her hand of out his, she stressed, "I mean it, Cade! We're friends, but I won't let you push me or try to tell me what to do. If you do, I'll manage to figure out the books myself, you can go back to working at your parents' place, and even our friendship will be over."

His smile dimmed by a few hundred watts. "Okay."

CHAPTER SIX

"Boy, where are you off to these days? Did you find another job after that Boyce female got you fired from Benavente's?" Mitchell was headed out the door with Knucklehead fast on his heels when Earl stopped him.

The Tucker patriarch surveyed his kingdom and his son from the seventies-era plaid, Herculon-covered recliner. He'd varied his dark-blue Dickies wardrobe with an old T-shirt that read MUSTACHE RIDES 25¢.

Mitchell had known his absence would come up sooner or later. Later would have been better. "I'm just out doing this and that."

The old man frowned. "Sounds like Darcy. 'This and that' usually amounts to a whole lotta nothing. You can't expect James to pick up all the bills around here. That air conditioner"—he nodded at the one in the living room window—"is gasping for breath like a rented mule. I want to see a new one in its place."

Mitchell's irritation began to grow. "You talk to the other boys about that. I pitch in, and you know it. I brought home seventy-five bucks' worth of groceries the other day. All Darcy buys is beer."

"If you aren't working, where's the money coming from?"

"I didn't say I'm not working; you did." He had cash that he'd stowed away to see himself through this, but his new job in Alpine helped, too. "Anyway, aren't you still getting money from your disability scam?"

"Yeah, but it's not my job to take care of y'all anymore."

Mitch resisted the great temptation to remind Earl that he never had taken care of them, mostly because he didn't have the time or energy for the old man's argument that would follow. Besides, it wouldn't change anything. If he was going to live here for a while, he knew it would be best to keep friction to a minimum. That didn't change history, though.

After their mother had left, Mitchell had to do some fast talking to keep them out of state custody. That and having a frazzled, overburdened caseworker had done the trick. He'd convinced her that he'd be responsible for all of them, but a little financial assistance would be ever so helpful, ma'am. They hadn't had much, but it seemed to Mitch that keeping them together would be better for them in the long run than letting the system split them up and send them off to one foster home after another. Earl had come back just often enough to prove that he was around now and then.

"Are you wanting for anything?" A sharp glare and the edge in his voice managed to shut off further complaint, Mitch hoped.

"You taking the dog with you?"

"Yeah. Any objections?"

Earl waved off the idea and made a big show of searching for the TV remote control. "Hell no. I don't need that flea bag around here eating us out of house and home all day. You go on. I got Andy Griffith to watch."

Mitch clenched his back teeth and reached down to pull Knucklehead against his knee. "I feed him, Earl. I buy his food and his flea stuff. We'll see you later."

He had to get out before his resentment got a good fire burning under it. He slammed the door behind him and put Knucklehead in the Skylark. The dog immediately bounced into the driver's seat. "Move over. It's not your turn to drive." The A/C worked only when it felt like it—not today—so he powered down the windows, and his companion was happy to ride shotgun with his head hanging out in the breeze, even if he liked to see out both sides of the car. Mitchell was pleased to see that with some decent food and care, the dog was filling out. His ribs were far less noticeable, and his ratty coat, after falling out in big tufts like a shedding buffalo's, was now growing in thick and shiny.

Inheriting Knucklehead was just a lucky break. Mitch felt closer to him than to any of his family. The animal was always glad to see him. This was the first time he was taking him along to Julianne's. She was jumpy around him, and it was plain that she talked to him only when she had to. He hoped Knucklehead would settle her down a bit.

He drove along the dusty road that would eventually lead to one of Gila Rock's paved streets, leaving a cloud of powder-fine caliche in his wake. An occasional lizard darted out from the clumps of grass alongside the trail, but there were no other cars down here. Across the dry arroyo, heat waves shimmered in the distance.

As for Cade Lindgren, after the first day he had met Mitchell, he'd hung around Bickham's like a persistent yellow jacket at a picnic. Anytime Mitch tried to talk to Julianne about the work that needed doing, Lindgren would buzz in and out, either to eavesdrop or to just butt in. Annoyance made him long for a rolled-up newspaper or a flyswatter. He didn't think Julianne was too happy about it, either, but she hadn't put a stop to it.

When he got to her place, he was relieved to see that Lindgren's truck wasn't there. Whether that meant he was just on an errand or not coming at all, he didn't know. At least he'd have some peace for a while.

But coming around to the back door, he stopped in his tracks. All the power lines coming into the building had been cut. The long, severed lines danced and popped on the ground. He grabbed Knucklehead's collar to keep the dog from investigating, and stepped around them. The short ones on the now-powerless store looked like they'd been neatly snipped with bolt cutters.

He climbed the steps and tried the doorknob, but it was locked. Since the bell wasn't going to work, either, he rapped on the door. "Hey, Julianne! Are you in there?"

He heard nothing, and knocked again. "Julianne, it's Mitch! Are you okay? Open the door."

At last he felt her footsteps vibrate across the floor inside. "You should know I have a shotgun pointed at you, Mitchell Tucker." Through the door he heard the muffled sound of the pump action.

Still gripping the dog's collar, he automatically moved to the side. "I'm not going to hurt you. Are you all right?" he repeated.

"No, I'm not. I'm sitting in a building with no electricity or telephone, as if you didn't know."

His sigh was impatient. "I *didn't* know. I just saw it now. Did you call the power company? Did you call the sheriff's department? Julianne, please open the door."

"What do you know about this, Mitchell?"

"I don't know anything, probably less than you do, for God's sake! I sure as hell would like to, though." Who was harassing her? How far would it go? And why? He understood why she was suspicious of him, given their past, but he had suspicions of his own.

A moment of long silence followed. He didn't know whether she was fine-tuning her blind aim or whether she was going to answer at all. At last the door opened no more than two inches, and he saw the muzzle of her shotgun and a section of her face above it.

"Where's Lindgren? I thought he was your guard dog."

"I knew he wasn't coming in. He couldn't get his sister's truck today."

Despite the grim situation, Mitch chuckled and shook his head. It was so ridiculous he couldn't help himself. The little man had to stay home because he didn't have a ride. "Look, Julianne, I don't know who did this, but it wasn't me. Do you believe me?"

Julianne gritted her teeth. On her side of the door, exasperation and the stuffy heat of the building pressed in on her.

Did she believe him.

She peered at Mitchell, the man who'd burned her husband alive in their barn, and she struggled with doubt. He had said he'd never lied to her, and when she thought back to their early days, she knew it was true. But now? What a clever ruse it could all be. He'd come to perform "community service" by helping her for no pay. Yet that gave him easy access to her, the opportunity to come and go around here, and to lull her into trusting him. She hadn't spoken much to him while they'd worked together—she wasn't all that nervous around him. But she didn't want to give him the impression that they were friends again. Maybe Cade was right. Maybe she'd made a foolish decision to let him get this close. *Did* she believe him? "I don't know."

"Will you at least open the door a little wider? You can blow my brains out if you decide I'm guilty—you've got the shotgun." Hesitating, she finally opened the door and saw that he had a real dog with him. When she looked at the shepherd mix, he gave her a wide doggy smile, and his tongue lolled out.

Mitchell nodded at her Remington. "No offense, but I'm getting kind of tired of having that thing pointed at me." The dog sat beside him and continued to smile up at her.

"Get used to it because no one is exempt."

Absently, he rubbed at a scar on his right arm. "It's not the best way to live—on the defensive all the time."

"Yes, I know, but I'm not sure who my enemies are. That's not a good feeling, either."

He considered her and released a breath. "Yeah. I can understand that. Do you want to let me in so we can get this straightened out? If you really think you need to call the sheriff on me, well, get him on your cell phone."

"*Tsk.*" She stood aside to let him and the dog come in.

The fresh-paint smell was still faintly detectable, although Julianne had bought low-VOC paint to guard against volatile fumes. It would be worse if she hadn't.

"Wow, it's hot in here."

The plastic drop cloths had all been removed, and the empty space was ready for shelving. Between her loss of security and her worries about turning the store into a going concern, her stress level had climbed into the red zone.

She put down the weapon and pulled her hair into a ponytail. "Of course it is. The air-conditioning runs on electricity," she said, more sharply than she'd meant to. "I can't even turn on a fan. This has been a horrible morning."

She explained that she didn't know the power was out until she woke up and realized that her clock radio hadn't gone off. "The sun was way too high, and it was getting stuffy in here. I didn't think I should open the windows upstairs—that would only make it hotter up there. And down here, alone, I didn't want to leave the doors open." She glanced at the dog. "Who's this?"

He reached down and scratched the animal's ear. "Knucklehead. He was hanging around the mobile home when I got there, but no one was taking care of him, and I think Darcy was kicking him around some. Since I have to share my bed with a dog, I thought I'd better look out for him."

"Knucklehead. That's an insulting name. It's demeaning. He looks more like—like a Jack." She held out the back of her hand to him, and he sniffed her whole arm.

"*Jack?* He's a dog."

"It works. If he were mine, that's what I'd name him. Is he a good watchdog?"

"As good as any, I suppose."

She rubbed Knucklehead's soft fur and smiled. "I've thought about getting a dog since this trouble started."

"You've already got Lindgren."

She gave him a sour look. "Mitchell, that isn't even close to funny."

"Yeah, I know. He watches every move I make and tries to order me around. But, really, he's your PITA, not mine."

"Pita?"

"Pain in the ass."

She straightened her shoulders. "Cade has worked for me for a long time. I can trust *him*. He knows what I've been through."

He didn't have a quick, smart-ass answer for that, she noted. After a beat, he replied in a winter-dry voice, "I don't think the last ten years have been good for any of us."

It crossed her mind to ask, *Whose fault was that?* But it wasn't so simple. She'd played a part in it, too. Her fault. Mitchell's fault. All the things done wrong. Changing the subject, she said, "The power company is coming to turn off the juice to the live wires, but I had to call an electrician to get the building hooked up again. Another expense I don't need."

"I'd bet you didn't get coffee or anything to eat yet," he said.

"No."

"All right. I'll go pick up breakfast for you."

"Really, you don't have to do that. I can make a peanut butter sandwich—"

He went on over her feeble protest. "I'll leave Knucklehead with you. He's a good dog—it might make you feel better to have him around. When I get back, we can start putting some of the displays together. We don't need power tools for all of them, and anyway, there might be a little life left in the cordless ones."

After years of looking out for herself and having to direct others, it was so tempting to lower her defenses against someone who said all the right things. Tempting, but dangerous and out of the question.

He was out the door, and she found herself making friends with a dog who was still smiling at her. She crouched down beside him and studied him. "Yeah, you're a 'Jack.'"

Mitchell walked into Do-Nut Delite to order something for Julianne. The pink-and-white walls with black trim suited the aromas of eggs, yeast, sugar, and fresh coffee that filled the place. Though they sold only coffee, doughnuts, and—in a radical update—bagels the rest of the day, in the mornings they also served breakfast. He placed a double take-out order of ham and eggs for Julianne and himself, then sat with a cup of coffee at an empty table to wait for it. He scanned the pages of a *USA Today* while people came and went, an electronic *ding-dong* sounding every time someone opened the door.

The little place did a pretty brisk business, and eventually the constant *ding-dong* worked its way into his head. Since he couldn't tune it out, he turned his attention to the Texas Rangers' early-season stats in the sports section until the bell rang again.

"Well, look who washed up on the bank. Mitch Tucker."

He looked up. Oh hell. "Hey, Cherry. Here for breakfast?"

She wore a variation of her usual clothes: tight jeans and a snug, sparkly white top that showed off her cleavage, and high-heeled sandals to display her red-painted toes. Looking at her was like staring into the face of a blazing noon sun that could melt a person's eyes. "No, I finally convinced Ernie to upgrade some of the crap we sell at the Captain Gas. So we get our doughnuts from here now. But Gila Rock is in luck—we still have day-old hot dogs and fossilized bubblegum."

She pulled out the chair across from him and sat. "I thought I'd hear from you again long before this. You pretty much left me hanging in Lupe's parking lot."

He ran a hand across the back of his neck and concocted a lie on the spot. Just because he wasn't a liar didn't mean he couldn't if he needed to. "Yeah, I'm really sorry about that. I was in the john when I got a call from an old friend. Like I said that night, I had to split right away. I'll make it up to you." He didn't expect to do that, nor did he think she'd wait for the day. In fact, he had the feeling she would go on hounding him until she had him lassoed to her bed in four-point restraints, even if she had to find a way to get him there herself.

"When?" She leaned forward, almost purring like a mountain lion, and he felt cornered. "It's Friday; let's plan something for tonight. I get off at three. Maybe we could drive over to Marfa for dinner at that fancy-ass place in the hotel, Jett's Grill, and then . . ." She waggled brows at him, suggesting just about everything under the blue yonder.

"It sounds great, Cherry, but not tonight. I'm working." The lies were mounting.

She sat back, purr off. "Working—at what? I didn't think you'd had anything to do since Benavente canned you."

"I'm busy with odd jobs around hereabouts." He was getting pretty damned tired of people asking about this. He wasn't going to tell her about helping Julianne, and no one knew about his part-time job in Alpine. It had to stay that way.

"At *night*?" she demanded.

"Yep, tonight anyway. Sorry."

"Look, Mitchell, if you don't want—"

"Cherry, here are your doughnuts, honey," a woman called from behind the counter. She held two big pink boxes.

Cherry got up and took them. "Thanks, LaDeen. Send the bill to Ernie at the store, as usual." She turned back to Mitchell and looked him up and down. "I'll catch you out one of these times, darlin'. Darcy told me all about you." She smiled when she said it, but her tone implied something dark.

He took a sip of the coffee he'd ordered before he sat down, mostly to hide his sense of unease. "I wouldn't put too much stock in what he says. He loves the sound of his own voice almost as much as he does cheap beer."

"Hmm, I think he's right this time. You just don't know it yet. See you later." She winked at him and walked out, making the bell ring.

Mitchell drew a deep breath. What the hell did that mean? Darcy was *right*—his brother was rarely right about much of anything. What did he know? That Mitch was in touch with Julianne? He needed to settle this business between Julianne and him, and be gone.

Just then, LaDeen, the counter girl, brought out his order in a big white paper bag. "Careful of the coffees. They're hot."

"Thanks." He gave her a dollar tip and headed out the door.

"What's the good word, Cherry?" Darcy lazed beside Cherry in her bed, thin bands of sunlight coming through the slats of the partly closed blinds. He blew smoke rings, trying to aim them at the ceiling fan to see if he could encircle the center of it. But the wall-mounted air-conditioning unit sent them flying to the other side of the room. Cherry held the ashtray on her belly.

Where the sun hadn't freckled and baked her like a dried apple, she had a redhead's skin—cream-colored and unmarked, except for the tattoos, one of butterflies on her butt cheek and another of one of those horses with a single horn on its forehead, near her hipbone. "What the hell is the deal with that horse, anyway?" He poked at it.

She craned her neck to look down at the tat. "It's a unicorn. They're magic."

"They aren't real." He lifted his arm to show off the viper on it. "At least a snake is real. If I had to go around all the time with a thing like that sticking out on me, I'd be cross-eyed."

She lifted the sheet and glanced at his deflated dick. "I wouldn't worry. It hasn't happened yet," she observed.

He frowned and tapped his cigarette on the edge of the ashtray. "You're a smart-mouthed female, y'know that?"

"Yeah, I know. It's one of the reasons you like me."

His laugh was smoke-rough and eroded into a cough. "Could be."

"These things are gonna kill you." She plucked the cigarette away from him and took a long pull.

"Not me. Bullets bounce off me."

"Uh-huh. I saw Mitchell at Do-Nut Delite this morning. I was picking up stuff for the Captain Gas, and he was there sitting at a table."

"That's not exactly a news flash," Darcy replied.

"It might be. I left first, but I was still sitting in my car when I saw him come out with a big to-go order. I got curious, so I tailed him. I stayed back far enough so he wouldn't see me."

"Yeah?"

"He went to Bickham's."

He propped himself on his elbow and stared at her, now alert. "Bickham's! You mean the dime store?"

"Yep."

"I'll be damned." This *was* a news flash. "What's he doing there?"

She gave him that flat, dry look that could wither a man with less juice. "Since I left my X-ray vision glasses on the kitchen counter, I wouldn't know. But he carried that order inside."

"He's gone a lot, but he's been pretty tight-lipped about what he does with his time. We can't get him to come out partying with us, or do any of the stuff we did in the old days." He flopped to his back again and sucked down another lungful of smoke while he pondered the problem. "Jesus, I wonder if he's working there. I saw that flyer the Boyce bitch plastered all over town. Naw, he wouldn't do that. It would go against everything the old man taught us, everything Mitch went to jail for."

"Maybe you should go ask him yourself."

"Not there. I'll have to catch him at home. We've pulled a few pranks on Julianne that weren't really anonymous. I'm sure she knows we did it."

"What else have you done?"

He wasn't about to tell all, not even to Cherry. "Just a dumb-kid stunt—burning dog-shit bags. Nobody got hurt."

A whoop of laughter exploded from Cherry. "Really? *Really?* That's the best you could come up with?"

"It was good enough to get her to call Gunter. He rolled by the trailer that afternoon and wanted to know what the hell we were thinking. Naturally, we denied everything. But he lit a pretty hot fire under Earl. I haven't seen the old man that wound up in years. Gunter threatened to put him in the back of the patrol car unless he went inside to his recliner."

"Gunter blamed your dad? He can hardly walk."

"He blamed all of us, but Mitch wasn't there when Gunter stopped. He's trying to lay low after that seven-year hitch with the state prison. It was almost like he knew Gunter was coming." A gap of silence opened, and he slid his gaze to Cherry's. It was as if they both considered the same possibility at the same moment.

"You don't think—"

Darcy studied the ceiling. "He's changed a lot, but . . . *pfffft*, no, he wouldn't do that. Mitch is blood, by God, he's a *Tucker*. He might not be the same fun hell-raiser he used to be, but he can't have changed so much that he'd turn against us and in favor of her." He ground out the cigarette in the ashtray. "He just can't have."

With the power restored, Julianne and Mitchell spent time organizing stock and working on a display for the front windows. She wanted something attractive and welcoming, not just a pile of sun-faded junk like Uncle Joe had put there, then forgotten. She also wanted window boxes on the outside, planted with red geraniums. Cade finally had gotten his cast removed, but the doctor had told him he still couldn't do any heavy lifting. So he remained at his post on the computer, and he was there every day now. Because he had to commute from Cuervo Blanco, he'd again hinted broadly about sleeping on a cot in the storeroom. She'd ignored it—that was at the bottom of the list of last things she needed.

One morning, Julianne stood looking at the front part of the store. Mitchell had just walked in carrying a Do-Nut Delite coffee cup. "I don't think paint really helped this old, crummy window-display shelf," Julianne commented. "I'd like to build a new one."

Mitchell reached for the tape measure on his belt. "I can do that. Hold the end of this tape."

When she reached for it their hands brushed, and she flinched. "Sorry."

He took her fingers and closed them around the yellow metal measure. "No cooties, okay?"

She felt a hot blush work its way up her neck, and she looked up into his face. Still attractive, damn him, and worse, she felt as tongue-tied as a girl. "Well—no, I didn't—let's just—"

"Hold it to the edge of the old shelf and read the numbers to me," he instructed, so she did. She studied him as he wrote down the dimensions on a piece of scrap paper he'd pulled from his pocket and saw lines fanning from the outer corners of his eyes that hadn't been there before. The scars on his arms had faded over time, but burn scars never went away. Her memory pulled up a scene from that horrible night—that horrible *sight*—Mitchell carrying Wes, both of them burned, smoke rising from them, a ghastly, indescribable smell overlaid with the odors of whiskey and gasoline. That event had been the culmination of years of half-truths and desperate secrets, exalted, heartbreaking romance, and lives forever changed.

Mitchell was two years older than she, and she remembered sitting in the bleachers at the high school, watching him play baseball. She'd also heard talk about the "wild Tucker boys," and not just at home. Their mother had taken off, and even though Earl Tucker came home once in a while, most kids knew that they were pretty much raising themselves. Julianne had been just a nobody-freshman and hadn't realized he'd even noticed her.

But he had. And so it began . . .

100

"You want a shelf just like this, right?" he asked, looking up suddenly.

Yanked back into the moment, she felt foolish, getting caught staring at him. "Uh, yes, yes, I like that shape and the height."

"Okay, now put the tape blade here." He guided her hands to the end of the shelf, and she read those numbers to him as well.

He took back the tape and hooked it to his belt. "I'll head over to Carver's for the plywood. What about the window boxes?"

"I guess we might as well measure for those, too," she said. They started to head out the front door.

"Julianne? Could I get your help here?" She glanced toward the back-room curtains and saw Cade standing there, watching. For how long, she didn't know.

"Go on," Mitchell said, "I can manage this." He took the tape from her and went outside.

"All right." She headed to Cade with an odd, guilty feeling of having been seen doing something wrong. "What's up?"

He inclined his head toward the front. "Was he bothering you? It looked like it."

"No, nothing like that. If he were, he'd know it and so would you. So far, it's working out."

"Considering how much trouble you've been having with vandalism and those other problems, I can't understand why he's even here. It's an open invitation."

She sighed and tucked a loose strand of hair behind her ear, then crossed her arms over her chest. "I can see why you'd think so."

"But you don't think so."

"I don't think it's Mitchell. It would be so obvious. We've talked about this already, Cade, and believe me, my antenna is up. He already knows that I've got the sheriff's department on speed dial."

"The doc said I'll be back up to snuff in a couple of weeks. Then you can send him packing."

"Uh-huh, great." She didn't sound convincing, even to her own ears.

"You said that's why he's here," he continued. "Because I was stove-up with this busted wing and you needed the help." The newly healed arm looked thin and pale compared to his other one.

"Yes—right. So you didn't really have a question when you came out here?"

"No. I was helping you get out of a tight situation."

Julianne was beginning to feel suffocated. "Okay, then we've all got work to do."

While Mitchell worked outside, he looked at the condition of the casement and pictured what would look good for window boxes. Julianne might be better off going with planters resting on the pavement pushed up against the wall below. There was no real way to gauge the soundness of the windowsill, considering how old this building was. Window boxes, heavy with soil and water, might not hold. He had no idea what a geranium was, but he could imagine plants lined up under the window. It would be a nice touch.

In the store, that Lindgren was hassling Julianne again. He was always around. He half expected the guy to pee around the perimeter of the store to mark his territory like a dog. Mitchell wanted to tell him that he had nothing to worry about, that he had no romantic intentions toward Julianne. But it would be a lie. His feelings for her had coming roaring back to life—well, if he were going to be honest with himself, they'd been there all along. He'd managed to push them to the back of his mind and a quiet, secret corner of his soul. Time had ripened the girl he'd known into a full-grown, mature woman, more beautiful and interesting than he'd envisioned her during those long, dark years in prison.

Behind him, he heard the clunking sputter of an engine with a bad timing belt. He glanced over his shoulder and saw Darcy behind the wheel of one of his junkers, a sorry-looking Ford. James was in the passenger seat. Both of them wore angry, disapproving scowls. They cruised by slowly, giving him the evil eye.

"Hey, *brother*, you're busted, man!" Darcy yelled, then hit the gas. The car's tires squealed on the pavement, leaving a blue cloud of exhaust and burning rubber.

Oh man. He'd known it would happen—the family would find out about this one way or another. He'd hoped for more time, but he wasn't going to get that kind of break.

Julianne stepped outside in time to see the back end of the Escort fishtail around the corner.

"What was that?" she asked.

He felt the burden of fate resettle itself on his shoulders, digging in and getting comfortable for a long ride, as he gazed at the dissipating cloud. "Nothing."

In truth, he knew it was hell coming to kick his ass again.

"I just came back to get my stuff," Mitch said to the three angry faces that greeted him at the trailer.

"Gonna go shack up with *her*?" Earl sneered, his rocker-recliner moving at top speed, an indicator of his fury.

"Nope, I'm just moving out."

"I can't believe it. You turned against your own flesh and blood," James complained bitterly.

Knucklehead, obviously mirroring all the negativity, joined in. Four male voices, yelling at the same time, along with the barking dog, stirred up a high-volume din that made Mitchell remember the bad old days of his youth. Darcy, swearing at the dog, planted a foot in the animal's ribs that sent him across the room, squeezing a yelp out him.

Mitchell turned on Darcy, grabbing him by his shirtfront and pulling him up close, filled with an icy fury at his brother that he'd always felt in his gut. Darcy was a mean, sneaky bastard with a talent for spotting those weaker than himself. "You *ever* touch that dog again, I'll tie you down and let him eat your balls for breakfast." His fist still wound in the shirt, he roared, *"Everyone shut up!"*

They all looked him, caught off guard.

"Now you listen to me! I've never known what caused that feud between the Boyces and the Tuckers, only that I was supposed to defend everyone against it. Well, I'm goddamned sick to death of it. The one time I asked you about it, Earl, you gave me a whack that threw me halfway across the room. But *I* went to prison for burning down Wes Emerson's barn, not any of you, even though James and Darcy were with me that night. *I* served seven years for manslaughter, not any of you." He caught both of them in his sights. "No one ever knew you two were with me. I took the full blame because you were young and I didn't want your lives ruined, too, although it doesn't look like I saved y'all for much good." He looked around at the tobacco-stained walls and ruptured, dirty furniture. "If I want to look at it from your viewpoint, I'm the one with the biggest bitch against the Boyces, but I'm tired of dragging it around like a dead tree branch stuck in my undercarriage. I don't care anymore. I'm over it!"

He paused to take a ragged breath. He released Darcy with a shove. "I came back to Gila Rock to do one thing. And when it's done, I'm leaving again. I don't belong here. This is not the way I want to live the rest of my life, fighting a battle that you probably started, old man." He stared at Earl. "Fighting a ghost, always looking backward and never to the future."

The three men gave him surprised but bitter looks.

He called the dog with a short, sharp whistle, and Knucklehead regained his feet and followed him to the back bedroom. He jammed his few belongings into his duffel bag and grabbed the dog's food. Before he left, he reached into his pocket and pulled out a fifty-dollar bill that he wadded up with one hand and threw at Darcy's feet. "For the crappy Skylark. I hope it isn't stolen." Then he was out the front door, Knucklehead next to his knee, letting the screenless screen door flap in the breeze. Just before he started the engine, he heard the shouting begin again among them and was glad to be out of it.

CHAPTER SEVEN

Julianne rolled over and stared at the dark ceiling above her bed. The window was open, but at this hour, everything outside was quiet. For now. She glanced at the clock, and the dim, green digital numbers read 2:37 a.m.

Even when she worked herself to the point of utter exhaustion, Julianne's nightmares about Wes still invaded her sleep. But sometimes, like tonight . . . oh, sometimes when she lay between the two worlds of sleep and wakefulness . . . dreams of Mitchell invaded her mind. Feverish dreams of the way his lips and hands had felt on her before Wes came into the picture. Worse, these dreams were even more vivid than those of her late husband. Maybe that wasn't surprising. She and Wes had been married only a few months. Her history with Mitchell went back much further.

She'd known she was supposed to regard him as an enemy—her father had told her over and over that the Tuckers were no damn good. His resentment had seemed to increase after her mother died suddenly from an aortic aneurysm. Julianne had carried the seeds of his bitterness in her heart, too; it was part of her family tradition, along with ham, not turkey, on Thanksgiving, attending every Fourth of July picnic in the town park, supporting Future Farmers of America and visiting family graves on each deceased's birthday. Every family had its quirks—hers included this grudge of unknown origin.

She remembered clearly the first sign that she'd caught Mitchell's attention. One spring evening just before dusk, she'd gone outside to collect the wash from the clotheslines. With her mother gone, all the housework had fallen to her by the time she was twelve. Against one of the clothesline posts, she'd discovered a bouquet of wildflowers tied with a long stalk of grass. She'd looked around but had seen no one in the sorghum fields beyond. When she picked up the flowers, she'd realized that a small square of paper had been jammed down among the blooms. It bore a couple of squiggly ink marks—*J from M*. Julianne had been truly baffled. At fifteen, she'd been shy and not very interesting to boys. There was no one around the farm with the initial *M*, not even among the hired hands. She'd brought in the laundry with the flowers but didn't mention them to her father, who kept a sharp eye on her activities.

At school, she considered and discarded possible admirers, eventually deciding that it must have been just some weird, random event. Then one day on her way to biology class with Melanie Sanchez and Kristin Gruelin, she found herself face-to-face with Mitchell Tucker in the hall. He was with a bunch of his rowdy friends, but he caught her gaze and held it until he passed. It was a straightforward look, not threatening, not rude or disdainful. But his scrutiny had made her squirm, and automatic, inborn resentment had flooded her while scalding her cheeks.

"Ooh!" Melanie piped up, grinning like a cat with a pint of heavy cream. Her glossy, blue-black hair nearly reached her waist. "Did you see how he looked at you?"

"Yeah, Juli! He's a *b-a-a-d* boy!" Kristin giggled, her braces gleaming briefly in a sunbeam that came through a window. "I didn't think you knew him."

"I don't!" she muttered, her face hotter still. She wrapped both arms around her books and hunched her shoulders.

"Hey, that's right—your family and the Tuckers have that grudge," Kristin added. "Oh, it could be like *Romeo and Juliet*. So romantic!"

"Shut up, both of you! I don't like him, he doesn't like me, and that's the way things are."

"If you don't know him, how can you know you don't like him?" Melanie pushed.

Losing her patience, Julianne hurried her pace and tried to lose the teasing girls, cursing Mitchell Tucker with every step for making her the object of major embarrassment. Where did he get off, that Tucker loser, thinking he could examine her that way, like—like a specimen on a microscope slide? After he'd blended into the rest of the students in the hall, she heard his laughter rise above other voices, and she'd thought of the brilliant retort: *Take a picture; it'll last longer.*

But the flowers at the clothesline appeared again three more times over the coming weeks, usually at that hour before dusk. Still, she told no one, and she didn't know why he was doing it. If it was him.

The mystery was solved one evening, when a fourth, straggly bunch of late-season flowers showed up. She looked around, not expecting to find anyone. Then she saw him and pulled in a startled breath. He was leaning against the big live oak beyond the barn. There was no mistake. She glanced back over her shoulder at the house, but no one was watching. She recognized his dark, curly hair and his usual T-shirt and jeans. There was nothing special about his clothes—lots of guys wore the same stuff—but on him they were different somehow. Better.

With another cautious scan of the windows, she picked up the flowers and darted toward the tree. When she got closer, she slowed. He just watched her, still leaning against the tree with his hands in his back pockets.

"Are you—you're the one who's been leaving these?"

He nodded. "I wondered if you'd figure it out."

She frowned. "What do you want? I'm not supposed to talk to you. You're gonna get me in a lot of trouble."

He shrugged. "You can go back anytime you want. I'm not keeping you."

"Why did you do this? *How* did you do it?"

"This is a good time of day. Not dark enough to make dogs bark, but easier for me to stay out of direct sight." He gave her a smile. "As for the *why*, I didn't think that would be hard to figure out."

"You could get into a lot of trouble, too. If my dad sees you here, he'll probably sic the farmhands on you and blast you full of shot."

"Only if he knows. Are you going to tell him?"

No, she had never told her father. Somehow they'd kept their secret for two years.

Julianne rolled to her side, trying to shut out the memories and quiet her busy mind. If she'd had the gift of foresight, if she'd known what would happen, so many things would have been different.

But she was faced with the here and now, and morning would come soon enough. In the darkness, she rummaged around in the drawer of her night table and found a bottle of over-the-counter allergy medicine she saved for times like this. It would make her drowsy enough to sleep for another four hours.

She hoped.

The next morning Julianne slapped the snooze button on her alarm twice before finally dragging herself out of bed. While the coffeemaker dripped, she pulled on her clothes, brushed her teeth, and ran a comb through her hair. She'd never been one for dressing up much, but she wanted to present a better image than jeans and a tank top—eventually. When the coffee finished brewing, she poured it into a vacuum pot and took it downstairs along with the shotgun, hoping to get a couple of hours to herself before Cade came in.

She flipped on a light switch, and the fluorescent tubes overhead sputtered to life. Her arms loaded with ledgers he'd already entered in the computer, she kicked aside an empty box to reach a back corner of the storeroom. She called this area The Tomb for the time being. All the strange, old junk she didn't know what to do with ended up here.

Cade. A thought of him buzzed around in her mind again like a fly bouncing against a window—not a flattering image, she knew. He hadn't pressed her for an answer to his proposal, but whenever she was around him he watched her with what seemed like alert expectation, as if that moment was *the* moment. *Now? No? Okay . . . now?* Every time she thought about marrying him, a little part of her cringed. That wasn't a good sign. But neither did she want to deal with a big scene right now. He would just try to convince her that everything would be great, and she wasn't so sure. She didn't want to lose his friendship. It was selfish, she supposed, but they had been friends before he'd gotten all swoony about her and messed things up.

Just as she emerged from The Tomb, she heard a knock on the back door. She glanced at the wall clock. It was only 7:15. Immediately on guard, she crept to the window and peeked around the edge of the curtain. She saw Mitchell.

Opening the door, she said, "What on earth are you doing here at this hour?"

He looked rumpled and haggard. The dog sat to his left, and a bag of dog food was on his right. "I'm glad you're up. I waited until I thought you would be."

Wary, she stood aside to let him in. "What's the matter?"

"Julianne, I need a favor."

Wishing she'd left him on the porch, she pulled back and gave him a suspicious look. So now they were coming to the real crux of the matter. She'd always had the distinct feeling that he was worming his way into her life for more than just "community service." "Favor?"

"Can you keep Knucklehead for me? I, uh, decided to move out of the trailer and I don't think I'll be able to find a place to live that will let me keep him. If I left him behind, Darcy would probably kill him." He walked over to the vacuum pot and poured coffee for himself.

"Dear God, kill him! Why?"

"Well, you know, Darcy's got a mean streak in him. I just don't want to live there anymore. It isn't working out and I need to do something different." She wasn't sure she was getting the whole story. "I spent the night in the car out here. I need to find a cheap apartment, but they won't usually let you keep dogs. Besides, I think it would be good for you to have him around."

"But—"

"Julianne, will you please take in Knucklehead? I brought his food."

She looked down at the dog, whose tail was thumping against the door as he smiled up at her, and her heart melted. That Darcy was a stupid man with a taste for cruelty. She wasn't surprised that he'd abuse animals, too. She'd like to kick him from here to the county line. "Yes, on one condition."

Mitchell rolled his eyes. "What?"

"I refuse to call him that dreadful name. He's Jack."

"Fine, fine," he replied, surrendering. "He's Jack. I'll be back after I find a place."

Over the next few days Julianne began receiving the inventory she wanted to add to the store, including a new cash register that networked with the computer. Mitchell returned. He'd found a rent-by-the-week motel room down the highway a mile or two, and they did allow dogs, but he didn't ask to take Jack with him. He said he thought it would be better for both her and the dog if he stayed here. She agreed. Having Jack around made her feel better, and it didn't take long for her to get attached to the happy mutt.

They were able to get the display shelving arranged the way she wanted it. Cade cleaned the Glass Wax off the front window, and she put a decorative **OPEN** sign in the corner. The terra cotta planter boxes lined up under the window, overflowing with red geraniums and white alyssum, really dressed things up.

She officially opened for business, although there was still work to do. Waiting any longer wasn't an option. A sign painter had repainted **BICKHAM'S** over the door, in an old-fashioned script she'd chosen that reminded her a lot of the Coca-Cola logo. Black-and-taupe-striped awnings had been installed the day before. At the back of the showroom, she and Cade replaced the ugly brown curtains with drapes that matched the awnings. Though still nervous about her situation, Julianne was proud of how things had turned out so far. She'd had the hardwood floors refinished, and they gleamed softly beneath all-new, fashionable lighting.

The local paper, the biweekly Gila Rock *Viewpoint*, sent someone around from its business section to take a photo and interview her. After the story appeared, she cut it out of the paper, framed it along with the first dollar bill she took in, and hung the picture behind the counter.

"I tell you what, this place sure looks a lot better than it did when your uncle had it." Mary Diller had stopped in one morning to look around. "You've made everything look wonderful, Julianne."

"I hope so. It's been a lot of hard work, but I wanted to stock nicer things than laxative and motor oil. I've got some gift items, too—a few porcelain teapots, handmade soaps, jewelry, bird feeders—things like that." She pointed to the section that featured what she thought of as "fun stuff." She'd put out a couple of demilune tables Mitchell had made from particle board with dowels for legs. Covering them with small, lace tablecloths, she'd created a pretty, feminine shopping nook.

"Well, it's great," Mary said, looking around at the new paint and decor. "You did a bang-up job. Since the chamber of commerce put up that sign on the highway, tourist traffic has picked up in Gila Rock. I've been trying to convince Leonard that we should spruce up the drugstore, too. We have our own share of laxative and oil. But he's as set in his ways as Joe was."

Julianne lifted her brows. "I didn't know about a sign."

"Lord, girl, with all you've had to handle I'm not surprised. It went up about three months ago. It wouldn't have made any difference to you when you were still on the farm, but I thought that was why you moved into town. Since we're close to one of the highways going to Marfa, I guess the chamber figured they could detour some of the traffic for a visit. It's about time."

"That's wonderful news!" *For a change,* she thought but didn't add. Her mind was already turning over ideas and possibilities.

"There's even talk about some targeted advertising, whatever that means. Maybe in *Texas Highways* and *Southern Living*, I think. And a massage therapist is opening a studio down the block from us."

It was difficult to imagine. Gila Rock had always been a quiet, simple outpost, seemingly on the way to nowhere. Just about everyone knew everyone else by name or, at least, by reputation. Keeping a secret was hard work. Now they were getting tourists and a massage studio?

Julianne caught a glimpse of Mitchell coming in through the back door and prayed he'd stay out of sight. She didn't want to have to explain his presence to Mary. Or anyone else, for that matter. He'd taken Jack outside, and the dog trotted right through the curtains to say hello.

"Hey, who's this doll?" Mary asked. She extended her hand to let him sniff.

"This is Jack. He belonged to someone who did some work for me, and he couldn't own a dog anymore. He's a sweet dog, but I'm going to have to find a way to keep him out of the store. Not everyone would appreciate a big galoot like him wandering the aisles."

Mary petted him with a sun-speckled hand. "He looks familiar, but I don't know where I've seen him."

Julianne sidestepped. "I think he was a stray for a while."

They moved on to another subject, and Mitchell abandoned his eavesdropping to pour himself a cup of coffee from a big insulated airpot that sat on a rickety corner table. Julianne didn't want the smell of brewing coffee floating out into the store, so she made enough to fill this thing every morning.

Mitchell let his memory wander back to the days when he'd still had some hope for getting out of Gila Rock and taking her with him. He wasn't stupid, but he'd been a lousy student. The only thing that had kept him in school and out of jail was baseball. It was supposed to have been his ticket out of here. Scouts had come to watch him play. His coach had ridden herd on him to squeak out enough passing grades to let him stay on the team. He'd been so close . . . he might have gone to the show . . . he might have been a success. Then it all had gone to hell, and he'd ended up playing catch in the exercise yard in Amarillo. Shit.

Julianne appeared in the doorway between the curtains with Jack trotting in behind her. She looked a little less anxious than she had the past few days. "Hey, Mitchell. Thanks for sending Jack to the front."

"Sorry about that. As soon as he saw you, he headed right in." He paused. "'Jack' . . . well, I guess it *is* better than Knucklehead."

"Of course it is. Who gave him that name, anyway?"

"James did, and Darcy said it fits."

"It fits Darcy and his opinion."

Mitchell chuckled. "That's the truth."

The bell on the front door rang, and she ducked back through the curtains. He heard a man's voice this time.

"Heck—"

"Julianne, I have your mail for you here. But the Domestic Mail Manual states that, 'Other than as permitted by 2.10 or 2.11, no part of a mail receptacle may be used to deliver any matter not bearing postage, including items or matter placed upon, supported by, attached to, hung from, or inserted into a mail receptacle.'"

Mitchell peered through the small break in the two panels to see retirement-age postal carrier Heck McKinnon. He'd been delivering mail around here for as long as Mitch could remember. The man's impressive ability to quote mail regulations like a fire-breathing preacher quoting scripture had always amazed him. He sure as hell was in a lather. Out front, he'd left his mail truck idling.

"What?" she demanded. "Heck, what are you talking about?"

"I'll deliver inside this time, but only as a courtesy, beings that you're Joe's niece and all. It puts a knot in my schedule if I have to get out of that truck more than once or twice a day for signatures and such. If that mailbox isn't cleaned up, your mail will be piling up at the post office."

He stormed out again, leaving Julianne looking baffled, her hands full of catalogs and envelopes. "What was that about?" she muttered.

As Heck was pulling away from the curb, she put the mail on a counter and went outside. Mitchell turned his attention back to stacking the paint cans.

Then he heard her shriek.

He raced through the store and out the front door. He found Julianne standing in front of the mailbox, her hands pressed to her open mouth, her eyes wide with horror. "What—?" When he stepped off the curb to learn what had her upset, he saw a dead chicken in the box, its throat cut. Congealed blood pooled around the bird, drenched its buff-colored feathers, and dripped off the edge of the opening. Its head, hanging by a thread of flesh, dangled. "Julianne—"

She transferred her horrified gaze to him with her hands still pressed to her mouth, and she backed away as if he were El Chupacabra, sprung straight out of the ground.

"You know I wouldn't do this!" he protested.

Just then Cade pulled up in his blue Dodge, back from an errand. Great. He stopped in front of the store, his bumper within a foot of Mitchell. He looked at the hen hanging out of the mailbox, then at Julianne, then climbed out of the truck.

"Julianne? What the hell is this?" he demanded, putting himself between Mitch and her.

"I-I don't know. Heck McKinnon came in and told me there was something wrong with the box. He said he wouldn't deliver my mail if I didn't clean it up. I didn't know what he was talking about, so I came out to look. And . . . and . . ." She gestured at the mess.

He rounded on Mitch. "Is this one of your stunts?"

Mitch gave him an even stare. "No, Lindgren. I don't perform *stunts*. I don't know when it happened." Neither of them looked convinced.

Cade put his arm around Julianne's shoulders. "Come back inside. I'll clean this up." She let him escort her back into the store. He glanced over his shoulder to throw a look at Mitchell that was both triumphant and haughty.

Mitchell swore a blue streak under his breath.

Mitch sat alone in a windowless interrogation room at the sheriff's office, studying the painted cinder block—pale green, like every institution he'd seen—and very aware of the camera lens up in the corner of the room. The floor was covered with a dizzying checkerboard of green-and-white asphalt tiles. It had a stuffy, closed-up smell of fear, time, and stale coffee.

No more than ten minutes after he'd heard Julianne scream, she'd gone back inside with Lindgren. He'd still been outside hooking up the hose to the front faucet when Dale Gunter and a deputy had appeared in a cruiser with the light bar flashing blue and red. She'd called them, as she'd threatened. Mitchell was put in the backseat and driven over here for questioning.

He didn't know who'd put that chicken in Julianne's mailbox, but he had strong suspicions. So where did that leave him? Was he still bound by family loyalty to keep his mouth shut about those suspicions? He knew he wasn't about to take the blame for this, even though he was almost certain that Darcy or James was guilty. Apparently they didn't care that he'd be the first suspect. Trouble was, he couldn't prove their guilt or his own innocence. And unless the county wanted to put a lot of time and money into forensics over a dead chicken, there was no way to identify the true culprit.

Finally, after sitting alone with his grim thoughts for what felt like hours, the door opened, and he recognized Detective Jimmy Ortiz, the same detective he'd faced all those years ago after the barn fire. His dark hair was now flecked with gray, and his body looked a little more lived in—he had a paunch around the middle and probably a bigger pants size.

He threw a yellow legal tablet on the table opposite Mitchell and sat in a metal chair. "So. First you burned down the Emersons' barn and killed Wesley. You went to prison and got out about a year ago. Now, you come back to town and Julianne Emerson begins calling in complaints of harassment and problems with vandalism. Today she finds a chicken in her mailbox with its throat cut, bleeding all over the damned place." He leaned forward in his chair. "What do you know about this, Tucker?"

Mitch was tempted to put his elbows on the table and lean forward, too, but he knew better than to antagonize the man. He did look him straight in the eye when he answered. "Not one thing."

"You can see why you look like the prime suspect."

"Yeah, but I don't have anything to do with the problems she's been having."

"Mrs. Emerson said that you came to her and asked to help her out with her new store. For free."

"That's true. She posted flyers all over town."

"No one works for no pay unless they're volunteering or kids on an internship. What were you planning to get out of this deal?"

"Just like I told her, I saw it as community service. A small repayment for the past."

"Wow, aren't you the humanitarian," he said with great skepticism.

"Julianne agreed to it and everything has been going fine."

"Until now."

"I've seen some of the vandalism. She's had her electricity cut, there were the flaming dog-poop bags, now this chicken. But I've had nothing to do with any of it."

"You were already on *our* shit list, y'know."

That was no big surprise.

"What about your brothers? Sheriff Gunter told me he paid a visit to the old homestead and things got pretty heated. Even Earl got into the act."

"You'll have to talk to them. I don't know what they do."

"You're living there, aren't you?"

Mitch sighed. "I moved out a few days ago. I realized I like my own company better."

Ortiz leaned back in his chair and studied Mitchell like he was trying to see into his brain. Mitch knew he was really trying to psych him out. But he'd been worked over by better psychologists than Ortiz.

"I really want to believe you, Mitch."

Spare me, he thought. That sympathetic routine wouldn't fly, either. "I'm staying at the Satellite Motel. You can confirm that. The county has nothing on me and you know it. I'd like to leave now."

After a few moments of tense silence, Ortiz threw his pen on the legal tablet, like an opponent laying down his sword in defeat. "I'll check out your story about the Satellite Motel."

117

"Fine." Mitchell pushed back his chair, and Ortiz followed. "I'll be around."

He waited for Ortiz to open the door to the interrogation room, then strode down the hall to the front.

Back outside in the glaring late-afternoon sun, he faced a three-mile hike to Julianne's to get his car, since there was no one to call for a ride. He reconsidered for a moment . . . he supposed he could call Cherry . . . No, he really didn't want to get into that again. She'd be after him, asking nosy questions, trying to hook up—it didn't sound like fun. He checked the time on his cell phone. Damn it, he had to be in Alpine in an hour for his paying job.

Deciding he'd just have to suck it up, he turned west and started walking, double-quick.

CHAPTER EIGHT

"Julianne, I hate to leave you alone, but I've got to go to El Paso on business for the family store," Cade said, leaning over her as she sat at the computer on the desk, inputting the new merchandise she'd just received. She didn't feel like working—she was still unnerved by the mailbox episode two days earlier—but she also knew it was the best way to keep her mind busy. It seemed to her that Cade's family had found a lot more for him to do now that she no longer operated the farming operation. But she wasn't paying him, either, so that might have been part of the reason.

She peered at a packing list, trying to decipher its tiny font. "It's all right. I'll be fine. I've got the dog with me." Jack had given her a sense of security. He was a smart, alert dog, and friendly. But he also barked at strange noises and some people. She'd bought him a bed but learned quickly that he was much happier sharing hers. Lucky for her, she had a queen-size mattress. "And he's good company."

"I just don't feel right about it," Cade continued down the same track, "considering what happened the other day. You need a male presence around here, a show of strength. I know it sounds old-fashioned, and I know you're a smart, capable woman. But some things don't change much."

Obviously, he was agonizing over this trip more than she was. She looked up at him. "Cade, just go ahead. It will be all right." She wasn't sure about that, but she was determined to not let the Tuckers scare her off. "It's not like before when I was out on the farm. It was more iso-lated out there. I live in town now. The police are close by." And Sheriff Gunter had made good on his promise to send a patrol car around more often. She'd seen it at night from her upstairs window, rolling slowly down the street.

Cade picked up her pen from the desk and fiddled with the click button until she had to take it out of his hand. "Please?"

"Sorry. Julianne, while I'm gone would you give some thought to, well, my marriage proposal? I know you've been busy, but I hope you'll have an answer for me when I get back in a week."

She put aside the packing list. "You asked a sincere, honest ques-tion of me and you deserve an answer. Maybe with some quiet time now, I'll be able to give it the attention it deserves." To her own ears, it sounded like they were talking about a job application or buying a car. She'd already refused him, but he wasn't getting it. Now wasn't the time to get into it, though.

Grinning, he replied, "Okay. I have to go." He leaned down and gave her a swift peck on the mouth.

When she heard the back door close behind him, she exhaled. Theirs was not a relaxed relationship any longer. At least she didn't think so.

She put the packing list into the scanner, then once the file appeared on her screen, put the paper document into the shredder. Keeping clutter and records organized and minimized was one of her goals. Eventually, she'd have to go through The Tomb and see whether anything in there was worth saving. With Cade gone, maybe she could begin to tackle it, a bit at a time.

So far, business had been pretty good. Not blow-the-doors-off busy, but not bad for just the first few days. A lot of people came out of curiosity, just to see what she'd done with the place, then stayed to buy something. She'd taken "before" and "after" pictures, and when she compared them, the store did look totally different.

Julianne knew that she couldn't have accomplished it without Mitchell's help. If only that incident with the hen in her mailbox hadn't happened . . . She didn't quite believe that he was responsible, but as a group, the Tuckers were still a trouble-making lot with no respect for others and a sense of self-righteousness that baffled her. They had no love for her, either, and even if Mitchell knew nothing about the latest episode, his brothers did.

It hadn't taken much insistence from Cade to make her call 911, and early on she'd promised Mitchell she'd do just that if something happened that made her uncomfortable. Still, in a corner of her heart she'd felt guilty and a little ashamed when she saw him manhandled into the backseat of the patrol car. She hadn't expected that to happen.

With her thoughts elsewhere, her computer had taken advantage of the peace and turned on its screen saver. When she bothered to look at it again, she found herself looking at crisp, professional photos of the Grand Canyon and decided to quit for the evening. She glanced at the wall clock—it was 8:00 already.

"Jack?" she called, and heard his thunderous footfalls on the stairs to the apartment. He appeared at the bottom and came to sit at her knee. "What do you say to dinner and a movie?" He jumped up again—she guessed it sounded fine to him. "Maybe a glass of wine for me and some cooked hamburger chopped up on your crunchies?" Chicken feed, dog food, cat food—to her, all dry kibble was *crunchies*. That sounded good to him, too. "Okay, let's go."

Suddenly, he pointed his nose toward the back door and started barking. She froze. Then there was a knock, and Jack's barking increased. Just as she closed her hand around the barrel of the shotgun, she heard,

"Julianne?" The sound was muffled by the walls. But the dog's frenzied barking turned to happy whining and tail-wagging, and he looked up at her.

She heaved a big sigh. "Mitchell, what do you want?"

"I brought another bag of food for Knuck—um, Jack."

Mitchell's fault . . . her fault . . . Mitchell's fault . . . her fault . . .

She released the shotgun, gripped the knob, and opened the door about four inches. His eyes reflected his weariness, and he seemed to have aged five years in the last three days. He carried a big bag of dog food in his arms. "I don't expect you to keep feeding him," she said.

Jack pushed his muzzle through the opening, and Mitchell stroked his nose. "I can't do much for you. At least let me do this for him."

That struck a deep nerve in her. She tumbled from her lofty tower of injured party to the uncomfortable position of doubt. That picture of him in the back of the patrol car flashed past her mind's eye again, and guilt nudged her again. She opened the door wide. "Come in. I was about to fix dinner for me and Jack. Would—do you want to stay?"

"What, no Lindgren to cook for? Thanks, but I already ate."

She flinched. "A beer, then?"

Mitchell gave her an even stare. "What's going on? I've gone from accused villain to invited guest in such a short time? No offense, but this is a one-eighty after the other day."

She ducked her head. "Yes, I know. I-I'm sorry about that. I didn't think Gunter would take you in."

A short laugh escaped him. "What did you think would happen? I'm Mitchell Tucker, one of the Tucker clan, ex-con, washed-out baseball player. You have nine-one-one on speed dial. Nine-one-one has us on the usual suspect list." He shrugged and added quietly, "Not without reason, I admit." He put down the bag of dog food.

The warm night air floated in behind him. "Since I didn't pay you for your help, I wanted to thank you."

"Like I told you, Juli, community service." Her brows hitched up her forehead. He hadn't called her *Juli* since the old days, before either of them had even heard of Wesley Emerson. He shifted his weight from one hip to the other. "There's still one thing to settle between us, but it can wait for a while."

Her head came up and so did her chin. "If you've got something to say, you might as well speak up. I hate having that sword hanging over my head."

"Not tonight." He looked around the office area and toward the store, where a couple of dim lights burned. "Where's the other guard dog, the two-legged one?"

She hesitated. How much should she tell him? "*Cade* is away on business. Anyway, he doesn't live here, you know."

"Did you get everything finished in the store?"

"Almost. There are still a couple of painting jobs and some shelving to finish."

"I can do it, that is, if you want me around and promise not to call the law on me again."

She knew she should decline, but those words didn't come out. "Okay, yes, that would be great."

"Then I'll see you tomorrow." He went out the door and down the back stairs. She heard his boots pounding across the path to the curb, then the sound of his engine. And he disappeared into the hot, still night.

"I haven't had anything this good for a long time," Mitchell said as they sat at a card table in the back, drinking soda and eating roast beef sandwiches Julianne had made upstairs. He'd spent the morning doing those painting jobs she'd needed finished. She listened for the brass bell on the front door—business picked up every day—but she might make it through the whole sandwich first.

"The food around town isn't *that* bad."

He shrugged. "Eating in diners and grabbing takeout gets old after a while. I can't remember the last time I ate a home-cooked meal."

"This isn't cooking. I just sliced up a loaf of sourdough bread and put some lettuce and tomatoes on roast beef. I bought everything at the Shoppeteria. It's not fancy cuisine."

"But it's great, Juli, thanks. I never got to taste your cooking." Mitchell downed half the soda in one gulp. "You know, I thought you would have remarried by now."

She paused, sandwich halfway to her mouth, surprised by the comment. It wasn't like him to pry. That was more Cade's speed. "The first time I lost so much. I just didn't . . . haven't . . ." She shook her head. "I'm not really comfortable talking about this."

Julianne couldn't bear to think of everything that was lost because of Mitchell's thoughtless act so many years ago. Even so, sometimes when he was around, she felt the hard, cold shell around her heart loosen a bit. There was still an air about him—a sizzle, a familiar vitality that could pull her in too easily if she let it.

"Sorry. I didn't mean to drag up bad memories." The expression in his eyes was sincere. He let a couple of moments pass before he spoke again. "Have you ever wondered what started the feud between our families?"

She nodded. "Yes, but I never could find anyone willing to tell me." She replaced a piece of fallen lettuce in her sandwich. "I've thought that the true reason was forgotten along the way and the thing developed a life of its own. Like a monster in a horror movie."

He chuckled. "It's a monster, all right. Years of time and energy have been wasted on it. It caused a lot of trouble and made some of us do things we wouldn't have otherwise."

Julianne waited. Where was he going with this?

"I want you to know that I never meant to hurt you, Julianne. Not ever," he continued. "When you married Wes Emerson, I sort of lost my head for a while. Nothing mattered anymore. But I never meant to hurt him, either. I was just so jealous."

She'd put down her sandwich. Her throat began to feel tight, and she didn't think she could swallow any more of it. "Mitchell—"

He pushed on, as if trying to get the words out before she could stop him. "I went to prison and served my time. People have asked me why I didn't get out sooner on parole. The truth is, I didn't think I deserved a break, so I didn't try for parole when it came up. But even that sentence didn't wipe out the guilt I've carried around in me all this time."

She stared at him, barely able to speak. Her throat was as dry as the caliche. "Why are you bringing this up? To make me relive it? To make me feel worse than I already do?"

"God, no, girl!" He leaned forward and reached for her hand, but she snatched it away. "I just want to—I mean I hope that someday you can forgive me."

He'd come far too close to a raw nerve for Julianne. "This is the unfinished business you've been talking about?"

He looked down at his plate, now empty except for bread crumbs. "Yeah, I guess it is."

"No apology is going to bring Wes back to life or put Erin in my arms! I lost my baby, my sweet little girl, right after that trial."

"I-I heard a little about it. I didn't know until I got back to town."

She hadn't wanted to analyze this memory again, but Mitchell had pulled the top off its hiding place in her heart. "She was stillborn at twenty-four weeks. The doctor was in tears when he put her in my arms because he couldn't find anything wrong with her! She was perfect and she was innocent of her parents' blunders, and she died." She grabbed her napkin and swiped at her eyes. Loss, loss, and more loss.

"God," he muttered, the color drained from his face, "I'm sorry. I'm so sorry."

"I don't talk about it. Ever. But I think about it every day."

He slid from his chair and dropped to his knees in front of her. "Juli, you might not believe me, but I never wanted anything bad to happen to you. I was angry when you married Emerson because I just couldn't believe you'd throw *us* away."

"I didn't 'throw us away.' Why did you string me along all those years ago? You knew I wanted to marry you."

"I was ready to grab you and get us out of here. I was only waiting to hear back from those baseball scouts. When I got turned down, I didn't have a backup plan. All I could see in my future was slaving away at a place like Benavente's. I didn't know how to do anything except play ball and be a grunt worker. When you married Wes, well, after that I didn't much care what happened to me. I ran around with Cherry and let myself get carried away by Earl's hate and my brothers' knack for making trouble."

"Don't you try to blame me for any of that. You strung me along with a lot of stardust and pie-in-the-sky. With my father dying and— and other problems, I had to do something."

He bowed his head for a moment, then looked into her eyes. "I'm not blaming you, Juli. I just couldn't bear the idea of you married to someone else. A couple of months later, I saw you in town, pregnant, and something in my screwed-up brain flipped a switch. When I left here for prison, I swore I'd never come back."

She wadded up the napkin. If he hadn't come back, her heart wouldn't feel as empty as it did now—and she'd already thought it couldn't feel any more barren. The longing that had slept uneasily in the hollow of her loneliness would have remained undisturbed. His return had dredged up all that.

She glared at him. "Why did you, then?"

126

He put his hands on her knees. "I came back to Gila Rock only to see you. To ask for your forgiveness."

"Really?" she demanded, furious now. "So you can sleep at night? Why do you deserve that luxury when there is no one I can ask forgiveness of for my own guilt? I'll forgive you the day that Wes and Erin do!"

She pushed out her chair and escaped up the stairs to her apartment and slammed the door. Then she pounded back downstairs, swept past him, and went into the store to lock the front door and flip her **OPEN** sign to **CLOSED**. She raced upstairs and slammed the door again.

Mitchell swallowed hard and let her go.

The rest of the day and that night were rough for Julianne. Tortured by jumbled pictures of the past, she spent the afternoon alternatively swearing at fate, Mitchell, and events in her past, and crying for all of them. She kept trying to move forward, but something—or someone—always seemed determined to pull her back. She was tired of having no one with whom to share her burdens, but when Cade's face rose in her mind, she found no comfort in the image or the idea of him. Wesley's memory left her feeling just as empty. Only one man came to mind, and she viciously steered her brain away from him.

When evening came, she ate the other half of her dried-out sandwich and finished a bottle of wine she'd opened two nights earlier.

Jack watched her, puzzled but somehow comforting, and never left her. When she sobbed against his big, furry side, he didn't move an inch but let her cry on him. "You're the only friend I have," she wailed, fueled by old grief and stale wine.

At last she wore herself out and fell asleep. Jack took his usual place beside her on the bed and stayed close.

Mitchell went "home" to the Satellite Motel, but restlessness put him back in the Skylark. He drove aimlessly, passing a patrol car once. The officer gave him a piercing look, and he waited to be pulled over, but it didn't happen. After a while he found himself looking at the old high school baseball diamond again, reliving the brief, heady days when he'd believed he'd escape Gila Rock, take Julianne with him, and head for the bright lights of the stadiums. Instead, he sat in the parking lot, using the dashboard lights to see the crummy burger and cold fries on his lap, wondering if his real life would ever start—or if this was it. Julianne's earlier words kept replaying themselves in his mind.

. . . *there is no one I can ask forgiveness of for my own guilt . . .*

What had she meant by that? He crumpled the white burger sack and drove by a garbage can to toss it in. She wasn't the guilty party of anything. He was.

Toward sunup, he made his way to the edge of town, chugging along in a fire-bright dawn through the gates of Desert Rest Cemetery. He parked along one of the paths and got out of the car, surrounded by headstones and modest statuary, searching the names carved upon them. If he couldn't get a pardon from Julianne, maybe he could explain himself to a dead man. After walking between graves decorated with silk flowers, Texan and Mexican flags, and the occasional unopened beer or melted candy bar, he found the headstone for WESLEY J. EMERSON, BELOVED SON AND HUSBAND. He sat down in the weedy dust beside it and looked at the dates. Wes had been twenty-two when he died, probably fifty or sixty years too soon. And he, Mitchell Tucker, convicted felon, was responsible for putting him here.

"Wes," he said aloud. "I'm sorry for this. I've been eaten up with guilt since the day this happened, something I never intended. I was crazy about Julianne." He shrugged helplessly. "I still am. When her father convinced her to marry you, I just about lost my mind. It wasn't your fault you got into the middle of this. I was young back then, kind of a screw-up, and I guess she felt that she had no options. I wanted to marry her, but I wasn't ready—hell, I was barely nineteen, old enough to know better, but not smart enough. She's doing pretty well, I think, but she's not ready to forgive me." He pulled a dandelion leaf from the weed next to him and began shredding it. "I was hoping you might, since you've moved on to something better."

But he knew that forgiveness was not the same as forgetting, and it did not absolve the wrongdoer. Most of all, he realized, it wasn't always easy to give or to get.

On the other side of Wes's grave, Mitchell noticed a very small headstone with a lamb etched into it. The morning sun sparkled on the flecks of mica in the stone. ERIN BRETT EMERSON . . . BELOVED DAUGHTER. Wait . . . Mitchell read the name three times. Oh God—could it—it was—

He swallowed and took a deep breath. He got up and stumbled back to his car, hoping he could find a pen.

Julianne didn't sleep well, but when morning came, she dragged on her clothes and started again. She had a slight headache but nothing too horrible, certainly not as horrible as the day before had been. Trying to come to grips with yesterday had made the muscles tight in her neck and shoulders. She'd made several concessions she thought she never would when it came to Mitchell—after all, she'd never expected to even speak to him again. But forgiveness? No, that was too much. Let him go to a priest or ask God, or whatever. She didn't have to forgive him.

Her thoughts, though, carried her a bit further along, and suddenly she remembered something she'd read in high school English class years earlier.

The quality of mercy is not strain'd,
It droppeth as the gentle rain from heaven
Upon the place beneath. It is twice blest:
It blesseth him that gives and him that takes.

Yeah, blah-blah, easy for Shakespeare to say, she argued with herself. He'd probably never faced the sort of dilemma she was looking at.

After getting her coffee and since it was still early, she decided to take a peek at The Tomb. Even though she'd been in and out of that corner many times over the past few weeks—sometimes with her own things that she'd moved from the house—she hadn't stopped to really look at the stuff back here. Now she set her coffee cup on a nearby peach crate and plowed in.

Some of what she found surprised her, although she knew it shouldn't by now. She discovered rubber-banded stacks of old, yellow carbon copies of customer receipts going back to the 1960s, created with real carbon paper. Lifting another box lid, she discovered three dozen rolls of adding machine tape and the heavy, ancient dinosaur of a machine with a crank that had probably used them. The thing might even qualify as an antique to someone who liked collecting that sort of junk. She excavated more of the same as she poked around, then came to a box that she had put here herself. On it, she'd used a marker to write, MOM'S STUFF. She remembered vaguely that most of the contents had come from the back of her own closet, things that she'd never noticed and had probably been there for many years.

She tore the tape off and lifted the box flaps. She flipped through photos of her mom in a funny, old-fashioned-looking dress and platform shoes with wooden soles, a recipe file, an empty perfume bottle—Jōvan Musk—some old costume jewelry, and . . . a journal.

Julianne sat down on the floor and looked at the cover. It wasn't fancy—no leather-bound, gilt-edged treasure. In fact, it might have come from this very store. It was the kind of thing that a person found in greeting-card sections. The binding featured color drawings of stylized butterflies and bumblebees with smiling faces on a pale-pink lattice background. One thing she knew for sure—it wasn't her own.

She opened the cover and found the first entry dated shortly after her parents' marriage. Her heart leaped when she saw her mother's handwriting. Losing her mom had been so hard, and she missed her. The entry contained chatty, mundane information, such as what she and Paul, Julianne's father, had eaten for dinner, how she'd spent her day (canning), and the people she'd talked to on the phone. Julianne realized her mother would have been just about her own age now. There were many similar entries, not written every day, until Julianne reached one that stood out from the rest.

I will never forget this day. I wish I could go back to yesterday and somehow change what was coming, but I can't.

Today, a woman came to our door while Paul was in town. She had long brown hair with stringy ends. Her black eyeliner and mascara were so heavy, her eyelashes stuck together to look like spider legs. She was just a little wisp of a thing with big boobs and a few freckles across her face. I didn't know her, but she asked to see him. I told her he wasn't home, and she handed me a letter, folded in half with no envelope, and told me to give it to him. I thought it was pretty danged strange and pretty danged nervy. Then she walked back to the road and was gone.

I stood there, holding the note, trying to decide what to do. I could have read it, easily. But I didn't. I put in on the kitchen table and waited for Paul to come home. When he did, he figured I knew what was in it. I didn't say anything. He told me that it had happened before he met me, when he and Earl

Tucker were dating the same girl, Tammy Lindgren from Cuervo Blanco. At the time, she wouldn't tell either of them whose baby it was. Then I said I hadn't read the letter. He stared at me with his mouth open, knowing he'd just given away a secret he'd kept from me all this time.

The journal entry went on to say that in the letter, Tammy revealed that Paul Boyce, Julianne's father, had sired the baby. Tammy had named him Cade, and she'd left him with her own parents to raise while she took off for parts unknown, never to be seen around here again. Just like Mitchell's mom. Julianne's father and Earl had been bitter rivals at first, then bitter enemies.

Julianne stared at the journal with her mouth open. She gasped for air, but it felt as if steel bands encircled her rib cage, keeping her from getting a deep breath. Her heart pounded against her breastbone, and a flood of adrenaline poured into her veins, constricting them and making her hands icy.

Oh my God!

She and Cade had been fathered by the same man? *Cade?* Who did Cade look like? That meant she had a half brother. But to think of him as a relative? She couldn't—at least not yet. Cade Lindgren was her half brother. *She had a half brother.* And he wanted to marry her.

She finished the rest of the journal. Apparently things between her parents had never really been the same after that, although they'd stayed together and had had Julianne. They'd both taken this secret to their graves. Even on his deathbed, her father had not revealed this to her, or the true reason for the Boyce-Tucker feud. She would bet that none of the Tucker boys knew about it, either. In this isolated case, that blockheaded Earl had kept his clacking dentures shut.

And those people Cade thought were his parents were really his grandparents. His sister Carol was his aunt. It explained so much—why they were so old, and why they hated him working for Julianne. She *couldn't* marry him—and he couldn't ask her anymore.

She leaned back against the wall, the journal in her lap and shock still coursing through her. This might partly explain why kissing him felt so, well, icky. She thought of his face and decided he must take after the Lindgrens, because she could see no resemblance to her father.

She rummaged through the rest of the box but found nothing else of much interest beyond the sentimental. Finally, she got up and dusted herself off, then went upstairs to change into a skirt and sandals to begin her day as the proprietor of Bickham's.

Mitchell paused outside the front door to Bickham's and took a deep breath. Exhaling, he leaned against the push plate, making the brass bell ring to announce him.

Julianne hurried out to the front, saw him at the counter, and her steps slowed.

"Hi, Juli." He gave her a tentative smile, trying to see if she was still mad. "How are you doing?"

She nodded. "Business is pretty good."

"No, I mean how are *you*?"

"Fine." She relented then. "If you want to know if I'm still angry, no, I'm not."

He waited a moment, wanting to talk about what he'd learned, but his courage deserted him. Then he responded, "Okay. I'll finish those shelves for you, if that's all right."

"Yes, it's great. Thanks, Mitchell. Oh, by the way, I'd like to hang a valance over the window that matches the back curtains. Could you help me with that? It's really a three-handed job."

"Sure." He glanced around. "It looks like we're the only ones here. Maybe this would be a good time."

He fetched the ladder, and she climbed up the steps with a ruler to check the placement. She held it with two hands to make sure it was straight. "I think the rod should extend out just here, three inches."

Watching her with her arms raised and seeing the graceful curve of her body stirred memories in Mitchell as nothing else had—of her as a young girl in his arms, of warm summer nights when she slipped out to be with him, of a time long before Wes and the fire and prison. When she stepped down he pulled her into his arms and gave her a fierce, desperate kiss. Her mouth was soft and yielding, slick and warm. For an instant she responded, then struggled to get out of his embrace. They stared at each other, breath coming fast, she with angry fire blazing in her eyes. He looked at her, and all he knew was how good it felt to hold her again.

"Mitchell, we can't do this."

"We're adults, both unattached, with a history that goes back further than Lindgren or Wes or any of that stuff. There was you and me."

She shook her head. "No . . . it's not . . ." She put the heel of her hand to her forehead. "Think of what—"

"Julianne, we can't keep living in the past. That's what my brothers and Earl are doing. Darcy and James learned to hate from Earl and it's corroded all of them. They can't think of anything else. Don't let that be us." He held out his open hand to her and willed her to take it. "Please."

Just as she began to reach for it, the bell on the door rang. He swore softly.

"Well, this looks cozy!"

He turned around and discovered Cherry Claxton standing behind him. Damn it all.

"Cherry—what brings you here?"

"I heard so much about Julianne's new version of Bickham's, I thought I'd better take a look for myself."

"Um, thank you. Feel free to look around. I'll be at the counter if you need anything," Julianne said, then walked back to the cash register.

Cherry was dressed as she usually was, in a low-cut, white top and second-skin, dark-blue leggings. No curve was left untouched.

She ran both hands up his arms to his T-shirt sleeves and down again. He backed up a step. "Mitchell, honey, I haven't seen you for a while. I've missed you."

"I've been pretty busy helping Julianne get this together."

"So I heard. I'm glad you're making all this money. You still owe me that dinner at Jett's Grill in Marfa you promised."

His temper began to heat up. He could feel Julianne's eyes on him, and he knew what Cherry was doing. He wasn't about to let her make Julianne believe there was something cooking between them. "Cherry, I seem to remember that was your idea. I didn't promise."

"Oh, Mitch," she pouted. She grabbed at his little finger and linked hers with it, swinging their two hands high, like they were eight-year-olds. He pulled his hand away. "I'm still waiting for that good time we talked about at Lupe's. Remember how much fun we had that night?"

"Look, I hate to cut this short, but I'm working on a project in the back. I'm sure Julianne would be happy to help you out here."

A cloud of genuine hatred crossed her face. It was very brief, but he knew he'd seen it. And he didn't think it was directed at him. She looked over her shoulder at Juli. "Okay, sure, Mitch. I'll see you around—eventually. Don't worry, I'm not going to let your job get between us. I've never let the Captain Gas interfere with my love life."

He knew he was being a coward, but getting away from her was the only way to stop the damage without a full-on confrontation, which he knew would be ugly, and unfair to Julianne considering this was her place of business. He headed toward the back with a grimace on his face Cherry couldn't see, but that he hoped Julianne could.

"Were you looking for something specific, Cherry?" he heard her ask.

"Yeah, but I'm not going to find it here. I'll have to wait for the right place and time."

Mitchell heard the bell ring and poked his head out between the striped drapes to the back. "She's gone?"

"Yes." Her answer was clipped.

"I'm sorry about that," he said, emerging. "I didn't mean to leave you here alone to deal with her, but she's been after me ever since I got back to town. I have no interest in Cherry."

"I seem to remember that you two were an item for a while after I married Wes."

"Yeah, *after*. Think about that. We ran with the same crowd in high school, but it was never a romance. You know what Cherry is like. She's been married two or three times and never lacks for male attention. I think that's one of the reasons she's after me—because I'm not interested."

Sighing, she said, "I hope she doesn't come back."

"Huh, so do I. She's got a vicious streak in her."

He went back the task of hanging the valance and tried to brush off the uneasy feeling that Cherry's glower had given him.

That night, Julianne listened to someone pelt the storefront with three dozen eggs while Jack barked his head off. She was fairly certain of the count, because the guilty party also left the egg cartons in her doorway.

"Okay, ma'am, that ought to take care of it."

The installer from SAF-T Security Systems came to the counter with his metal clipboard. The oval name patch on his shirt read Mark, and he was pretty dirty from crawling around under the building to run the wiring. "You've got your camera over the back door, and another up there that covers the front. They're pretty hard to see, to help avoid the risk of someone spray-painting over it." He gestured with his pen. "But even so, I put up the one in that corner that covers this whole interior. Then you've got your alarm system on both front and back doors, with motion detectors. If an intruder makes his way past the locks and windows, the alarm will sound, we'll get the alert on our equipment just like that." He snapped his fingers. "The system will call the police even before we call you." He'd been at the store all day, and this was a big expense, but Julianne needed to feel safer. After all the things she'd been plagued with the past few months, she wanted to know just who was hanging around here at night, or when she wasn't looking. Now anyone who decided to pester her would either see the cameras and think twice or be recognized.

"Thank you for your help." She wrote him a check. "And it's set up to go?"

"Yes, indeed. I'm leaving the manual with you, which is written for just about anyone, and we have live twenty-four-hour phone and online help. I showed you how to access the computer display for the cameras, right?"

"Yes. I appreciate it."

"Okay, ma'am. If you have any trouble with the system, just call us."

She nodded, and it was just about closing time when he left. She set the alarm, locked the front door, and flipped her **OPEN** sign to **CLOSED**. There was still plenty of daylight left, but she had a special task to complete, one that she performed every month.

She got into her truck and drove to her destination with a small bunch of flowers she'd picked up at the Shoppeteria. It was odd. For as many times as Julianne had made this journey to the edge of town, she'd never encountered anyone else. New graves appeared, and she visited at different times of day, but she had yet to see another visitor or a funeral. She was always alone here in this necropolis.

She came up here for one reason, to see Erin. It was such a tiny grave, and the lamb on her headstone, the one she had chosen herself, always made her throat tight and her eyes burn. Only she remembered that her child lay out here. Poor little soul, her poor baby, forgotten by everyone but her mother.

Today, though, something was different. Flowers didn't last long up here because of the heat, but she spotted some fairly fresh ones at the base of the headstone. She got out of the truck and headed straight for the grave. When she reached it, she picked up the wildflowers that had been tied with a long blade of grass, and saw a note among the stems. A shiver went through her. This was just like the notes she used to find . . .

Erin, your mama can't forgive me. I hope you can. I'm sorry for everything. I wish I had known you.

Love from your father

It was written on the back of a receipt from Captain Gas, leading her to believe his visit hadn't been planned. Maybe he hadn't even known that she'd see it. She pushed a hand through her hair. Why had he come up here? How, *how* had Mitchell figured out this secret, one she had shared with nobody? She looked at the headstone again and realized how easy it would have been for him. She'd never expected him to even come back to Gila Rock, much less to this cemetery, so she thought he'd never see Erin's lonely little resting place. She hadn't told him where the baby was.

Oh, Mitchell . . . Tears filled her eyes, making everything look swimmy, and ran down her cheeks. The closer he got, the more she cried, it seemed. But these weren't tears of despair—not exactly anyway. He'd made her begin to feel something besides anger and loss. How odd that he, of all people, should be the one to do that. Reaching down, she pulled a couple of weeds that grew in front of the little headstone.

Neither Wes nor Mitchell had known she was pregnant when she'd gotten married, and neither had she. She'd thought that stress and worry had made her late. The truth came to her a week after the courthouse wedding when morning sickness had set in. But when the baby was born and she was an orphaned widow herself, she gave Erin her father's middle name to share. No one would know except her, in the private hell of her own grief and guilt. Until now.

Mitchell knew.

That changed everything.

She laid her own bouquet next to Mitchell's and, her stomach as tight as a fist, she briefly ran her fingers over the etched name on the stone. Then she walked to her car and drove back to town.

CHAPTER NINE

The following morning, Julianne stood at the computer in the back, reviewing the images her new security system had captured on the cameras. They were crisp and sharp, for which she was glad. Often when the TV news showed security videos of thieves or attackers caught on cameras in parking lots or convenience stores, the quality of the images was so poor they were downright useless. Then viewers were urged to notify authorities if they recognized the pixelated, moving blobs. Apparently, it had been a quiet night. The only thing she saw was a coyote running down the sidewalk past her front door.

Mitchell had washed down the front of the building and cleaned up the egg mess, and she had dutifully called the sheriff's office. She felt pretty certain that he wasn't responsible for this. While he was outside, Darcy drove by and yelled insults at both him and Julianne. This was really becoming a problem, but she knew that Mitchell's brothers would continue to plague her even if he were gone. And the sheriff was no help in a case like this. They could drive past and yell ten times a day, if they wanted to. The Tucker brothers had all sorts of protections under the law. She had none.

But Mitchell, he was a different story.

After all he'd done for her, and all she'd read in his face and heard in his voice, the ice around her heart shifted. She couldn't forgive him, but she would let him know she appreciated the gesture of his apology. When he walked in fifteen minutes later, she stopped him on his way to the back.

"I thought you were done with everything."

He glanced at her. "Well no, not exactly. I've still got a couple of door pulls to install and I was wondering if there was anything in the apartment that needs help."

"Yes, in fact, there is. I've got two sticky kitchen drawers and I think there's a leak under the sink. But just a second."

She went to the front door, locked it, and put another decorative sign in the window that read BACK IN 15 MINUTES. She used it when she had to go to the bank or run some other quick errand. Since she had no other help, she had to leave sometimes. "Come on back," she said, waving him toward the work area.

She sat in her desk chair and motioned him to pull up the other one that she'd put by a door set on top of cinder blocks that she was using as a table. He gave her a hesitant look, as if he were expecting bad news or an ass-chewing. "What? What did I do now?"

She smiled ruefully. "Nothing." She took a deep breath. "A few days ago, we sat here and you asked me if I knew anything about the feud between our families. I really didn't."

He nodded with obvious caution.

"I learned something that you'll want to know. I was digging through The Tomb and I found an old journal that belonged to my mother." She went on to explain what she'd discovered.

"They dated the same woman? Really?"

"Yep."

"That doesn't sound like a reason for something that has lasted this long," he said, shaking his head. "This seems like the kind of thing we should be discussing over drinks."

"But we're here now." She took another deep breath. "There's more, and this is, well, pretty strange. Much more for me than for you. That baby the woman had—it was Cade."

His eyebrows flew up. *No shit?*

"No shit. He's my half brother."

He continued to stare at her. "No one knows?"

"We didn't and I know he doesn't. I'm not sure even your father knows. Only his family does, as far as I can tell."

"I'll be go to hell," he said, shaking his head. "This *is* strange. It's incredible." He looked up. "So he's family now?"

"I guess. It doesn't feel like that, though. It's just—well, bizarre. Like finding out I was left on the porch at birth or something. Except I'm not the odd one out here. He is."

"Are you going to tell him?"

She thought about what sort of conversation that would be. "Yes. I'll tell him."

A brief, private smile pulled up the corners of his mouth. "I guess you won't be dating him anymore. I have to tell you, I'm not sorry about that."

"I never dated him. Anyway, Cade isn't a bad guy," she protested.

"Let me tell you something about Cade Lindgren. His interest in you is stronger than you realize. He almost peed on this entire place like it's his territory when I was around. But he's like an eighteen-year-old. Still living with his parents at his age?"

She knew he was right, but she lifted her chin. "He's just being a good son. Or grandson. Whatever." She didn't believe that, but she felt compelled to defend him. "Besides, what makes you such an expert on human nature?"

His laugh was not one of amusement this time. "Are you kidding? I spent seven years studying it."

They were quiet for a moment. Then she said, "I'll take care of it. I have to." He gave her a questioning look. "I just do. He deserves to know." She wasn't sure how to go about it. The impact it would have on his life would be even more profound than her own, since he'd confessed his feelings for her. No matter how she approached it, it wouldn't be easy.

He lifted his hands wide in concession. "Okay, okay. I wish I could be a fly on the wall."

Just then, someone knocked on the back door. Upstairs, Jack began barking. When she opened it, she saw Cade. Wow. What timing. Her altruistic determination to reveal his parentage to him stumbled, but she set her jaw and took a breath.

"Hey, Julianne, I'm back!" He walked in and started to lean forward to kiss her when he saw Mitchell sitting there. "Oh. Tucker," he acknowledged.

"Lindgren," Mitchell returned. "I guess I'll get to those kitchen drawers. I haven't seen Jack for a while." He got up and climbed the stairs to her apartment.

Cade watched him go. "Was I interrupting something?"

"No, we were finished. How was El Paso?"

"My sister ended up going. I needed to hang around and help the folks. They're getting on and she likes one of us to be there."

"Um, uh-huh." She went to a filing cabinet and pulled the journal out of the back of the drawer. "Sit down, Cade. We need to talk."

"Hey, how's my favorite dog?" Mitchell said when Jack practically launched himself into his arms. He knocked him down onto the sofa and sniffed him all over, as if to make certain he was real. He yipped and barked and licked his face. Mitchell laughed at the squirming, happy mutt. "Is Julianne taking good care of you? It sure looks like it. You've been brushed and shampooed. Do you love your new mama? She's great, isn't she?" Julianne was right—Jack was a much better name for him. And he'd filled out with good food and good care. "Maybe she could do the same for me, if I had the same chance you got."

Suddenly from downstairs, he heard raised voices. He knew he shouldn't do it, but he wanted to make sure she was all right. He tiptoed to the door and opened it a crack.

"—didn't want to marry me, you could just tell me so without making up this bald-faced whopper."

"Cade, it's not a lie. I wouldn't make up something like this. Look."

There was a moment of silence while she must have been showing the journal.

"It's bullshit!" Cade said. "I don't believe it. Do I look like your old man? I never met him."

"No, I'm guessing you look like your mother, or someone else on your side of the family. You really ought to talk to them about this."

"Talk to them! This would probably put them in their graves! This is a low blow, Julianne. And after all the years I worked for you and took grief from my family about you. They were right. I should have listened to them."

"How do you think *I* feel, to learn this the hard way? But we're related now, I have family I didn't know about. Cade, I'm sure you're upset—"

"Upset!"

Mitchell heard a crash and pounded down the stairs, followed by Jack. Swiftly, he took in the scene. The wobbly corner table and a chair were overturned and the coffee airpot lay on the floor, broken. All the coffee things that usually stood next to it—a pitcher of half-and-half, sugar, ceramic mugs—were scattered and shattered. Julianne was chalk-white, Lindgren was as red as a turkey, and Jack started growling at him, the fur along his spine standing on end.

"Is there a problem down here?"

Cade didn't look at him, but pointed in his direction. "You just want to go shack up with him, that ex-con who killed your husband. Fine, you do that. I thought I knew you."

Julianne stared at him with her mouth open, clearly insulted.

"Your bad manners are showing, Lindgren," Mitchell put in. "Maybe you should tell her how you broke your arm." He threw it out on a hunch, just a gut feeling he hadn't shared with Juli.

"What the hell are you talking about?" Cade asked, rounding on him. "She knows I broke my arm when I was trimming a tree at home."

"You broke your arm when you fell off this back porch, spray painting that message on the door with black engine paint."

"What?" Julianne demanded.

"I-I did not! I told you how that happened."

Mitchell pressed on, knowing he'd struck a nerve—and the truth. "At first I thought my brother did it. He's got lots of old cars parked out at the mobile home. Until I found a used spray can of black engine paint while I was stacking the other painting stuff back there." He nodded at the corner where he'd put the interior paint.

Julianne whirled to face him. "Cade! Is that true?"

The muscles in his jaw worked, emphasizing his agitation. "I just— I only wanted to prove to you how much you needed me."

Now her cheeks blazed, too. "And that was how you went about it? By trying to scare me half to death? I don't need any man!"

"You're nothing but a slut after all, just like my parents told me."

Mitchell, the much taller of the two men, grabbed Cade by the back of his collar and the waistband on the back of his jeans. "Okay, that'll do. I think I hear your mama calling, Lindgren. She wants you to go home now because you're being rude and acting like an asshole. Watch that first step—it's a doozy." He steered him toward the back door and put him out on the stoop, then slammed the door and locked it. Outside, they heard him yell a couple more insults before he got into his truck and peeled out.

"I guess that didn't go very well," Mitchell said.

Julianne let out a big breath, and she put a shaking hand to her throat. "How did you know he was the one who sprayed this door?"

He shrugged. "I didn't, at least not for sure. I did find the can of spray paint the other day. But it was a bluff—I wanted to see how he'd react. He didn't disappoint me."

She got a pursed-lip look that he'd seen a lot of lately. "You never mentioned it."

"I didn't say anything to you because I thought you'd just blow me off and tell me again about what a great guy he is." He bent over to retrieve the coffee pot. "Maybe not so great now, huh?"

Her pinched expression turned pensive. Then her brows went up as another thought occurred to her. "I wonder if he did any of the other damage around here. I didn't expect a scene like that. I'm not sure what he was going to do before you came down. I've never seen him so angry. His eyes were just, well, black, like there was no other color in them. There's angry, and then there's dangerous." She looked at him. "I'm really glad you were here. And Jack! My wonder dog, Jack!" She crouched beside her "wonder dog," rubbed his ears and put kisses all over his face. Lucky dog.

"Do you think he's gone for good?" he asked.

"Considering what I told him, I don't think he'll want to bother with me again for quite a while." She seemed very confident.

He looked out the back window a long moment. "I do."

That night, Julianne checked all the locks downstairs and made sure the alarm was set. The scene with Cade had shaken her to her core. She and Mitchell had cleaned up the mess of broken cups and spilled sugar and cream. With the mopping and wall-washing, it had taken nearly an hour. The mild-tempered hired hand had showed her a side to his personality that she didn't recognize and behavior she never would have suspected. He'd kicked that table with a force that would have launched a beach ball over a house. Cream had sprayed the walls, and the sugar made surfaces glitter. When she tried to imagine what might have happened if she'd been alone with him, it frightened her. She hadn't been keeping the shotgun as close as she once had—after all, she had trusted Cade and she did trust Mitchell. What a turnabout from a few months ago.

But besides the scare Cade had given her, she was devastated by his treachery. She had known him for so long. She'd realized he had a crush on her, but she hadn't grasped the depth of his attachment. It gave her the creeps to discover what a controlling personality he had, and what lengths he'd go to in order to get his own way. She had seen no hint of that until recently, and then today, well.

The next morning, Julianne came downstairs and opened the back door to let Jack out. On the porch was a bouquet of flowers tied with a stalk of grass.

"Oh my." Just as she had so long ago, she looked around as if expecting to see who'd brought them. She saw no one. While she waited for Jack to finish his business, she examined the blooms. These weren't typical grocery-store flowers. There were sprigs of blue curls, huisache daisies, purple nightshade, and coreopsis. They grew in West Texas, but they were spring flowers. It was too hot for them now. Where had they come from? There was no note in them, but they were so like the flowers Mitchell had left for her long ago.

Then she remembered. The camera—she could look at the recordings of the last few hours and see if it had been him.

"Jack, come on." He came bounding up the steps, and she went inside to look at the images. On her computer monitor, she scrolled through all the images—nothing else had happened last night, fortunately—looking for whoever had left the bouquet. At last, she discovered the right one to confirm her suspicions. The timestamp was 4:30 a.m. It was still dark outside, but the light captured the image of an approaching man. A man she knew well.

"Mitchell," she said, shaking her head in wonder. "How did you find these flowers at this time of year?" For a moment she was a girl again, filled with the delicious, forbidden thrill of finding an anonymous bouquet from a totally unexpected and semisecret admirer—the dangerous bad boy of Gila Rock High School, the one all the girls had giggled over. She had wanted to brag to them about her exciting sort-of boyfriend. But of course, that had been impossible, and it had to become a romance to cherish in her heart.

Then everything had changed.

Now, through years of betrayal, disappointment, and loneliness, they seemed to have come full circle.

A search in The Tomb yielded a pretty vase, and she put the bouquet on the glass case where she displayed nicer pieces of jewelry and vanity sets. At nine o'clock, she unlocked the front door to begin the business day.

Mary Diller had been right about the tourists. She saw faces she'd never seen before, people who talked about driving in from Colorado, Oklahoma, North Dakota, and California. Others flew in to El Paso and rented cars to come over on US 90. Outside, the city had put hanging baskets on the light poles with a drip watering system, and that really dressed things up. Business was better than she'd ever imagined it would be when she'd taken over Uncle Joe's old wreck of a store. Proudly she'd carried a loan payment to the bank every week since she'd opened for business, to pay it off faster.

And things were about to improve even more, it seemed. Today, she'd heard a comment that had piqued her interest and imagination. A woman with hair that made Julianne think of Lucille Ball had remarked, "We came over to see the Martha Lights and decided to look around the country a little." Julianne didn't correct her mispronunciation; she'd heard it before. "I thought there might be a bed-and-breakfast here, but

I couldn't find one. I'd love to spend more time here, but there aren't any nice places."

So far, no one had even inquired about the farm she was trying to sell. What if the farm began paying for itself? What if . . . ?

Late that afternoon, when things had quieted down as people went off to dinner, Mitchell came through the front door. "Hey, Julianne. What nice flowers. Where did you get them?"

She gave him a wry smile. "I double-checked the video from the security camera out back."

"I—uh—well, I didn't realize there was one out there, too. Good thinking."

She couldn't help but laugh. "That doesn't mean I didn't like them. Where did you find wildflowers at this time of year?"

He put on a lofty expression. "I have my ways." Then he dropped it and reached out to take her hand. This time she let him. "Would you like to have dinner with me tonight? Say at the Paisano Hotel, in Jett's Grill?"

Her brows rushed together. "I thought that was supposed to be your date with Cherry."

"But I never wanted to go with her. I want to go with you. Beats the vending machines at the Satellite Motel."

"I'm sure it does," she said, smiling again. "Don't we need reservations?"

"Done, seven o'clock."

She studied his face for a moment. "Mitchell, I suppose it's none of my business, but I know Jett's Grill doesn't have diner prices. How—are you sure you can afford this? I'm not paying you." The Satellite Motel wasn't the Ritz-Carlton, but it wasn't free, either.

He gave her an even look. "I manage."

"Independently wealthy?" she tried to joke.

Smiling, he replied, "Yeah, that's it. Can we take your truck?"

"It isn't exactly a limousine."

"It is compared to the Skylark."

Yes, she had to give him that. That old Buick barely had any upholstery left and a faint cloud of exhaust trailed behind it, like an old man. "Okay. Give me an hour?"

"At your service, ma'am." His mood had improved considerably since he'd left the trailer and begun living at the Satellite, even if it was kind of . . . well, "run down" would be a kind way to put it.

She closed a few minutes early, having earned her sales quota for the day. Things might change by winter; it was hard to say. But they'd probably get the snow birds down here, and that would help.

She went upstairs and took a shower, shaved her legs—she didn't want to sound like a cricket when she walked—and hurried through hair and makeup. This was a real treat. She hadn't been to the Paisano for years. There had never been a reason to go, or anyone to go with. Now, there was Mitchell. No one in town had mentioned their relationship to her face, although she'd expected it. People couldn't resist a piece of gossip like this. *Tough,* she thought, spritzing her hair with a light mist of spray. It wasn't anyone's business, as much as they liked to think it was.

Rummaging through her closet, she found a white peasant skirt with a matching top with an elasticized neckline, which she pulled down around her shoulders. After she hooked a pair of hoops in her ears and gave herself a faint whiff of Miss Dior, she was satisfied with the result. She hadn't been this dressed up since she'd applied for her bank loan, and even then not as nice as this.

Jack watched her with a look that said, *You're going to leave me here, aren't you?* "Yes, honey, sorry. No dogs in restaurants."

When Mitchell came to the door to pick her up, she was pleased to see him in a jacket, bolo tie, and a Western shirt. So far, his wardrobe had consisted of jeans and T-shirts.

"Mitchell, what a nice surprise," she said, looking him over.

"You look pretty special yourself, girl," he replied, with a frank inspection of her outfit and hair. "Very edible."

She laughed. They drove off in her truck, not a stylish vehicle, but clean with no dents and a decent paint job.

In Marfa, the Hotel Paisano had a lovely, ornate historic exterior and a red tile roof. Its most notable claim to fame was that the cast of the movie *Giant*, including Rock Hudson, Elizabeth Taylor, and James Dean, had stayed there during filming. Next to the parking lot, a few people were scattered around the courtyard with their drinks.

Inside, Julianne looked around at what she thought of as Old West–casual luxury—a mounted buffalo head hung on the wall in the lobby, leather furniture, and multicolored tile floors. Gift shops occupied at least a third of the main level. One of them continually screened the film and showcased movie memorabilia.

Mitchell put a light hand on her elbow and guided her to the restaurant where they were seated in an intimate, quiet corner with a view of the courtyard. With its white tablecloths and pretty table settings, it was a welcome change from eating alone in her apartment over the store. They placed their drink and dinner orders, and it almost seemed like a vacation to Julianne after the weeks of work and worry.

When the drinks had been delivered—a margarita for her and a double Tennessee whiskey for Mitchell—he lifted his glass to her. "Here's to old friends."

She touched her glass to his and gave him a pensive smile.

Old friends. They'd shared so much more than just friendship. "Mitchell, now that we've reached this, well, truce, I guess, I think it's time we talked about what happened before I married Wesley. You think you know what happened, but you don't."

He sat back in his chair, with one hand steepled over the top of his drink, his expression wary. "Okay. You first."

"I know you didn't understand why I married him."

"Not then I didn't. I can't say it bothers me less now, but I get it."
He considered her. "Why didn't you tell me you were pregnant back
then?"

"I didn't know until after the wedding."

"Did *he* know she was mine?"

Julianne dropped her gaze to the salted rim of her glass. "No. I
would have told him before she was born. But—you know how that
went."

He sat silently, obviously waiting for her to continue.

"You know how my dad fretted over my future in the last months of
his life. I had to do something, even if it was the wrong thing. I thought
I owed him that." Absently, she folded a pleat in her cocktail napkin. "I
wanted to marry *you*. But you were so distracted with your own life, I
didn't think you'd be able to make that kind of commitment."

He took a swallow of the whiskey. "Just so you know, I did have
a plan. And you probably remember I was waiting for the green light
from a baseball scout. I really thought I had a good shot at going to
the bigs—eventually. I pinned all my hopes on getting an offer to play
minor league. I was so sure about it, I was going to tell you to pack up
all your pretty things and be ready to go. I would come to pick you up,
and we'd leave Gila Rock as soon as I got a 'yes.' But it didn't happen
that way. Oh, I had it all mapped out."

"You didn't bother to tell *me*. You just kept talking about *someday*.
I didn't have a 'someday'—I needed a 'now.' I couldn't understand why
you didn't get that."

He looked up. "I did. But I was pretty damned cocky. I thought I'd
just slide right into a sweet deal. It didn't work out that way. I was good,
they said, but not quite good enough. 'Sorry, son, keep at it and maybe
you'll get another chance someday.' Shit, I knew that wasn't going to
happen." He sighed and tapped the ice in his drink, making it bob. "I
didn't have a Plan B. I just let everything slide after I was turned down.
I'd hung all my hopes and dreams on that single thing. I thought I

needed it to make everything else work." He shrugged. "That's how kids think—I couldn't see beyond it. So you married Wes, and I got pissed off. It was just another slap in the face. Then I realized I'd been fooling myself. Why did I think I could get away from that life? I'm a Tucker, by God. I was born to it and it was all I'd ever have. I wasn't going to have the pretty wife, or the kids and nice house." He laughed, as if at his own foolishness. "I'd live the same kind of life I always had, the same life that Earl had, and who knows how many generations before that. I didn't realize it was going to get worse—I didn't even know it could." He didn't sound bitter, but he spoke with the weary surprise of a much older man reviewing many decades of life instead of just three. "But a baby . . . man . . ." He shook his head in a kind of gut-punched astonishment.

She touched her finger to the salt crystals on her glass. "When I realized I was pregnant, it was too late. I had to stick with the life I'd allowed myself to get. Anyway, what would you have done if we'd found out about the baby sooner? Not much, I don't think. And maybe you'd have come to resent me, and her, too, for tying you down."

"I loved you, so much. I didn't have much to offer you, but I'd have done everything in my power to take care of you both."

She caught his gaze, and her heart wrenched. "So if you'd known about her, it would have made a difference?"

His shoulders dropped slightly; his voice more so. "Oh yeah. It would have made all the difference in the world. At that sentencing hearing, the judge told me to spend the time in prison thinking about how I wanted to live the rest of my life. I did that. I also got some perspective on my past. I thought you just didn't care anymore. I was a loser."

"I didn't think that." They fell silent when their waiter stopped at their table with a basket of bread and butter.

Mitchell signaled him to bring them another round. "But it was the truth as I knew it," he continued when they were alone again. "My big fantasy dried up and I couldn't seem to get out of my own way. I was an ass—I made a mess of things." He stated this as fact, not in a way that made it sound as if he hoped she'd disagree with him. "I sure as hell would have given you my best, though."

"I wish I'd known that. But I suppose I had my own baggage, too," she admitted. "I had to grow up fast and I was expected to carry on the tradition of the hog farm." She took a sip of her tart, slushy drink. "I love that house and the land, but I hated hog farming. *Hated it.*" She couldn't believe she'd finally admitted that to anyone, including herself. The idea had flitted through her mind, but she'd always pushed it away, feeling disloyal to the earlier Boyces who had worked and sacrificed to keep that farm together for the next generations.

"So you got married, your dad was at peace, and Wes thought it was his baby you were carrying."

She rolled her swizzle stick between her thumb and index finger. "You took up with Cherry and burned down the barn," she replied.

That pretty much summed up their past at the end, and they sat at their table, looking across the years at each other.

"I've never stopped loving you, Julianne. I tried everything to get you out of my mind. None of it worked."

Hearing the ghost of long-buried emotion in his voice sent a quiver through her that made itself felt despite the relaxing glow of tequila. She looked down at the tabletop. "I never loved Wes. I was fond of him—he was a good soul who did his best to save the farm in the few months he worked at it. When he died I was racked with guilt." She lifted her gaze to meet his. "I've loved just one man in my life."

The more personal and urgent their conversation became, the closer they leaned toward each other at the table, until finally he pushed aside a slender bud vase of baby's breath and carnations along with the alcohol-burning candle. He reached out a hand to her, and she took it, holding on while the world she'd known for the last eight years tilted and fell away.

"You told me you came back to Gila Rock for one reason—to get my forgiveness."

"I guess that was pretty selfish of me, considering what you went through. I don't deserve it."

She maintained unwavering eye contact with him. "I promised myself I wouldn't budge on that, too. But when I found your note and the flowers on Erin's grave I realized I must do that—appreciate your gesture. I didn't expect you to go looking around out there. I didn't think anyone would know." She turned her face toward the courtyard, where a tiered fountain burbled water into its lower levels.

Feeling as if a benediction had been laid upon his life-scarred soul, Mitchell tightened his grip around her hand. Her acknowledgement wasn't the absolution he hoped for, but it was something anyway. His voice turned low and rough with emotion. He felt as if his heart had climbed into his throat and lodged there, pulsing, aching, immovable. And Julianne . . . God, poor Julianne had been left alone to deal with her grief. "*We* know. We're her parents and we know. That's what counts."

She nodded, still looking at the courtyard. "We created a child together, and we lost her."

"Maybe it's not too late. We could take another shot at it. We're grown up now, and smarter, I hope." He squeezed her hand to make her look at him. "And that fever I had for you—Juli, it's still in me."

"I-I know," she uttered just above a whisper. "I feel it. I didn't expect this at all. I never thought I'd ever be—"

Just then, the drinks and their entrees arrived, and they sprang apart. If their waiter had any sense of the intimate conversation he'd interrupted, he gave no hint of it as he launched into a chatty series of questions about who wanted fresh ground pepper, whether they were from out of town, if had they visited the local attractions, and so on, until Mitchell was ready to escort him back to the kitchen. He appeared to be about college age, and his maneuvers to earn a bigger tip were pretty transparent. Finally, Mitchell smiled and peered at the name tag pinned to the man's vest. "*Jeff*, there's an extra five dollars in this for you if you run along right now."

Jeff bumbled to a stop in his empty gab, then grinned and gave Mitchell a leering *gotcha* wink, as if he actually understood what was going on. "Sure."

"Smart ass," Mitchell muttered after the kid was gone, and Julianne laughed. The disruption had derailed their conversation but not the intensity that had sprung up between them. While she speared her southwest salad and he cut into the rib eye steak he'd ordered, Mitchell felt a moment of dreamlike peace that he hadn't felt in years. Briefly, he let his memory light on a scene from his not-too-distant past: a grim, institutional hall flooded with fluorescent glare, bad food of questionable origin, anger, and hopelessness. He didn't dwell on it, though. That was behind him, and the hope of Julianne was in front of him, a situation he'd never even dared to hope for.

As they ate and talked, Mitchell learned more about Julianne's struggles over the years, and he shared with her some of the facts of life behind bars. He left them purposely vague—the details would just throw a bucket of cold water on their evening. And while he'd never once doubted he deserved a different fate for causing Wes's death, he didn't want to dwell on that. He concentrated on Julianne, even more beautiful now as a full-grown woman than she had been as a girl, and he felt the core of himself jitter with love, anticipation, and plain old lust. Her white top accentuated her slim neck and exposed her shoulders, where her sun-streaked hair fell in a smooth, sleek drape. Right now, Mitchell wanted to press his lips to the pulse he saw throbbing on her throat.

At last the smirking Jeff returned. "Anything else tonight?" He'd just cost himself five bucks with that smirk, Mitchell decided.

Mitchell glanced at Julianne. "No," she replied to him only. "I have a nice bottle of Malbec at home that I've been saving." He didn't know or even care what Malbec was, but it gave them a good reason to leave.

Jeff left the check in a black vinyl folder. Mitchell felt like he couldn't hustle her out of there fast enough, but didn't want to seem obvious about it. He looked at the total and threw down some twenties. He let Julianne walk ahead of him, partly to enjoy the view. Her long hair swung loose down her back, and he wanted to sink his hands into it, letting the gleaming strands slide through his fingers. Once outside, she let him catch up with her and tucked her hand into the crook of his arm. He folded his hand over hers.

At that moment, free man Mitchell Tucker felt ten feet tall.

The drive back to Gila Rock seemed interminable and yet too short to Julianne. The blistering sun of midday had dialed down to a backburner simmer as it rode the western horizon. It colored the sky a dark pink along that border and threw long shadows across the highway. Somewhere—Moscow? Hong Kong? Timbuktu?—that same sun was making a rosy appearance on an eastern skyline.

"Hey, look at that!" he said, pointing at the wide-open landscape.

She glanced but couldn't see what he was pointing to. "What? Where?"

"Pull over."

She slowed and brought the truck to a halt on the side of the road. As far as she could see, they were surrounded by miles of the flat, open Chihuahuan Desert. "Do you see a garage sale or something?"

"Ha ha. Come on, let's go look."

"At *what*?" But she shut off the engine and took the keys when she got out. He waited for her and took her hand when she came around, then led her out a few paces into the landscape, through patches of spreading moonpod, Missouri milkvetch, and pink sand verbena.

"There, see?" He pointed again.

On the periwinkle eastern horizon, a golden moon, full and heavy, climbed the sky. Between it and them stood a giant saguaro cactus, a traditional symbol of the American West.

"I've never seen one this far east!" she said. "They don't grow here." Their sole habitat was the Sonoran Desert in Arizona. But there it was, not that far from the road, with its unmistakable pitchfork arms stretching toward the sky. "This is an old one, too. Somehow it's survived all this time and in this place."

"Isn't that something?" he marveled. "I saw a few of them in Arizona last year when I was bouncing around."

Mitchell pulled his cell phone from the inside pocket of his jacket. He hit the keypad, and from the small speaker she heard Willie Nelson singing "Waltz Across Texas."

"Ma'am, could I have this dance?" Mitchell held his hand out to her. She laughed and looked around. "Here?"

"Sure—a big yellow moon, an old-man saguaro, and Willie."

Up on the highway, an occasional vehicle flew past, but they seemed far removed from that picture. She stepped into his embrace, and they moved around the desert floor to the sweet old ballad, between a rising moon and the sunset. Under her hand his shoulder was strong, and she felt the muscles move. "We never got to dance much," she said.

"That's because we had to sneak around. Now we don't. But this is more fun than Lupe's, don't you think? And I don't have to worry about some other guy trying to cut in."

"*Pfft.*" As if that would happen, she thought. But she was pleased and tucked her chin down for a moment, feeling bashful. He tightened his arm around her, and her long skirt whisked over the sparse, low-growing vegetation as the moon arced up into the sky. This was probably the most romantic thing she had ever done—of course, her few romantic experiences had all occurred with Mitchell.

When the song ended, he slowed their steps to a halt. "Thank you for having dinner with me," he murmured. He took her face between his hands and looked into her eyes. Julianne thought she could get lost in a gaze like his, just fall in and drown.

"Thank you for asking," she whispered.

He lowered his head to hers and covered her face with tender kisses before he consumed her mouth. A part of Julianne that had slumbered all these years—the sense of true joy, thrill, anticipation—woke with the energy of a firecracker. She looped her arms around his neck and kissed him back while she breathed in his scent and the dry, clean smell of the desert.

Mitchell reached into his inside pocket again. This time Waylon Jennings sang "Waltz Me to Heaven." He took Julianne's hand and pulled her along under the first pale stars that began to twinkle in the eastern sky.

She smiled with her cheek resting against his shoulder. "I haven't heard that song in years." She thought back to a time when she'd heard it often. Now, it was a bittersweet memory.

"Remember when we used to park out there behind Bill Rogers's sorghum field?" he asked, leading her across their outdoor dance floor.

"Yes, I do." She remembered the CD player turned down low in the darkness of his front seat, and this song, so perfect for them, then and now, floating from the speakers. "It was a long time ago."

"It's here and now."

"We didn't dance, then," she pointed out. Their steps grew closer until they were moving in a small circle.

"That's because when you're younger, everything is in a hurry. Time, life, cars, sex, fun, trouble. Everything is turned on full blast. We're older now. We know better about what matters. We'll just live this moment, dancing in the desert with only a magic saguaro for company."

They danced beyond the passage of time and bad memories until the song ended.

"Maybe we should be going," he said at last.

"Hmm, maybe," she agreed, languid and comfortable.

They walked back to the truck with just enough bright sunset to light the way. She got into the driver's seat, happy to leave behind the past and worries about the future for tonight.

Right now her thoughts were on this time, this place, and the man sitting in the passenger seat. She and Mitchell had rolled down the truck's windows, and locks of her hair flew around her head in the warm evening breeze as the tires raced over the pavement. She didn't think her senses had ever been as acute as they were right now. She smelled a faint whiff of whiskey and motel-provided soap coming from Mitchell's side of the truck, and the dust of the hardscrabble landscape. His left hand rested easily on the back of her neck, a gesture of affection and intimacy that she realized was exactly what she had found lacking in Wes and the very few other men she'd known since Mitchell. Now, his touch raised goose bumps on her scalp and arms, the kind she used to get when he'd brush a long blade of grass across her ear.

She put a little more pressure on the accelerator under her foot.

They didn't talk. There was no need for words right now. Their only communication was the comfortable presence of each other and the feel of his hand on her neck.

Without warning, a dark-silver GMC Yukon appeared in her rear-view mirror, the front end so close to her bumper the SUV's headlights weren't visible. And its windows had such a dark tint, she couldn't see much of the driver beyond a general shape that told her nothing.

"Who is that back there?" she wondered aloud.

Mitchell craned his neck to see from his side-view mirror. "I don't know, but you'd better slow way down. I don't like the look of this."

She took her foot off the gas, stuck her arm out the window and waved the vehicle around. "Just pass me, you jerk, and get off my butt!"

Instead, she felt a bump and realized they were speeding up. "They're pushing us!"

"Let up on the gas," Mitchell directed and twisted in his seat to look at whoever was behind them.

"I did!"

"Then *carefully* steer over to the shoulder."

Before she could do that, the aggressive SUV fell back a bit, then revved up and bumped them again, this time much harder, making the truck swerve a little. Her seatbelt caught and held her in place. "My God! Mitchell, they're going to run us off the road!" she said, fear gushing through her body as if from an open hydrant. Adrenaline made her palms prickle, and she gripped the wheel to keep their very lives in this truck and on the road.

He turned in his seat again. "Who is that son of a bitch? I don't know anyone with an expensive rig like that."

"I can't even see the license plate, they're so close. And the truck bed is in the way."

They were headed for a sharp curve in the road that Julianne knew well. Drunk drivers tended to miss it on dark nights and go crashing through the scrub and creosote bushes, then down a thirty-foot embankment. Even sober drivers had flown over the edge and rolled their vehicles, especially if it was raining. "Damn it, I'm not going to let us get pushed off the ledge." Her arms and legs felt boneless and weak, but she mashed both feet on the brake pedal, hoping that would help. The steering wheel shuddered in her hands. Blue smoke poured off her tires, creating a dense veil between her truck and the SUV.

She expected another impact.

Suddenly, their pursuer fell back just enough to swing around, then went flying past them like a rocket. All the windows were dark, and she couldn't see inside. Julianne skidded to a dead stop on the side of the road just short of that deadly curve, her dry mouth open as she watched the late-model GMC disappear into a pair of distant taillights. It had no rear license plate, or even a plate frame.

"Are you all right?" Mitchell asked, running a hand through his hair and pulling at his tie.

"Yes, I think so." Her fingers still gripped the wheel in a spasm of fear. "God, Mitchell, what happened? Was that road rage? I wasn't driving like some old granny out for a Sunday ride."

"Not road rage. I don't know who it was, but they knew you. Or us."

She looked at him. "You mean we were singled out?"

"It seems like it. We've pissed off some people lately."

He was right. They had. "You mean your brothers?"

He unbuttoned his shirt collar. "Maybe, but there might be one or two others."

"Who? Really, Mitchell, don't they have anything else to do?"

It was a rhetorical question, but he answered it. "You'd think so. We sure do." He unfastened his seatbelt.

"They could have killed us!"

"Come on, trade places." He motioned for her to get out. "I'll drive us the rest of the way."

Ordinarily, Julianne would have refused, unwilling to reveal weakness or show any face but a brave one. Now, though, she was glad to lean on Mitchell for a moment. He was with her in this situation; she'd grown so accustomed to facing trouble alone, with others looking to her to solve problems and avert disaster. To be able to surrender the responsibility for a while was a relief, and her sizzled nerves appreciated it, too. She climbed out of the truck and walked around to the other side where he waited for her. Shaken to the marrow of her bones, she leaned against him, and his arms closed around her. It felt good, familiar, to be sheltered by him. She exhaled.

"We're okay," he comforted her. "We're okay." He said it as if to reassure himself as much as her. He put his hand on the back of her head and pressed it against his shoulder.

When she was in her seat, he closed the door and took over.

"You sure you're all right?" he asked again.

She took a couple of deep breaths and nodded.

He squeezed her wrist, then put the truck in gear and pulled out onto the highway. "What's Malbec, anyway? Some kind of Australian beer?"

"Wine. From South America."

"Have you got anything else?"

"A bottle of whiskey."

"Better. That's what we need—snake-bite medicine."

Back in Julianne's apartment, Mitchell watched her arm the security system, still spooked by their near miss on the highway. He flopped on the sofa, pulled off his tie, and opened the top two buttons on his shirt. Julianne had called the police about what had happened, although she didn't think it would do any good and told him so. It wasn't a secret that she was seeing Mitchell, even if just on a work-related level, and he figured that had probably cost her any credibility she had with the sheriff's department. She brought out a tray with the whiskey and two glasses, only one with ice, and a bottle of water.

Mitchell reviewed a mental list of people who might be angry enough, or crazy enough, to pull a dangerous stunt like the one they had just gone through, and really, he could only come up with Darcy. He said as much to her as she settled beside him.

"I guess that doesn't surprise me, but I don't know why he'd bother." She poured his drink and handed it to him. "Is he willing to go far enough to put his own neck on the block just to get even? Even for what? I'm sick of it." She took a sip of her own "snake-bite medicine." "And where did he get a fancy truck like that?"

"He either borrowed it or stole it. I'm just not sure who would trust him with an expensive rig like that." He took her free hand for a moment as he recalled scenes from the old days, lots of yelling, swearing, and threats carried out. "Earl was hardest on Darcy—when he came home, anyway. I wasn't sure why, except Darcy had a smart mouth and never knew when to keep it shut. He still doesn't, really. James isn't nearly as bad, but sometimes he goes along with Darcy, maybe just to *get* along. We all got our share of the belt and Earl's ridicule, and once my mother was gone, he cranked up his temper to 'high.' But Darcy got more than his share, and the strange thing is, the worse Earl treated him, the more Darcy became like him. He's not a kid anymore. He could have left home years ago to get away from that. But he stayed and took it until Earl's imprint was forged in his brain." Absently, he rubbed at a small scar on her wrist, then looked up at her. "It's strange—in some ways he's even meaner than Earl was at his worst."

She set the tray on the end table. "He hit on me once."

"*Darcy* did?" he asked, horrified.

"Yep." She told him about how she'd run into Darcy at the Shoppeteria after Mitchell had gone to prison, and Darcy had suggested they get together. "I couldn't believe it."

"Wow." It was all he could think of to say. Though Mitchell didn't tell her, he suspected that Darcy hated women.

She poured two fingers of whiskey for herself—neat, he noticed— then kicked off her sandals. "I hope he never has kids of his own. To pass on that cruel treatment to innocent children? What would he produce besides cringing, broken people or, worse, some kind of Super Earl?"

The bare-bones concept of that wasn't funny, not at all. But fried nerves and a little alcohol made Mitchell picture a King Kong sort of monster in his mind's eye, stepping on FedEx delivery trucks and kicking overpasses out of the way like cobwebs. He chuckled, then started laughing. "Super Earl! The thing that came from the arroyo."

Julianne gave him a serious look, then said, "In a world of evil relatives and bitchy in-laws, one stands out among them all: Super Earl, the spawn of an unholy alliance between Darcy, the Dark Brute, and She-Beast, a female Gorgon from the Chihuahuan Desert."

Mitchell had a sip of whiskey in his mouth and let it drain back into the glass to keep from choking on it when he laughed his head off. She started laughing, too, and the two of them rolled around on the sofa, tears streaming, whooping with a kind of crazy, hysterical howling. Just when they'd start to settle down, one of them would get going again, and they went on like that for a good five minutes.

At last Julianne flopped back against the upholstery, gasping and exhausted. "I think we've lost our minds." She dragged her fingertips under her eyes to wipe away the tears, and sniffled.

"Not yet," he replied, still chuckling. "God, I forgot how good it feels to really laugh like that. I can't remember the last time I did."

"Me, too—or me neither." She took a careful taste of whiskey, as if afraid of slobbering it down her white top in case she got the giggles again. "We used to laugh a lot, the two of us."

Her fit, long-legged teenage body flashed through his memory. She hadn't changed. If anything, she had ripened into a more lushly tempting woman. He lifted her hand and kissed the inside of her wrist. "Yeah, when we weren't busy with other things. You always brought out the need in me, Juli. No matter what was going on in my life, you were there in my mind, making me want you. True, I got sidetracked with the baseball thing, but my plans always included you."

She leaned into him on the sofa and put her hand on his jaw. Her touch sparked a flame in him that was familiar and urgent, an echo calling from the past that had appeared right beside him. He pulled her onto his lap and kissed her. She tasted of whiskey and smelled faintly of a spicy, floral fragrance—not the heavy kind of scent that burned off a person's eyelashes and saturated his lungs like a toxic gas. That was Cherry's style, not Juli's.

The kiss deepened, and despite all the things that had happened in the intervening years and the toll exacted by those experiences, he felt seventeen again, kissing the hog farmer's blonde daughter behind a live oak on her daddy's place. But now they didn't have to worry about getting caught. She fitted into his embrace perfectly, her breath coming fast, stoking the candle flame into a blaze. It was as if only a week instead of nearly a decade had passed.

When the kiss broke, she surprised him by pushing him down on the sofa and climbing over him to settle her body on top of his. She gathered her hair in one hand, then let it fall like a curtain around their faces. He groaned and automatically pushed his hips against hers. No other woman felt as comfortable in his arms or as welcoming to his touch as she did.

He worked a hand up between them and managed to unbutton his shirt and inch down the elastic neckline of her blouse until their flesh touched, chest to breast. She drew back for a moment and looked him straight in the eyes. That look pierced his heart as no other had. In it he saw the forgiveness she'd already given him and the promise of something much greater and even truer.

When he reached up to kiss her again, the fever between them climbed toward a white hotness. He pushed her to her side and looped one leg over hers, but the narrow cushions restricted their movements.

Frustrated by the constraints, he rolled off to the floor, then grabbed her wrist and caught her in his arms.

"Oh!" Julianne's breath hitched when she landed. His lovers' choreography called to her as he did, wordlessly, with an irresistible pull. Their kisses were urgent, desperate—taken and given by two people who'd felt the burden of so many empty years. She felt as if she'd been holding her breath, waiting for Mitchell to fill the emptiness in her soul.

Everything about him that felt so right seemed lacking in other men she had known. He'd been her first lover, and she had forgotten until now how utterly male he was compared to Wesley. But she didn't want to think about Wes now. Nothing had been Wes's fault, and he was long gone. Mitchell summoned the female in her. Long-buried memories of how they once were—together—came roaring to her. She buried her face against his neck and inhaled the scent of him. His arms, sinewed and scarred, embraced her. Pushing her to her back, he traced a line of leisurely kisses along her shoulders and collarbones that made her nerves hum with anticipation. Like a conjurer, he whisked away her skirt and blouse, and he let his gaze roam over her bare breasts and torso. She would have felt self-conscious with any other man taking in the features of her body. But Mitchell's expression was introspective.

"You're so beautiful, Juli. Even more beautiful than I remembered," he murmured, and outlined her upper lip with his finger. "I've missed this. For years."

"Mitchell." She closed her eyes briefly while a surge of emotion flooded her, washing away the sense of time and place, except for this moment, this room, this man. "I missed *you*." There it was. She hadn't realized it before, but it was true. She'd missed him. The empty space in her heart, the one beside Erin's memory, belonged to him.

He lowered his head and closed his lips around her tight nipple. She squirmed beneath his attentions, even as his hand crept up the inside of her thigh. He hadn't forgotten. He knew exactly where her sensitive places were—the curve of her ear, the tender underside of her breasts, the center of her palm—and he planted soft kisses in each spot. Automatically, she reached for him and closed her hand over the hard length of him. His heat radiated through the fabric of his pants. Impatient, she pushed his shirt off his shoulders and kissed him, nibbling along his collarbone and his jawline.

Groaning, he stood, pulled her up from the floor, and dropped her on her bed. She bounced into her white comforter and pillows as if they were clouds swelling around her. Then he yanked open his belt, which hit the floor with the clank of its buckle, and shucked his boots and pants.

There were no delicate pauses or questioning hesitation. She opened her arms. "We've been alone too long."

Uttering a low, inarticulate sound, he covered her body with his own and pushed a knee between hers. She knew him and had thought she remembered what he felt like inside of her. But this true moment of their joining was new and unexpected. They met and parted and met again in an ancient rhythm that drove them to seek completion.

Julianne thrust her hips toward Mitchell's, and the storm brewing within her gained more power than she could contain. Fierce spasms gripped her, and she muffled a sob against his neck as they overtook her.

"I love you so much," she said, and clung to him limply.

She heard Mitchell's breath rush through his lungs like a sirocco. This was where he belonged—here with her.

When his own completion shook him, he called her name.

Julianne rolled over in the darkness, under the hum of the air-conditioning unit, and flung the sheet up over them.

Mitchell pulled himself up to one elbow and looked at her with only the reflected streetlight to illuminate them. "Did you mean what you said?"

"Yes." She turned her head and smiled at him. "Mitchell, I realize I never stopped loving you. That's only one reason why I was partly responsible for Wes's death."

"Julianne, you don't really believe that."

"I never loved Wes, but I tried hard to be a good wife to him. The night of the fire was his birthday and I'd fixed a special dinner for us. But my pregnancy made me pretty crabby sometimes, and when he told me he had to work on the tractor rather than come in to eat, I got into a huff. He asked me to bring him a thermos of coffee, but I didn't." She sighed. "My last words to him were just bitchy. If only I'd taken him the coffee, I might have seen you, or the fire before it got out of control. I'd have been able to call nine-one-one." She looked at the ceiling. "Of course, I never should have married him at all. I don't know what would

168

have happened to me or the baby, but Wes would probably still be alive if I hadn't crossed his path."

"*I* should have married you," he said. "You've owned my heart for more years than I can count."

Now she was up on *her* elbow. "Mitchell, you never even proposed—everything we talked about back then was always 'someday' and 'maybe.' You couldn't decide what you wanted. You wanted to play baseball, you wanted to hang out with your friends—you weren't ready to grow up. When my father was diagnosed with pancreatic cancer, I agreed to that arranged marriage, because I wanted him to die in peace. He was so worried about leaving me alone in the world. And I couldn't tell him about you."

"That's not exactly how it happened. Baseball scouts were coming here to see me play. I was trying to get things lined up so we could leave Gila Rock behind and start a new life." She heard a defensive tone in his voice.

"But I couldn't just walk away from the farm. It goes back five generations. Wes was willing to take over the responsibility. You wouldn't have wanted that."

"Hell no. What I know about hog farming could be written on the head of a pin." He flopped back down to the mattress.

"That didn't stop you from going to work at Benavente's," she observed.

"I needed the job, and no one else was willing to hire an ex-con. Besides, I wasn't about to hang around the trailer with my old man, like Darcy does. Anyway, I got fired."

"I suppose that was my fault," Julianne said, sighing.

"Well, no, honey, how could it be?"

"I was so mad when I saw you that day at Benavente's."

"Yeah, I probably should have thought twice about how I handled that. I should have found a better way to talk to you."

They were squabbling like five-year-olds over who was guiltier, but Julianne couldn't seem to stop herself, and Mitchell gave as good as he got.

"I made a big fuss—"

"It's okay." There was a long pause; then he said, "Anyway, I found another job."

"I'm sure Benavente's paid better than I do."

"I wasn't going to tell you this—I wasn't going to tell anyone. This has to stay between us."

She turned her head to look at his profile. "What?"

"I have a part-time job in Alpine. I'm coaching baseball for a little team there. It doesn't pay much—those spots are usually volunteer, but they needed someone to help out."

"Why is that a secret?"

"Do you think I could have gotten within a mile of that baseball diamond if anyone knew about my past?"

"No, I suppose not. You still have a thing for baseball after all these years?"

"Didn't you ever want to do something that made you feel good about yourself? Or at least better? When I'm standing out on that field in the sun and clear air, sometimes I'm able to forget that I screwed up nine years ago. I had a chance and let it slide through my hands like water. I'll never get a full-time job doing this, but this little taste of it is good."

"Of course, I understand." That he trusted her with the information said a lot about his opinion of her. "No one will hear about it from me. Thank you for telling me, Mitchell."

He put his hand on her hip. "Juli, look—we're dragging years' worth of junk around with us. A lot has happened, to both of us. We aren't the same people we were back then." He took her hand in his and rolled toward her. "But we still care as much about each other. Can we just start over? Tonight—right now. It can be a clean beginning for us. I want to make a life with you. And we won't look back, ever again. All right?"

In the quiet darkness, Julianne's eyes stung. He was right. There was nowhere to go if they let the past drag at them. They'd be stuck in this limbo of rejection and painful memories. "Mitchell—"

"All right?" he asked again, pressing her hand.

She nodded and kissed him. "Yes," she choked out, emotion squeezing her throat.

He brushed at a tear that ran down her cheek, then let out a big sigh. "Thank you," he whispered, and she laid her head against his shoulder.

"What will—"

A thud against the building and an explosion of breaking glass stopped her cold. They both jumped; then Mitchell grabbed for his jeans and boots. The alarm shrieked, and Jack's wild barking only added to the chaos. Julianne pulled on a sleepshirt and clutched Mitchell's forearm.

"Dear God, what was that?" Julianne called over the racket.

"I'm not sure, but I'm going to find out."

The dog stood at the closed door, hackles stiff down the length of his spine, and he pawed at the panel to open it and charge down the stairs.

From the street below came the sound of squealing tires and an engine throaty with a glasspack muffler, growing fainter as it sped down the street.

"The police," she said. "The security company told me they're notified first. Then they'll call me." Just then the phone began ringing, but Mitchell pulled open the door—both he and Jack disappeared down the stairs.

"Wait! The police will be here." But he didn't turn around, so she shut off the alarm, then grabbed the Remington from its spot next to the door and followed him.

When they reached the first floor, the scent of latex paint, fresh from the can, blew through the striped curtains that separated the back office from the store. The night lighting that Julianne left on for security didn't reveal a great detail, but even from here, she could see a dark puddle spreading across the floor. Faint streetlight lanced the walls and highlighted glittering pebbles of what looked like crystals that were strewn everywhere. Only a jagged frame of glass daggers remained of one display window.

The dog struggled to break loose from Mitchell's grip on his collar. "Jack, no—you'll just make it worse."

He flipped on all the lights to reveal the extent of the damage.

"Damn it!" she snapped, and pushed past Mitchell with the rifle raised.

"Juli, don't go in there—you're barefoot," he warned. But she charged ahead.

A one-gallon paint bucket lay where it had come to rest against a table filled with shabby chic table linens and coffee cups. Shattered knickknacks lay in red paint that had splashed most of everything and created a scene that made Julianne think of a Jackson Pollock painting she'd once seen on TV. It made her think of blood. She uttered a small, anguished cry.

"Who did this?" she demanded, looking at Mitchell, and her voice rose to a wail. *"Who did this?"*

A muscle jumped in his jaw. "I don't know. Not for sure, anyway."

A patrol car pulled up then, its red-and-blue light bar flashing. Deputy Joe Porter emerged, his sidearm drawn, and he surveyed the wreckage. Jack directed his yapping at him. Stepping through the broken window and around the paint puddles, he made his way to Julianne and Mitchell.

All formality in the moment, he gestured at her weapon. "Please put down the rifle, ma'am." She did as he asked, and the deputy gave Mitchell a cursory once-over, apparently noting his shirtless torso. "Well—you've got yourself a hell of a mess here, Julianne."

His obvious double entendre made her back stiffen, and it was all she could do to keep from screeching at him. "Joe, this isn't just a prank. It's vandalism and it's getting worse. It must be a—a felony or some other kind of crime! Hasn't your office figured this out yet? I called earlier tonight—someone tried to run us off the road between here and Marfa."

"I heard. Is anyone else here?" The deputy glanced at Mitchell again with a dry expression.

"No!" Then she glanced toward the back office and thought of The Tomb and the downstairs half bath. Anyone could hide in those places. Her voice quavered as her throat clenched. "At least I don't think so." Why wouldn't any of these lawmen take her seriously? Would they finally rouse themselves from their apathy when she was dead? That thought alone shook her, and she pulled her mind away from it.

"I'll take a look around." He lumbered off, still clutching his service revolver.

Mitchell let go of Jack. "There's an old sheet of plywood out in the shed. We've got to cover that window until you can get it fixed tomorrow." He nodded toward the back. "I hope Sheriff Andy doesn't shoot me out there—maybe even in the back, with the way things go these days."

"Don't make jokes like that now. Take this." She handed him the rifle.

He grinned briefly. "Okay. Trade you for the dog."

Julianne took Jack upstairs and put on jeans and shoes, then helped Mitchell cover the gaping wound of a window. Deputy Porter found no one else on the property and dutifully took her statement. She made a copy of her surveillance file with the DVD burner and gave it to him. He didn't think it showed enough to be helpful, but he said he'd file a report.

With a mop and a bucket, Julianne did her best to clean up the paint mess and thought the one, tiny saving grace was that it was latex and not oil-based. There was more glass to sweep up, but it would have to wait until she had daylight to see it all.

By the time she and Mitchell dragged themselves up to the apartment, it was almost midnight. She'd rearmed the alarm system but didn't turn on the lights. It seemed safer to sit in the darkness, broken only by the full moon and a flickering streetlight. Mitchell was unusually pensive, but she didn't feel like talking, either. A heavy drape of gloom hung over Bickham's. Every time she thought things were looking up, something slapped her down.

She poured both of them a drink, and they sat side by side on the sofa, like two mannequins, not touching. Sleep didn't register in her mind as a possibility.

So much for their new start.

After several moments of silence, she said, "Your brothers did this, didn't they?"

He rubbed his forehead, a weary gesture. "God, I suppose they did, Juli. I think they're trying to get back at both of us now. And I promised you I wouldn't let that happen."

Julianne swallowed hard. "Maybe that feud is branded on us, and we'll never get rid of it. We let it come between us years ago, and now it's back. We can say we won't let the past strand us here, that we're starting fresh, but what can we do about everyone else? They're getting their *mail* delivered to those old days. Talk about stuck."

He uttered a vicious obscenity, then sat up and groped around in the dark. "Yeah, maybe," he agreed. "But I'm not going through that crap again. They don't have the right to steal my future, or yours, either."

"What are you doing?" she said, startled by his actions.

"I'm going to settle this once and for all."

"What? How? We don't actually have proof." She turned on the table lamp beside her and watched him gather the rest of his clothes. In just a few hours, he'd gone from a nicely dressed date to an angry, harassed-looking man with his shirttails flapping and his hair going in all directions. "Mitchell, are you leaving? Now?"

He jammed his bolo tie into his pants pocket and grabbed his jacket. "Yeah, I'm fed up with this feud bullshit. We can't even make love without it lying there like roadkill in the bed with us. Talk about getting a turd instead of a Tootsie Roll."

She followed him to the door, baffled and furious that he was going, unable to believe that he was leaving her here alone and putting himself in more danger. "Mitchell!"

He turned and grabbed her by the shoulders, then kissed her with an agonized desperation. "I love you, but we can't have this thing between us. I told Earl, and now I'm telling you, I won't drag that bad blood around with me anymore. I'm sick of this."

"But what are you going to do?" she asked again, worried about him starting an all-out war. "Don't go stirring up your father and brothers!"

He went out the door and down the stairs. "You'd better turn off the alarm, or you'll have cops all over you in a minute," he called. "Keep the rifle and Jack with you. I'll talk to you soon."

Hot-wired nerves and fear for the two of them came out as anger. She punched in the code to disable the alarm on the control unit in the apartment. She didn't want to admit that she was afraid to be alone. "All right, go! Just go! I don't need—"

But the door slammed behind him before she could finish what she was saying. After she reset the alarm, she went to the bed and slumped on the edge. "I-I don't need you or any man," she lied aloud and sobbed.

Then she called the police. Again.

CHAPTER TEN

A late-night visitor pulled up to Cherry Claxton's apartment and killed the headlights. His rumbling muffler must have tipped her off, because her door opened immediately, and the glow of the television behind her silhouetted her figure. She came outside, dressed in some filmy thing but still teetering in heels despite the hour. He had to hand it to her—she was always ready. She made a cranking motion with her hand, and he rolled down his window.

"How did it go?" she asked, leaning in, her forearms resting on the window frame. Her perfume filled the cab like a cloud.

"Better than I expected. Easy as pie."

"Julianne is bound to get tired of this sooner or later. She's pretty stubborn, but she'll cut her losses and go back to that pig farm, or wherever. And not a minute too soon for me."

"I don't think we're the only ones twisting her tail, either. I've seen the cops coming and going around there."

She smirked and gave him an offhanded wave. "Hell, bring them on. We can use the help, and I don't care what it takes. I just want her gone and out of Mitchell's mind."

He shook his head. "I don't know what women see in him, but they seem to follow him like teenagers after a shoe sale. What's so great about him?"

Cherry laughed. "Sometimes we want the peach on the branch that's hardest to reach. Anyway, honey, I think you're great at all sorts of things, too."

How did she do that, make that sound like a purring cat when she spoke? "You'd be surprised." He grinned in darkness, and she smiled back.

She straightened. "Well, it's getting late and I have to open at 5:30 in the morning. The Captain Gas waits for no one. You come around one of these days and I'll give you a *personal* tour—behind-the-scenes stuff."

He chuckled. "I just might do that."

He turned the ignition key, and the engine came to with that low thunder as he pulled away.

Mitchell pulled up to the trailer by the arroyo. It was one in the morning, but he knew everyone inside would still be up. He climbed the narrow wooden stairs and pulled open the screenless screen door, then turned the knob. Of course, it wasn't locked. They never locked this door. He walked in, and the room was mostly dark, except for the flashing TV picture that periodically lit and dimmed everything. The old air-conditioning unit still wheezed along.

Darcy sat on the disgorging sofa, looking at pictures in an old issue of the *National Enquirer*. His head jerked up. "What the hell are you doing here, you backstabber?" he demanded.

James lay on the other end with his head pillowed on a pile of clothes and a T-shirt thrown over his eyes.

God, it was disgusting here.

"I came to see the old man, not you." The response to that was a snore deep within the recliner. Mitchell stepped over and spun the chair around, startling his father awake.

Earl snorted. "What, what? Mitchell, don't bother me now." He'd taken out his dentures, and his face had a collapsed look to it.

"Earl, I want to talk to you."

The Tucker patriarch peered up at him and gave him a dismissive wave. "Now? Forget it. It's late, and no, you ain't moving back here."

Mitchell looked around at the horror show that was this dwelling. "I don't want to move back in."

"Then what are you doing here? We've already said everything there was to say. You've gone over to the enemy."

"Yeah, and that attitude ends now. I don't care if you all want to live here, rotting away in your own hate, but I'm done. You, though"—he pointed at his brothers—"you leave me the hell out of it. And leave Julianne alone. Tonight—man, you'll get arrested for that. She has security cameras, in case you don't know." She had glanced at the images and hadn't seen anything, but they didn't know that, either.

Darcy launched his rawboned frame from the sofa, all twitchy moves and defensive swagger. "Arrested for what? We didn't do anything! We've all been here the whole night."

"Give it up, Darcy; that dog won't hunt. I don't know if James helped, but you were there. I'm telling you, it ends *now*."

"I didn't do anything, either," James muttered from his spot on the sofa.

Darcy danced around like a boxer in the ring. "Are you threatening me, man? Don't you threaten me!" That edgy restlessness he often displayed had its high beams on.

Mitchell leaned over him—he and James were taller than the middle Tucker brother. "Don't forget where I spent seven years, Darcy," he said. "I learned more on the inside about fighting and killing than

178

you'll know in your lifetime, even if you make it to old age. Those guys make you look like a little girl. I saw a man killed over stolen *tater tots!*"

"Yeah, well, they ain't here now!" Faster than Mitchell would have guessed, Darcy landed two rapid-fire punches in the center of his face. Lights exploded behind his eyes, and his neck made a snapping sound like a cracking knuckle. He felt blood begin to stream down his upper lip and drip from his chin.

"Darcy, damn it!" James said. "Will you all pipe down? Some of us are trying to sleep."

"Go to bed, then!" Darcy barked.

James wadded up his pillow of dirty clothes and stayed put.

"You two take that shit outside!" Earl threw in. "I don't want things getting broken in here."

"You lousy bastard!" Mitchell raged. Equally swift, he grabbed Darcy by his skinny throat and shoved him hard against the ancient, brittle paneling that lined the walls. He saw hate in his brother's eyes. He saw fear, too. He smelled it on him. A red veil dropped over Mitchell's vision, and his fury grew. He dug his fingers in and felt sinew and bone. Darcy struggled in earnest and began to make strangled noises.

"Mitchell, you're gonna kill him," Earl observed with no great concern, but Mitchell barely heard the comment.

"Jeezum, Mitchell, let him go!" He felt James pulling at him.

"Don't you *ever* raise a hand to me again," Mitchell warned Darcy. "You do, and I'll snap that hand like a pencil. And work up from there."

Darcy swallowed under his tight grip, and Mitchell released him.

Darcy coughed and rubbed his throat. "Damn mofo ex-con! I'm not afraid of you!" he jeered, but with less gas.

"Seven years," Mitchell repeated, letting the insults slide, "and I remember every single day of it." He turned to include James in this conversation. He grabbed a towel from the sofa and swiped at the blood streaming from his nose. "Haven't you ever wondered what started all these years of bitterness with the Emersons? Did you ever bother to ask why we were raised to hate that family, or why they hated us?" No one answered. *"Don't you want to know what you're wasting your lives on?"*

"What the hell are you talking about?" James threw in. "They did us wrong, and that's plenty."

"Earl, why don't you tell the boys what's behind the legacy you left us? Do you even remember?"

Earl narrowed his eyes and scowled. "I remember just fine."

"It was about Tammy Lindgren, wasn't it?" Mitchell knew this topic was a potential powder keg. If emotions ran hot enough, the whole damn trailer might as well explode.

"By God, boy, you don't know how to leave something alone, do you?" Earl struggled to climb to his feet from the rocker, but he couldn't manage it and flopped back against the grimy cushions. "That story is none of your business."

"None of our business! You made it our business from the day we were born. You even made it Mom's business." Mitchell could feel his temper climbing and took a deep breath, hoping to settle it some.

"It was all a long time ago," was Earl's feeble defense. "Water under the bridge."

"Except it wasn't. It isn't. That living, breathing thing dragged at all of us—"

"What are you two talking about?" James repeated, sitting up.

"Are you going to tell them now, or shall I?" Mitchell asked.

The old man remained silent and gnashed his gums.

So Mitchell repeated the story Julianne had shared with him, including the evidence in her mother's journal.

"*That's* what this was about? Some woman?" Darcy asked, apparently stupefied.

"So long ago?" James added. "We weren't even born."

"There was more than that," Earl said, but didn't go on.

"Figures," Darcy muttered. "Some *woman*." Then he stuck out his chest and chin. "It don't matter; it's too late to change things now. You didn't defend the family honor and you're still a traitor."

The family honor. Mitchell's head and face throbbed as if a locomotive had rolled over it. Sweating like a prison fish, he sank into a hardback chair beside the TV after shoving away an empty pizza box. He didn't think his nose was broken, but he wasn't sure. Whenever someone got their nose hit in the ballfield, the coach would jam tampons into their nostrils. It worked, but he wasn't about to find any here. Bloodstains soaked the top half of his shirt. But if he'd felt better, he would have laughed the ironic laughter of the damned.

"Family honor! Darcy, does that balloon you're riding in ever land? What honor is there in any of us? Earl, here, carried a grudge all this time because some girl he wanted got pregnant by Paul Boyce. So he taught us to hate the Boyces. We burned a man to death in his barn because of it. How honorable is that? I guess since I took the blame for the whole thing, there was some kind of twisted virtue there." And he'd lost his baby girl in the bargain. Wearily, he stood up.

"I'm going to marry Julianne, if she'll have me. That's the way it should have been from the beginning."

"The Boyce female?" James hooted. "You're going to marry her? Well, give him your blessing, Earl."

His father scowled. "I'm not giving you anything. You're no son of mine. My kid wouldn't marry the enemy's brat."

Darcy added, "You tell him, Earl. I didn't get anywhere with him."

"I'm not going to argue about this," Mitchell said. He had better luck talking to Jack, and he was a dog.

"Then get out. You said yourself that you don't belong here anymore, and you were right. Your name might still be Tucker because I can't do anything about that, but you aren't one of us anymore."

Damn, wasn't *that* a shame, Mitchell thought, but in a way he was relieved. The break would be clean, or at least as clean as possible with this bunch. "You're right. I'm not one of you. Maybe my bad luck will end now that I'm free of this bad-luck family."

"Are you going to take that?" Darcy demanded, his hard-ass facade quivering. "I'm not!"

"Shove it, Darcy!" Mitchell barked. "And leave us the hell alone, because if you don't, you'll answer to me this time. You two should do yourselves a favor and learn to think with your own minds. But I have no reason to protect either of you anymore. I'll kick your head so hard you'll be looking at the world through your ass." Mitchell walked out, not bothering to close the door. Fury coursed through him like a jolt of electricity, giving him a sensation of unnatural power and life—one that would be hard to control if he didn't get away from here.

Cranking over the Skylark, he realized that now neither he nor Julianne had anyone to block their way. They'd make their own family. Bouncing over the deep ruts on the car's bad shocks, he recognized that he'd let his father run over him just to keep the peace, and he'd helped perpetuate that hate for a long time. He couldn't change their thinking, but he sure as hell could let them know what they were in for if they gave him or Juli any more trouble. He felt bad about leaving her—he shouldn't have walked out the way he had. But he hadn't been willing to let this go any longer. And maybe he'd finally settled the problem with his own loser family. At least he'd spoken his piece.

Driving toward Highway 90, he decided he wouldn't pester Julianne tonight. She had Jack to look after her and the security system. After a glance in the rearview mirror, he knew he'd scare the hell out of her if she saw his blood-soaked shirt. His face was swelling, too, and in an hour or two he'd look like a boxer who'd gone fifteen rounds and lost. He hoped his eyes didn't turn black, but that was a real possibility.

While he sat at a railroad crossing waiting for the eastbound freight train to pass, he examined his face in the vanity mirror. The red lights on the crossing gates competed with the glare flashing between the railcars, but neither let him see much, and the dome light wasn't at all kind. Goddamn that Darcy, he'd really done a number on him. Very gingerly, he placed his thumb and forefinger on the bridge of his nose and wiggled it. The knifing pain made him swear the worst string of words he knew, but nothing moved, so he hoped it wasn't broken. Groping around on the floor of the backseat, he found another towel and did his best to scrub the blood off his upper lip and chin.

When the train had passed and the gates began to rise, he saw a Presidio County Sheriff's car waiting on the opposite side of the tracks, headlights glaring. He held his breath as they passed each other, bouncing over the tracks. He followed the cop's taillights in the rearview mirror until they grew distant and turned down the road that led to the arroyo and the only dwelling there. He let out a deep breath. That scene would get ugly.

At least the Satellite Motel had an ice machine—he'd hit that before heading to his room. Maybe in the shower he'd be able to wash off the blood and the smell of stale beer and bacon grease.

Julianne didn't really sleep that night; she napped. Her anger at Mitchell's reckless confrontation with his family had fizzled away, and now she only worried. If he would just call and tell her that he was all right. She flitted in and out of one doze after another, several of which were long enough to feature chaotic, disturbing dreams.

Every creak and groan in the old building made her eyes snap open. At one point she woke to what Mark Twain had called the ticking of a death-watch in the wall—the expansion and contraction of dry wood after a day under hot sun. SAF-T Security Service called and assured her that the motion detectors on the first floor still worked. But with a sheet of old plywood nailed over the gaping hole that had been a window, and after Mitchell's abrupt departure, she felt very alone. Even Jack couldn't fill the emptiness, and finally he got so tired of her tossing and turning, he jumped off the bed and went to his own.

Lying there in the darkness, she thought of Mitchell beside her a few hours earlier, and she could barely believe everything that had transpired in the past few months. She still detected the faint scent of him in her bed, and that gave her comfort. To think that the man she'd loved, then hated for so long, she now loved again. Had always loved. But nothing to do with him had ever been easy or uncomplicated. He brought a hurricane with him—a storm of serious trouble and longing and joy. She had only to consider all the events of tonight alone to remember that. In some ways, that was part of his appeal.

And that he loved her.

Julianne was already up by the time the sun finally crept over the horizon and cast slats of light across her bedroom wall. In late August, the sun rose around 7:30, but she had enough work and worry to keep her busy and sleepless. After a shower and a jolt of hot coffee, she fed the dog, and made some phone calls to get the repairs underway. A rep from her insurance company was coming by in an hour. Then she went downstairs to look at her store.

With a box of black garbage bags tucked under one arm, she walked around the floor searching for anything that was out of place, covered with glass, or paint-splattered. The damage was fairly contained, and she'd worked hard to get the worst of it mopped up the night before. Where the paint had splashed and dried, though, it was bad. A pretty Belleek cup and saucer wore a gory spray of red paint. A stack of hand-embroidered, linen dinner napkins had been soaked with it. Disgusted, she yanked them from the display and shoved them into a garbage bag to catalog later. After pulling out other ruined things, she swept up all the glass she could find, then went over it again with a shop vac. The floor would have to be refinished again. It would be great if only the damaged part could be done instead of the whole thing, but she didn't know if that was possible.

Some other inventory and display items had to be tossed, and her insurance should cover those. All of it could be replaced and yet—and yet . . . Each of these events—the vandalism, the dead chicken in her mailbox, the destruction of her property—chipped away at her courage. Determination and the will to succeed still drove her, but how much could one person take?

The sheriff's department hadn't gotten in touch with her to say if they had discovered anything at the mobile home. And she still hadn't heard from Mitchell. She had no idea what had happened after he'd left here last night. But she remembered very well what had occurred between the trip home and this catastrophe surrounding her now.

In that brief spell between troubles, she and Mitchell had made love. They had been able to lock out the world. Her body and heart had been one again at last, joined with his.

Then real life had come calling again with a bucket of red paint.

She sighed and lifted her chin. She had no choice. She had to keep moving forward.

CHAPTER ELEVEN

Julianne screamed. The installers from Marfa Door and Window nearly dropped the pane of plate glass they were carrying, and gabbled a panicked burst of profanity. She'd been on the sidewalk outside Bickham's, watching them maneuver her new window with suction cups when she glanced to her left and saw Mitchell standing there. He'd turned his back to the street and to the men, then lifted his sunglasses to show her a face that looked sort of mashed, like it had been whacked with a skillet. She felt the pavement tilt beneath her for a second.

She clapped both hands to her mouth. Pulling them back, she uttered, "Mitchell! Dear God, what happened?" One eye was black, bloodshot, and nearly closed, and a raw-looking gash marked his left cheek bone. He had bruises the size of continents on a world globe. Even the window guys were staring.

"I went to the trailer, like I said I was going to." He tried to smile, then winced, then shook his head. "I think I made my point, but not before Darcy got in a good sucker punch."

"With what, a hammer?" She grabbed his arm and pulled on him. "Come on, come on, I need to take care of this." To the installers she called, "I'll be upstairs if you need me." He let her lead him into the cool dimness of the store.

"At least you didn't get the train-wreck version from last night. My nose bled like a faucet. I threw my shirt away—I didn't think it would ever come clean." He glanced around and gestured at the general mess. "Damn, this place looks pretty bad, too, Juli. Did you call your insurance guy?"

"You look worse. And yes, he came by first thing. He says I'm covered, especially because of the surveillance equipment I had installed." If this was some kind of karmic endurance test sending one problem after another, she was sick of it.

"That's something anyway, I guess."

Fortunately, she'd gotten rid of the old refrigerator that she had inherited with this apartment and had a new one installed. This one had an ice maker with a door dispenser. That had been a big leap forward in technology; the one on the farm still had stubborn metal ice trays that generally refused to work for anyone. She grabbed a towel and a plastic Ziploc bag from a drawer and made an ice pack.

"Sit, sit," she directed, and pointed him to the kitchen table. "Did you go to the hospital or see a doctor?" She set a glass of iced tea in front of him and gave him a straw.

He touched careful fingertips to his cheekbone. "Who, me?"

She made an impatient noise. "You could have a broken bone in there someplace. You should have at least called *me*." Standing over him, she tipped his face up to hers to inspect the damage, and her heart actually hurt in her chest. Those puffy bruises and cuts looked so painful. "Oh, Mitchell," she whispered. With difficulty, she pushed down tears. She'd never wanted to be a woman who cried over every broken nail or greeting card commercial on TV. But this was hard. Catastrophes were always hard.

"I put ice on it for an hour or so when I got back to the motel. If anyone had seen me digging through the ice machine near the office, they probably would have called the cops."

"Did you hit him, too?" Turning back to the cupboards, she found her first aid kit.

"Sort of—those jackasses seem to bring out the worst in me. He swore he was home all last night and didn't break the window. James said the same thing." He flinched when she touched the ice pack to his eye and cheek. "How can I believe them? They're fixed on a single target, like dogs being trained for the fight pit."

That image sent a quiver of revulsion through her. "I'm the target?"

"Not exactly, but they have pretty narrow lives. I did tell James and Darcy about Tammy Lindgren, though." He went on to tell her what had happened after he left her.

She took his hand and raised it to the ice. "Hold this right here. What did Earl say when you told them about Cade's mother?"

"He said it was no one's business and that it happened years ago. I told him that was bullshit—he made it everyone's business, and 'years ago' has always been 'now.'"

In the first aid kit she searched out antibiotic ointment and butterfly strips. "So they're going to hound us to our graves?"

"I told them this has to be the end of it or they'll answer to me. I think I actually scared Darcy." He let out a huff of a laugh. "Maybe it was when I had my hand around his throat. His eyes were about to pop out. When I left, I passed a cop car headed that way. You called them, I hope."

Her brows shot up. "Of course, but I didn't expect them to really do much about it. I haven't heard anything from them yet. If I'm going to." Pushing away the ice pack, she dabbed the ointment on the gash over his cheekbone. All the muscles in his jaw jumped at her touch. "Sorry. I'm trying to be careful."

They were quiet for a moment while she tended to him. From downstairs came occasional pounding sounds and a conversation in Spanish between the installers.

"You look pretty cute in those white coveralls," he said. "I wanted to tell you that the first time I saw you in them, but you were cranky."

She managed a faint smile. "I had the right to be cranky. Think about what you've learned about me since that day. Anyway, you had a chip on your shoulder, too."

His sigh made him sound world-weary. "Yeah. I still do sometimes. The world is a hard place. Believe me, I've seen the worst of it."

A question that had nagged at her for a while now came to mind again. It felt like an awkward one to ask, seeming as clumsy as inquiring about someone's bathroom habits or their private spiritual beliefs. But Mitchell had touched on the subject now. "Is—is prison really bad?"

A chasm of silence opened between them, and she thought he might not answer.

He cut her a sidelong look. "Just want to make sure I got what was coming to me?"

"N-no, of course not." Her face grew hot, and from past experience, she knew she probably looked blotchy. "It was a rude question. I'm sor—"

He pulled her hands away from his face and took them into his own. "How can I describe it to someone who's never seen it?" It sounded as if he were asking himself the question. "It's not like what they show on TV. Life in a correctional institution is constant chaos and noise. Slamming doors that rattle your teeth and the rooms, loud music, yelling inmates, fights between cliques and gangs, between individuals— like I told Darcy last night: I saw a man killed over stolen tater tots at breakfast. People get beaten or raped."

Her breath rushed out of her in a soft cat's-paw.

"A lot of the inmates are damned scary-looking, with so much ink on their faces and bodies, they're like monsters from a nightmare. Prison is zero privacy, constant danger, and small-minded, unpredictable corrections officers who like to yank inmates' chains just for the hell of it. It's easy to get into trouble over some rule made up on the spot, one that didn't exist the day before, or even the hour before. Some of those COs—the only real difference between the inmates and them is the uniform. It's lonely and boring. It's the loss of everything except your own thoughts. Sometimes even those are up for grabs. And that's on a good day." He let go of her and put the ice pack back on his eye. "On a bad day, someone gets killed, beaten to a pulp, or there's a lockdown. Another inmate decides he's going to challenge you or doesn't like the way you look—*just because*. Sociopaths make up about a quarter of the population. That only makes things harder. And the nights—sometimes the nights are endless." He stopped talking and gazed at the litter of cotton swabs and bandages in front of him on the table.

"I shouldn't have asked," she fumbled, her face now blazing. He got what he deserved, she told herself feverishly. It wouldn't have happened if not for Wes. But—

"Most people there will tell you either that they're innocent, or yeah, they're guilty but it's someone else's fault—someone *made* them do what they did. And I suppose that's true once in a while." He lifted his eyes to hers again. "But for the most part, we all got there under our own steam, because of bad decisions and bad choices. I sure did. And considering what those choices led me to do, you have the right to ask."

Julianne sank into the chair to his right and put her hand on his arm. "There's too much hatred and heartache in life," she murmured, feeling suddenly overwhelmed and worn out, despite the pep talk she'd given herself earlier. "Good things happen every day, but so do a lot of bad things." Looking at him, she asked, "Mitchell, do you really think your brothers will stop pestering me now?"

"They're just two forking idiots. Julianne, don't you let them spook you. Stand your ground. You have a right to be happy, and you're strong. They're nobodies, and they really hate that." He leaned toward her. "But they *are* nobodies."

"For nobodies, they do a lot of damage." She waved her arm in a wide arc to indicate the breadth of their crimes. "And I guess it's been a hard fight for me all these years, going it alone."

He kissed her then, softly, with such tenderness that her pent-up tears stung her eyes before she forced them back. His strong hands traveled up her forearm and down to her wrist, something she found oddly comforting.

"You're not alone now."

Mitchell walked into the Captain Gas and took off his sunglasses when he confirmed the place was empty of customers. The scent of buffalo jerky and single cigarettes piled in a candy dish on the counter floated in the air around him. But those aromas couldn't compete with Cherry's perfume or the desiccated muffin sandwiches sitting under the heat lamps next to the condom cabinet. He'd stopped here because he hadn't seen any cars in the parking lot or at the pumps right now. He wanted to talk to Cherry alone, on halfway neutral territory. This was the best way he could think of.

"God-a'mighty, what the hell happened to you?" Cherry demanded from her command post at the cash register, plainly startled. She wore her long red hair in a high, voluminous ponytail, and her form-fitting top clung obligingly to her shape.

Mitchell's face was still swollen, and the throbbing pain radiated to his whole head and down his neck. During the day he squeaked by on ibuprofen, but at night he wished for a prescription painkiller.

She leaned forward. "What does the other guy look like? You won, didn't you?"

He didn't laugh. "As far as I'm concerned." Her reaction to his appearance didn't surprise him. After hours of icing, and soaks with cold washcloths administered by Juli, the damage to his face had emerged as one-and-a-half black eyes, assorted bruises, and the nasty gash from a ring Darcy had been wearing when he'd slugged him. She'd screamed when she'd seen him the morning after the fight, scaring even him, and he'd already seen himself in the motel bathroom mirror. Now he was patched up with butterfly strips, but he still looked like a weird melon that someone had kicked around a parking lot and tried to tape back together.

"I expected Darcy to tell you all about it."

"Darcy—I haven't seen him or any of you Tuckers since late last week. He only comes in to buy beer and cigarettes, or gas for those shitty old cars. He and I aren't doing the nasty, y'know. He's just a customer, and someone I went to school with."

Cherry could be as smooth as a lake of molasses—dark and blank. She had one of the best poker faces he'd ever seen. But she fumbled this time, and he knew she had to be lying. Her lie told him more than he expected. He wasn't sure *what* she was doing with Darcy, but he knew it was something. "Ask him the next time he comes in. I'm sure he'll tell you a great story."

"Did *he* do that?"

He raised his brows and gave her a pointed look. "Yeah, but he learned not to do it again."

Her laugh sounded a bit forced. "You boys were always such hotheads, giving each other shit, or one guy and another. Do you remember that time—"

He wasn't in the mood for reminiscing. "I'm not here for another trip down memory lane, Cherry. Julianne and I were on the highway coming back from Marfa the other night and someone tried to run us off the road." He stared at her, and she blinked first. "We could have been killed. Then a few hours later, someone threw a can of paint through one of her display windows at Bickham's." He took a step closer to the counter. "Do you know anything about that?"

She dropped her jokey pretense and her voice turned gritty and defensive. "*Me!* I don't know a son-of-a-bitching thing, Mitchell. Why would I?" She lit a cigarette with short, fitful movements and squinted at him through the smoke coiling around her head. "Maybe your *girlfriend* has made some enemies. You should ask her." She exhaled smoke from both nostrils. Her surprising contempt turned "girlfriend" into a filthy word.

And he had his answer. That bristly defensiveness reminded him of all the "innocent" rapists, thieves, and murderers he'd come across in prison. Not a damn one of *them* was guilty, either, and a single question about it would get the same kind of response. Before they jammed a shank between your ribs.

"Keep your distance from me, Cherry. You and I don't have a reason to talk anymore."

"Now, Mitchie, don't say that," she began, her tone melting. "Why do you want to go and marry little Bambi? You need a real woman."

Another red flag went up in his mind. "Who says I'm getting married?"

Darcy knew it.

"Darcy might have mentioned it a while back. It seems like she got over you killing Wes—"

A Captain Gas regular walked in just then, and Mitchell put his sunglasses back on.

"Hey, Buddy Lee," she called, recovering her breezy persona with obvious relief. "How's every little thing?"

"Hey, Cherry. I'm on the number two pump for a fill. And ring me up for a case of PBR." Buddy Lee was heading for the beer cooler when Mitchell walked out.

He started his car and drove off, just catching a glimpse of the vehicle parked at the number two pump. He whipped his head around to confirm what he thought he'd seen—a big, dark-silver SUV. Like the Yukon that had tried to run Juli's truck off the highway? When he decided to turn back, he was on the other side of the railroad tracks, and a train was creeping past. By the time he got back to the Captain Gas, the SUV was gone.

Julianne sat at her desk inputting her list of damaged inventory. So far, the estimate had climbed to nearly $1,000, and that didn't begin to include the cost of fixing the hardwood floor or the plate-glass window, which had left her gasping. She was glad the installer had submitted the bill directly to her insurance company. At least she didn't have to fiddle around with that paperwork. She hated paperwork—she wanted to get back to fruitful activity, not push invoices around. Every passing car out front or group of voices made her antsy. It was Friday, a big part of a three-day weekend getaway. For tourism, it was a little gold mine. But potential business was passing right by her closed door.

Being closed meant no income. A small, artful barricade disguised the mess on the floor, and she'd rearranged the display tables with new merchandise. The hardwood couldn't be fixed until next week, and she'd have to close again for that. But the window was in and except for the red stain on the floor, it was hard to tell anything had happened.

"Julianne? Are you here?"

She jumped. It was a woman's voice, but one she didn't place immediately.

"Around this way!" she called from her desk. She got up and opened the back door. Hearing the crunch of footsteps on the side-street gravel, she waited and saw Darlene Gibbs come into view.

"Mother of pearl, Julianne, what happened? I saw the Closed for Repairs sign on the front." Darlene puffed her way up the steps while Julianne held the door open. "I thought your shop was up and running."

Julianne sighed. "It was." Briefly, she explained the vandalism without going into any detail about reasons or "perps," as Sheriff Gunter said. "I'll be open again tomorrow. Have a seat." She pushed out the desk chair next to her own.

Darlene settled her ample backside on the padded upholstery and fanned her face with a church bulletin she'd pulled from her purse. "What a world," she clucked. "You wouldn't expect that kind of crime in a small place like Gila Rock. I guess it's everywhere now, especially with the increase in tourists." She lifted her nose. "That coffee smells wonderful." The coffeemaker was just gasping out the last bit of steam and hot water into a fresh pot.

Julianne headed toward the new card table that held the cups. "I'll get you some."

"No, no. I don't like the taste, but I love the smell." Darlene was a short, round woman in her late forties, with a gray-blonde pageboy and today, a soft-blue, coordinated outfit of pants and a top. A grandmotherly sort who wouldn't strike a person as a real estate dynamo, she nevertheless had been the top producer in her office in Marfa for the past three years. "Anyway, I have some interesting news."

Hope fluttered in Julianne. She poured coffee for herself and loaded it with milk. "You have a buyer for the farm?"

"Possibly." The older woman motioned Julianne back into her desk chair and leaned forward eagerly, as if she were about to impart an exciting secret. "It's a couple from Dallas hoping to switch gears. They're in fast-paced jobs and after the husband had a little heart scare, they thought they'd like to get away from that."

"And go into farming?" Julianne asked, almost incredulous. "Talk about stress—"

"No, no, honey, they're looking for a property they can turn into a little resort. You know, like one of those guest ranches or a winery spa or something. There's the one south of Marfa, but that's pretty highfalutin. Some people just want a more down-home country trip."

"And they're interested in my place?"

"They could be after I show it to them. I told them about it, and they're arranging a trip out here to look around. I've got other farmland for sale, but none that is as right for this use as yours."

The wheels in Julianne's head began turning. She'd had quite a few visitors ask her about accommodations around Gila Rock. There were none she could think of except for the Satellite Motel, where Mitchell was living, and a couple of others like it. The sort with neon signs partially burned out, dusty pop machines lined up outside the offices, and dead flies on their window sills.

"I've heard that people are looking for more B and Bs around here. Customers have asked me about them, too, now that Gila Rock is attracting some combination of artsy vacationers and the Marfa lights crowd."

"So, there you go," Darlene said, and hoisted herself out of the chair. "I'll let you get back to work, and I'll go on about mine." She replaced her makeshift fan in her purse and dabbed a tissue at her sweaty temples. "Lordy, I just don't handle this hot weather the way I did when I was younger. I'll have to sit with my car's A/C blowing on me for a while before I see my next client. Anyway, I'll let you know when the Dallas couple is coming."

Julianne stood to see her out the back door. "Thanks, Darlene. I appreciate the visit. Come back when I'm open." She laughed. "The shop looks better than this back room." Once the woman was on her way back across the yard, Julianne went to her computer and pushed aside the tedious task she'd been working on before. With quick keystrokes, she googled bed-and-breakfasts around the southwest to see what they looked like. Some photos depicted rustic decor, embracing the traditional western-cowboy flavor under endless blue skies. Others had a quaint cottage feel, and a few others emphasized a luxurious Victorian theme.

She took a taste of her now-lukewarm coffee, imagining the farmhouse with a new, old-fashioned look and the possibilities spun out from there like streamers in the wind. It could be done. She'd need help, of course—it would be a big job. Then her bubble of inspiration burst.

Who was she kidding? she thought and rested her chin on the heel of her hand. Such an ambitious project would take *money*. A lot more money than the Bickham's facelift had cost. And although she and Mitchell had talked about a future and starting over, who knew what was coming?

CHAPTER TWELVE

Julianne bumped along a narrow, side-road shortcut that ran between town and the farm, past the scrub and occasional skittering lizard. Jack rode shotgun, and she was glad to have him along.

She'd asked Mitchell to come with her, considering everything that had happened lately, but he begged off, claiming to be busy with his coaching job. They'd argued over it, but he still wouldn't budge. That and her already-jumpy nerves made her irritable. His damned family was the reason she was having so much trouble, and even if he'd divorced them, it was still open season on her. The least he could do was come along in case one them decided to ambush her. She was just plain scared, and it irked her to admit it even to herself. She was tough enough to take care of herself. But it was nice having someone in her corner. At least she was headed in the right direction—back to town. And she'd feel better when she got there.

Out on the far distant hills, dark clouds crowded together in an expanding low ceiling. The wind had kicked up with them, but it was hard to tell whether those clouds would bring rain or just sit out there like crouching wolves, watching.

After the floor refinisher had completed the job, leaving behind a bill that left Julianne gasping, she'd decided she had to get out of Bickham's. There was still work to do, but her nerves were pulled as tight as they could stretch. She'd locked up, set the alarm, and taken Jack with her to check on the farmhouse.

Not too many people found their way to this back road, and the solitude suited her right now.

A few window shoppers had stopped by the property to look, but Darlene Gibbs still had her money on the Masseys from Dallas, the couple who wanted to escape big-city life. Of course, it didn't help that the FOR SALE sign kept getting knocked down. Kids, probably, the same sort that Mitchell had once been. The Masseys were due to fly in sometime next week, and she'd wanted to make sure everything looked presentable. God, that farm. She'd gotten another monthly mortgage statement for it. Her income from Bickham's made it possible for her to pay her bills, but with two loans there was precious little for extras.

Julianne hadn't been out here for weeks, but her agent had also told her that both of the spotlights had burned out on the exterior shop wall. She wasn't surprised—they weren't on a timer, although that had been a project she'd once meant to get around to *sometime*. They were on twenty-four hours a day. It was silly, she supposed, but she believed that having lights on made it look as if someone still lived there. If she'd had more time, she would have taken a quick look at the property, but these days she was short on money, time, and patience. It was enough that the parched front grass and weeds had been mowed, and that the mailbox was empty of flyers and shopping news. She'd have to thank Darlene for seeing to that. They'd never discussed grounds maintenance, but obviously, Darlene had thought about it. Julianne had seen no evidence of vandalism. What a surprise.

Now that she was headed back to town, the late-afternoon sun glared in such a blinding narrow ribbon along the horizon even her sunglasses didn't help much. Then she heard a hard thump from the undercarriage, as if she'd run over something or maybe even broken a part. Glancing over her shoulder, she saw sparks trailing the truck bed like the bottom end of a roman candle. After clunking around for thirty or forty yards, the truck ejected some beat-up thing that looked a big tin can. It bounced out, spinning away behind her.

"Crap," she muttered, and pulled over to take a look. After a quick trip around the truck, she couldn't find anything wrong. She trotted back down the road to see what she'd hit. Just as she reached it, she heard a familiar chugging. When she looked up, she saw Cade's Dodge nose out of a nearby gravel pull-out. Great.

The object in the road turned out to be an old oil filter, not hers. This one said Mopar, what little printing was left on it.

"Trouble, Julianne?" Cade asked, rolling up to her. He looked just about the same as always, this time wearing a feedlot cap and a blue-striped work shirt.

"No, I just hit a piece of junk. The sun was in my eyes and I didn't see it." She kicked the oil filter off to the side of the road, then eyed him for a moment. "Cade, what are you doing out here?" She hadn't seen him since their stormy encounter more than a month ago, and there was no reason for him to be out this way. Cuervo Blanco was in the opposite direction.

"We'd better have a look." He shifted into reverse and backed up to where she'd left her truck. Julie turned to retrace her steps and saw him get out of the Dodge and lift her hood. He poked around in the engine compartment, fiddling and prodding. When she caught up, he asked, "Are you sure you didn't break something?" From inside the cab, she could hear Jack growling low in his throat.

She tightened her ponytail. "No, I don't think so. It just made a lot of racket. This pickup has been through worse. Why?"

"Hm, you can't be too careful. You know it's pretty isolated out here." He pulled out the dipstick and looked at it without wiping it off, tapped on a hose or two, and strummed a belt. She knew that none of this would reveal anything about damage. "Follow me."

"Follow you where? I'm going back to town. The truck is fine."

"To the farm. I've got some tools with me—it'll be better than standing here in the road. There could be a problem, Julianne, maybe with the power steering or even the brakes. You know you don't want to get stuck out here with a breakdown."

She wasn't helpless when it came to machinery, but she didn't know as much about fixing cars as Cade did. She looked up and down the road. No one was out here but them. It would be a hassle to get stuck here, even with cell phone coverage. "Well, but . . . oh, I guess. All right. But I can't dawdle."

Julianne got back into her truck and turned it over. It sounded fine to her, but maybe that power steering thing . . . She wasn't going to follow him when she knew exactly where she was going. Checking the rearview mirror, she watched him turn around and fall into place behind her. Jack stood so he could see out the back window, that growl still rumbling. His ears were cocked, and his posture was rigid. A weird chill made her shudder, as if things were just, well, off. Or odd. Cade had been pretty scarce after the day she'd revealed their shared history. Mitchell had been certain he'd keep hanging around, but that hadn't happened. Maybe he'd gotten over his mad, although that still didn't explain why he was out here.

They pulled into the gravel drive that led to the farmhouse, and she stopped just before reaching the front porch. It was far enough. She got out. "Honestly, Cade," she called to him, "this is nice of you, but I'm sure it's okay."

He jumped down from his tired Dodge and grabbed a toolbox from the bed. "I'll have a look."

Jack uttered a couple of serious *woofs*.

Cade opened the hood again and looked around. She stood opposite him and looked, too. He held out a hand. The dog barked again.

"Give me the key and I'll start 'er up. I'm going to want to listen for noises." He scowled at Jack. "If I can hear over that damned dog. Do something to shut him up." She ignored his rude demand and started to give him her keys, but a quiet warning bell in her head made her pause.

To distract him, she asked, "Is that something?" She pointed at what she knew was only a grimy spot on the air filter cover and quickly slipped her keys into her pocket while he leaned in to look.

"No, it's okay."

"Hey, what about that?" She tapped a dent that she knew had been on the radiator for years.

"Nope, I don't think so."

"I didn't expect to see you again," she said, to keep the conversation and the distraction going.

It seemed to work. He bent to grab a socket wrench from the tools at his feet. "Yeah, well, some pretty rough things were said the last time we talked."

"Yes, they were." That was an understatement. "I was never called a 'slut' before."

He didn't lift his gaze from the engine, but his face turned blotchy red. "I admit that was kind of rude, but it wasn't my fault. I never had anyone tell me such a terrible lie before."

She gripped the edges of the fender, feeling less comfortable with this situation with every passing minute. "Cade, I wasn't lying. You saw the story with your own eyes."

"Story! Fairytale is more like it. Why should I trust some woman's old diary? What makes *it* the authority about how I came into the world?" So far he'd only held the wrench but hadn't done anything with it. In fact, he hadn't done anything at all to the pickup.

"Did you ask your—your parents about it?"

"Yes, I did." He straightened and now used the tool as a prop to emphasize his words. He pointed the butt end at her. "And they told me it's a lie, too. They said they weren't surprised to learn it had come from you."

She took one step back. This was just getting worse. "Is that why you stopped me on the road and dragged me here? So you could confront me about that day?"

"No." He lowered the tool and his voice.

"And I asked you earlier—what are you even doing out here? Did you follow me?"

He looked at her across the windshield washer tank. "Julianne, when you get your head out of the clouds and realize that Tucker is no better than you ever thought he was, you'll want to come back. And we'll live here."

The shivery feeling was back—the pale hair on her arms stood on end, and it felt as her if eyebrows nearly scraped her hairline. "You can't be serious. We're brother and sister!"

"That's bullshit! I don't believe that for a minute. I know you think you want to live in town and run the dime store. But you belong on the land. It's what you grew up with, and in your heart, that's what you really want. I worked with you long enough, I saw how hard you struggled to make a go of this place. You love it here. I do, too. And I still love you."

She stared at him. This was wrong, so desperately wrong, and her sense of peril grew. "Have you been pulling out the For Sale sign?" It was a blunt question, maybe not a smart one.

"No, I-I wouldn't do that. If visitors come around when I'm here, I make myself scarce. And I always park behind that big thatch of creosote down the road, not in the back."

"You're—are you living here?"

"Not exactly. More like before. Sometimes I come over and stay a few days in my old cabin when things get too tense at home. I like to keep an eye on this place."

The muscles in her shoulders began to cramp with tension. "I locked that door. I locked all of them."

"I have a key to the cabin. I didn't think you'd mind."

She frowned. "I certainly do mind! Cade, you're trespassing. This isn't your personal getaway. I'm trying to sell it."

He straightened up, all testy and put-upon. "Who do you think keeps things tidy around here, anyway? If I didn't cut the grass and keep the weeds down, this property would look abandoned."

"You're doing that? I thought my real estate agent had arranged to have it done."

He pulled on the hood and let it drop into place. "I guess I shouldn't be surprised that you wouldn't give me credit."

"Why on earth would I—" She broke off. There was no point in pursuing this. She had to get out of here. He'd come unhinged or something, and was spoiling for an argument. He must have been here, watching, the whole time she was changing the lights—apparently not one of the jobs he'd taken on. He'd known she was here and when she'd left. She thought about that oil filter. Most of its black paint has been scuffed off, but Mopar was the brand name of parts made for Chryslers and Dodges. She glanced at his Dodge truck parked behind her. He'd arranged her little road mishap somehow. He must have. And when he'd pulled out onto the road, it was at the point where creosote bushes grew tall.

Her throat was so tight with fear it felt as if someone had dug their thumbs into it. But she was determined not to show it. "All right, I'm going home."

"This is your home, Julianne." He grabbed her forearm in a fierce grip and began to drag her toward the house. "Yours and mine. We belong here." His eyes were angry, but blank, too, and that frightened her even more.

"Let go of me!" she snapped, trying to pull away. But she couldn't break loose, and the porch stairs were getting closer. If she wasn't able to get away, he'd drag her into the house and then do God knew what.

"Always in charge," he complained. "Always a firecracker, ordering me around. Not this time." With the two of them pulling in opposite directions, Julianne's forearm, the rope in their tug-of-war, wrenched painfully.

In her mind, an old memory jerked awake, letting her see a way out of this. A fragment of a 2:00 a.m. self-defense infomercial she'd watched one of those sleepless nights after Wes died . . . how to stop a playground bully . . .

"Cade, stop!" she shouted, a short, loud command that made him pause and turn toward her. She made a fist and rolled her arm up toward her shoulder; then she stepped forward and dug the fingers of her other hand into his palm. The maneuver loosened his grip. She was able to grab his thumb and give a hard outward twist to his entire arm, pulling him off his feet. He wasn't merely on his knees, he was down on the patchy, yellowed grass, holding his own forearm and groaning. That gave her just enough time to scramble around to the driver's side and jump back into the truck. She rolled up the windows and locked the doors, all while fumbling with her key chain to find the pickup key. Her heart thundered in her head.

The dog barked at full volume, so loudly that she could think of nothing else but *Go! Go! Go!* She thrust the key into the ignition and gave it a vicious turn. Slamming the gear shift into reverse, she looked up and saw Cade getting to his feet, cradling his arm. The fleeting realization that she had torqued his recently broken limb gave her a twinge of guilt, although *only* a twinge. She also knew that might have given her a better chance of getting away from a man who'd apparently lost his reason.

But his pickup was still parked behind her. She couldn't back out and going forward would only lead her deeper into the property. In an instant that seemed like an hour, she made the decision to cut left across the front yard, mowing down shrubbery and her mother's unruly cape jasmine. Cutting a sharp circle, she retook the drive and sped out to the road, leaving rooster tails of gravel in her wake.

Jack resumed his guard post at the back window, watching clouds of caliche while she flew back to Gila Rock as if a rabid pack of mythical chupacabras were bearing down on them. The sun had finally been overtaken by the dark clouds boiling up on the western horizon, and the smell of coming rain seeped in through the vents.

"Oh God, oh God," she intoned. Her hand trembled when she jammed it through her hair, trying to push it out of her face. She clung to the steering wheel, hoping to still her tremors.

She thought of that dead-eyed look she'd seen on Cade. She thought she knew him. Mild, eager-to-please Cade. She'd never detected even a hint of the man she had just escaped from. Mitchell had seen through his facade immediately. She hadn't, and she'd hadn't believed him.

She'd have to get all the locks changed at the farm. He could still stay there for the time being if he was so inclined, since she hadn't gotten her key away from him.

Call the sheriff—*again*.

She dug her cell phone out of her purse and began issuing directions to its voice assistant to make calls.

The first wave of rain hit the windshield and she wondered, how many enemies did she really have?

Mitchell faced Larry Tomlinson in the dugout with a leaden sense of doom. "Look, Tucker, all I know is that a woman named"—the school district assistant consulted his notes—"Juliet Emerson called the district office and told us about your record. I talked to her myself. She said we probably would want to know, and she was right."

As bad as this was, the feeling of betrayal was so much worse. And what could he say, that it was all a mistake, a lie, the satisfaction of an old grudge?

Tomlinson took off his cap to reveal a gleaming, bald dome of a head edged with a graying brown fringe of hair. The kids were out on the diamond where Mitchell had left them, doing ball drops. "I wanted to give you the benefit of the doubt, so I did an offender search at the Texas criminal justice website. You were on the list. To *double-*check, I even called their office in Huntsville. They confirmed what I learned—manslaughter, time served at the state prison in Amarillo. You're a convicted felon, Tucker, and we don't permit convicted felons to work around youngsters. But I imagine you know that, which is why you failed to disclose your past on the application. Maybe I should thank you. Our system screwed up when it let you slip through. We'll put the IT guys on it and that won't happen again."

So happy to help, Mitchell thought sourly. He tried to swallow the knot that had formed in his chest. The last time he'd felt this lousy was the first day a cell door had slammed behind him. Even though he'd paid that debt and was free, he was still serving a sentence.

And Julianne had turned him in. He'd known she was angry with him for not going with her to the farm, but he'd never expected this. Stress was wearing her down, and he understood why. Still, he hadn't thought she'd be so mad that she'd throw him to the wolves.

"I understand," he muttered, humiliation flooding him. He'd realized that he might be found out, but not this way. "I just—I used to be good at this." He waved in the general direction of the field. On the breeze, the players' voices floated to them, along with the solid *thwuck* of a baseball landing in a leather glove.

"And it's plain that you still are. But you can't do it here, mister. Not with kids. I'll take your locker key and your ID."

Mitchell gave him the key to the equipment shed, then pulled off the lanyard that bore his photo ID. "What are you going to tell them?" he asked, nodding toward the players he'd nursed along all summer.

Tomlinson looked at the field for a moment. "I'll tell them that you were called away on a family emergency. It's a lie, but in this case I think it serves better than the truth."

Mitchell nodded. "Thanks for that. And I'm sorry for everything. I just wanted to help them play baseball. A couple of them have some real promise."

"Right. Good luck, then." The district assistant dismissed him, obviously hanging around to see him walk to his car and drive away.

So he obliged him and headed to the Skylark, with plans to pick up a bottle of whiskey on the way back to the Satellite. The rest of the world could go to hell. The fine, sunny day wasn't so fine after all.

CHAPTER THIRTEEN

When Julianne got back to the apartment, she double-checked everything—the locks, the alarm, the cameras, and the Remington. She trembled to the marrow of her bones, and she couldn't seem to stop. That forced her to take extra care with the rifle. A weapon in shaking hands could be very bad. This time when she called the sheriff's office, they listened to what she had to say about Cade. She had solid information and a serious complaint: attempted kidnapping, and breaking and entering. She had tried to call Mitchell four or five times, but all she got was his voice mail. She'd left messages but still hadn't heard back from him. Jack followed her every step of the way, to the point that she nearly tripped over him a couple of times. Finally, she fed him, just to keep him busy for a minute. For her, dinner held no interest. Instead, she took a shower, shutting Jack and her rifle in the bathroom with her. At least if he barked she'd know something might be happening. God, she was sick of living this way.

Inches from pacing the length of the apartment like a trapped animal, she decided on a glass of wine for herself and settled in front of the TV to ponder her cable options.

The Hunger Games. That sounded appropriate. She'd seen it before, but she wanted to watch a movie about a strong woman overcoming an impossible situation. Yet only a few minutes in—just as Katniss and Gale stepped through the deactivated electric fence—she heard knocking at the back door downstairs and hit Pause.

Jumping up from the sofa, she crept to the window to see whether there was a car parked outside that she recognized. But her view wasn't the best from here, and she knew a vehicle could be in the blind spot she couldn't see. The knock sounded again, harder this time. She hadn't set up the security system on her laptop, so she couldn't even look at the camera images. Stupid, stupid—

Now it was pounding. "Julianne, open up!"

Mitchell! And he sounded furious.

With her hand on the stair rail, she glanced at the rifle but thought better of taking it with her. After all, she knew him.

"Julianne! I know you're in there."

"I'm coming, I'm coming!" she called. She disarmed the back door alarm and opened it. "What's—"

He pushed his way in and shut the door behind him. A sizzle of fear ran through her. He'd brought with him an unopened whiskey bottle he gripped by the neck. "Thanks for getting me fired again. Are you happy, now?"

"Fired—from where?"

He scowled at her and with his face still bruised, the effect was alarming. She took a step back.

"From the coaching job, like you don't know. I told you about that job because I thought I could trust you and that you weren't a snitch. This afternoon some fat-assed school district assistant came to the field and said you called them." Despair melded with his angry expression. "How much more do you want from me, Julianne? How much?"

She felt her jaw drop. The only other time she had seen him this mad was when she'd told him she was getting married. "Snitch! I didn't call anyone. I've never said a thing about it, *ever*."

They faced each other with no more than a forearm's length between them, both pulled as tight as fence wire.

"I . . . you . . . ," Julianne sputtered. She leaned in closer and shouted, "I was nearly kidnapped today! I was too busy trying to get away from Cade Lindgren to call anyone about you! I wouldn't do that, anyway."

"Kidnapped!"

"Didn't you listen to the messages I left on your voice mail?"

He groped in his pocket for his phone. "No, I had the phone turned off."

"It doesn't work very well that way!" This horrible day made her short-tempered and sarcastic. But then, so had his insulting accusation.

Dusk closed in, dimming the office where they stood with long shadows and pale-gray light. She motioned him over to the desk chairs, not in the mood to invite him upstairs for any reason. "Sorry, my hospitality has expired," she snapped, panting. Nodding at his bottle, she added, "Do you want a drink?"

"In a minute. I want to know about Lindgren."

So she told him what had happened that afternoon, about Cade's weird behavior and her tough-girl getaway.

"Shit. I guess I should have gone with you." He rubbed his chin and jaw, and his beard stubble made a scraping sound. "This is no good, Juli. We can't fight the whole world."

"You believe that I didn't make that call?"

He waited a beat before answering. "Yeah. But who did, then? No one else knew I had that job."

"I guess *someone* did, maybe someone with a grievance who saw you on that field in Alpine and put two and two together."

He looked up suddenly. "Cherry. I'll bet it was Cherry Claxton. She's still trying to cozy up to me, even though I've told her to lay off. And I think she's the one who got someone to try and force us off the highway. I thought I saw that Yukon at the Captain Gas the other day. Buddy Lee Crawford was there buying gas."

"So she wants to get rid of us both?"

"I think you're her target and she doesn't care who gets caught in the crossfire. So she called the school district about me, hoping that I'd blame you and break things off."

They fell silent for a long moment; then he rolled his chair next to hers and took her hand. "I love you and I want to keep you safe, but it's getting to be a lot worse than I expected. Even I'm not sure who all is involved."

"And so—what are we going to do?" she grumped.

"I don't think you'll like it." He looked up. "Juli, maybe we should go away."

"I can't do that. I have payments to make and I don't have any spare time."

"No, I mean *leave*. Leave town. For good."

She stared at him. "Leave Gila Rock? You're damned right I don't like it. Where would we go?"

"I don't know—anywhere."

She pulled her hand away. "But I can't do that! Everything I own is tied up here, this place, the farm. I owe money on them both and they're all I have. And I've never worked at anything else."

"You're in the retail business now," he pointed out, cracking the seal on the whiskey cap. He scrounged around the desktop and found an empty coffee cup, then poured a drink for himself.

"Because it's mine and I had no choice. Would you let your family run you out of town?"

He held the cup out to her, but she shook her head. "My only real tie here is you. You're the reason I came back—you know that. I couldn't get us away from here when we were younger, but I can now."

Julianne didn't feel one bit better than she had when he'd walked in. Distraught, she fiddled with a pile of receipts and grouped them with a paper clip she found. "Mitchell, you have no obligations or responsibilities. I do. The idea of letting those bastards chase me out of my home—" She threw the gathered receipts on the desk and jumped up from the chair. "I won't let that happen! Are you going to run?"

He took a drink and pressed light fingertips to his forehead. "I don't see it as running, Juli," he said quietly. "I see it as leaving trouble behind and getting on with our lives. Think about what they've done—what they might be capable of. We should just go."

"Mitchell." She crossed her arms over her chest, and suddenly years of suppressed resentment and disappointment came roaring out. "A while ago you asked me if I'd ever wanted to do something that made me feel good about myself. Then you explained what baseball meant to you. Well, someone has been telling me what to do most of my life. My father saddled me with his dream of carrying on the tradition of the pig farm, even though I didn't want it. And before he died, he saddled me with a husband I didn't love to supervise me. They claimed they knew what was best for me and nothing I said could change their minds. Now, no father, half brother, husband, *your* brothers, whoever, are going to make me feel like I can't stand on my own two feet and accomplish something in this world. I have my store and I'm going to make a go of it. I love you and I want you to stay here with me, but I can't and won't force you." She paced a couple of steps, then turned to look at him. An icy wave of uncertainty washed through her. "So is that what you're going to do? Get on with your life? Leave me here with the trouble the other Tuckers are causing?"

"We both have to go," he stressed.

"The night the window was broken you told me that they're nobodies, and not to let them spook me. You told me to stand fast."

"Yeah, and I think I was wrong to say that. Now Lindgren is a problem, too, and I can't be with you twenty-four hours a day."

"I think the police will get him."

He propped the coffee cup on his knee. "Huh. Like they've caught Darcy and Cherry?"

"I really think they will." She drew a deep breath and blew it out impatiently. "I don't want to leave. I'm determined and no one is going to get the better of me."

Bolting the last whiskey in the cup, he exhaled. "You can punch a cash register anywhere. There's nothing high and holy about where you do it."

Her brows shot up. "Is *that* what you think I do? Punch a cash register?" She unfolded her arms and dropped them to her sides, fists clenched. "I'm not just a shop girl here. I run a business! I thought you understood that."

He got to his feet, and she saw his frown. "I don't know why you think you have to prove that you're tougher than those nobodies! I get that—you're a strong woman and you don't need anyone. You've told me that. But I'm not going to argue about it and I don't want to fight with them. I'm sick of having to battle the whole world, I just want peace."

Lifting her chin to keep it from trembling, she said, "I can't stop you if you decide to go. Just like I couldn't make you change your mind about marrying me years ago. But if you go now I will think much less of you." It hurt her to say it, as much as she could see it hurt him to hear it. The sting of her words was plain on his face. Oh, Mitchell—she loved him so desperately. Why couldn't he see her side of things? It occurred to her that just about every one of her adversaries wanted to be rid of her. That she even had adversaries was alarming to her. It was also a lonely, frightening realization.

He got to his feet and headed toward the door. "I'm tired and I'm done. Just give it some thought, will you?"

She set her jaw. "I will, but I don't like it. At all."

He considered her for a moment, as if trying to see into her mind. "I thought I knew what you want. Maybe I got that wrong, too."

"And what do you think I want?"

"To be safe, and start life over again with me." He gripped the doorknob. "I didn't know that means staying here no matter what."

She groped around for a response. "I do want a life with you. And I'm sure in six or eight months' time, everything will settle down here. The sheriff can't let your brothers harass me forever. If I can hold out, can't you?"

He sighed. "Julianne, I've spent years waiting for things to 'settle down.' I marked off twenty-five hundred days on calendars. That really changes the way a person sees things."

She couldn't think of an answer to that.

"I'll be around for a while if you change your mind."

Then he was gone, and she stared at the closed door, angry and hurt.

Julianne dragged through the days, trying to bury herself in work to keep her mind busy and away from thoughts about Mitchell. Working was easy. Work came in a never-ending supply. Her thoughts were a different matter. She didn't think he really saw her side of things, even though he expected her to see his.

His absence dug a deep hole in her soul and kept her awake at night.

Early one morning before opening, she worked on inventory. No matter how she tried to concentrate on the shipping list she was study-ing in the back office, he wouldn't leave her alone. She craved the solace she felt around him, his energy and heat, the sound of his voice, the sense of completeness. Damn him, she thought, as she plowed through sheets of bubble wrap and packing peanuts. Once or twice she'd seen him drive past, but he hadn't stopped. *Fine*. That was just fine with her.

Frustrated, she flung a handful of packing peanuts toward the floor. It was a singularly unsatisfying way to vent. Half of the foam objects only fluttered away from her fingers, and the other half clung to her with a static charge. Slamming a door would be better.

She pulled a stack of ceramic coasters from the box. Why did he think that she could just walk away from the only security and source of pride she had? It was a snap for him; he had nothing here. The farm and Bickham's represented the sum total of her life's work. They represented personal success and her ability to jump over every rock that had been thrown in her path.

Mitchell said he was tired of fighting the world. So was she—he'd been right about that—but it didn't mean she'd give up.

Mitchell lay propped up against the headboard in his room at the Satellite Motel, pillows jammed behind his back. He held a week-old copy of *USA Today* open in front of him, trying to read an article that once again flogged the case for bringing a major league baseball team to San Antonio. He'd started the same paragraph three times before he realized he wasn't really concentrating on the subject. For a moment, the print blurred on the page. He saw himself standing at bat in an imaginary stadium under a sticky-sweet midafternoon sun. Sixty feet away the pitcher stared him down, wound up, and fired a white, round rocket at him. But it would all be good. In the stands, his beautiful Julianne rose from her seat, her light hair gleaming in the sun like a candle. He swung and felt the crack of the ball when he struck it. It arced, clear and pure, over left field to bounce off the railing on the upper deck.

Look, Juli, I did it. I made it because of you . . .

The soundtrack from *The Natural* kicked in, and he dropped the bat to take the bases, the home run hero of the day.

He wasn't really part of this daydream, and neither was Julianne. When he'd left her the other night, he'd been so tired and fed up he'd really considered driving out of Gila Rock on his own. But he just couldn't manage that.

He'd driven by Bickham's with every intention of stopping. He'd lost his nerve both times. Strange that he could ask for her pardon for killing Wes but couldn't make himself apologize for not understanding why business somewhere else was different from her shop here. On the other hand, she didn't seem to get that a better life could be theirs in another place, where no one knew them or their histories.

What did it matter what town they lived in if they were together? They'd be rid of the nightmare tangle of people's memories, of his relatives, of these small-town cops with their small-town minds. Why did she think she had to prove herself to anyone?

A sharp knock on the door startled him out of his reverie. The maid had already been here today, so who the hell was that? These days, anything was possible. He slid off the bed and looked through the peephole. He sighed when he discovered the tall, dark-haired guy standing in front of it. Wary but hoping for the best, he opened the door.

"James," Mitchell acknowledged his youngest brother. "I didn't expect to see you again so soon." He and James, dark-haired and green-eyed, favored their mother. Darcy was a lanky, unfortunate knock-off of Earl in his younger days.

His brother stood with his hands jammed into his pockets and fidgeted a bit. "Yeah, well—you know how it can get over there." He tilted his head in the general direction of the arroyo where the single-wide stood.

"I do."

James peered at his bruises. "Wow, Darcy really did a number on your face. Is anything broken?"

"No, just my patience with him."

"Look, I don't feel right about the way things ended the night you came by. You always took care of us when Earl wasn't around and now, well, I don't see any of that old feud shit quite the same way now. Um, can we talk?"

Mitchell stood aside. "Sure, come on in."

James glanced into the room and gave him a quick once-over. "How about if I buy you a beer at Lupe's?"

Mitchell considered him. He hated to even think about it, but he couldn't help wondering whether this was some kind of setup. Just as he pictured the baseball diamond, it was even easier to imagine the possibility of Darcy or one of Cherry's admirers jumping him, with Earl egging them on. He hadn't survived seven years of incarceration by being careless. He backed up and grabbed his boots, then pulled them on. "Okay, even better. I have an errand to run a little later so I'll follow you over there in the Buick."

"Sounds fine." James turned from the doorway to walk back to his truck.

Mitchell grabbed his keys and closed the door behind him.

He wondered whether he really knew anyone anymore.

They walked into Lupe's together, but that didn't catch much notice from the few guys whiling away their afternoon in the roadhouse's dark-paneled confines. In the kitchen, Lupe could be heard arguing with her current cook in a firestorm of angry Spanish. George Strait promised anyone listening that he'd be in "Amarillo by Morning." So it was just a typical day here.

Mitchell and James sat on the red-vinyl upholstered stools at the far end of the bar, away from two old farts who were watching a bullfight on ESPN. Lupe emerged from kitchen combat long enough to sell them a pitcher of Lone Star and hand over two glasses.

After some awkward preliminary chitchat, Mitchell said, "I know you didn't meet me here to yap about the weather."

James put his elbows on the bar with his shoulders hunched. "Was that stuff you told us about Earl really true? That whole revenge thing was about some woman from years ago? Just because she chose Boyce over Earl?"

"In the end it doesn't sound like she chose either one of them. Or if she did, I didn't get the impression that Boyce was interested. I couldn't tell from what I saw. He told Julianne's mother it all happened before they met and got married. But yeah, that's about the size of things."

James stared at the beer mug between his hands, as if pondering some great problem. "Damn. It doesn't seem like that was worth all the trouble we went through."

"It wasn't."

"But Darcy won't let go of it. If anything, he's more pissed off than before."

Mitchell shook his head. "I still don't understand why any of you would want to waste your time on something like that. And Darcy, you'd think it was *his* girlfriend who ditched him. I just don't get him. Sometimes I have the feeling he's not firing on all eight cylinders."

James glanced off to the side and rubbed the back of his neck. "I get that. I *really* get that. For what it's worth, I wasn't as stoked up to keep that thing going all this time. I just went along to get along. But I'm done. I'm just done."

"Yeah?"

"It was never my fight. I should have left a long time ago. But Darcy"—he turned to face his brother—"there's something you should know about him."

"What, he hates me now? I'm not surprised."

"Yeah, he probably does, but I think he hates everyone, including himself." His brother drained his glass and took a breath. "Here's the thing. You remember that night the Emerson barn burned down . . ."

Mitchell made a disgusted sound. "I'm not likely to forget that, James. I might not remember the whole night, but I sure as hell know what happened afterward."

"But Mitch, what you don't know—" He closed his eyes for a moment as if seeking strength. Or courage. "Mitch, you didn't start that fire. Darcy did it. You were already passed out." He gabbled the words in a rush.

Mitchell stared at his brother. The sound of the jukebox faded to a dull mumble. The cheering crowd at the Mexico bullring washed away. In Mitchell's mind, all he heard was the slow, warning clang of a single bell, like a death knell. He jerked upright, as if he'd been poked with a hot wire. His hands turned cold, and his heart mule-kicked his ribs. "What . . . *what are you saying, James?*"

Don't kill the messenger.

Don't kill the messenger.

His brother's face faded to a sickly white, and fear flashed through his eyes, but he plowed on. "You passed out before any of the gas was poured, before Darcy sparked that damned Zippo lighter of his. He left me with you and snuck around to the barn. He came back a minute later and he was laughing to himself like he'd just heard the best joke in the world. Then he looked at you laying there and said he'd have to do this job himself. And that's when it happened." A gleam of sweat shone on James's forehead, even though Lupe kept this place as cold as a meat locker. "He started sloshing that gasoline out of the can." He broke off.

"And? *And?*"

"I tried to stop him, but he punched me." He pointed at his left brow, which sagged a bit lower than the right, something Mitchell hadn't noticed until just now. "He broke this bone in my face and I could barely see." He pulled in a hitched breath. "He started that fire. I watched him light it, and—and I know he saw Wes Emerson in that barn before he set it."

Jesus Christ. Holy Jesus Christ! Blistering, white-hot rage filled Mitchell—a mammoth rage he'd never known before. "He *knew* Wes was in there? A man who never did anything to him? He killed him in cold blood! And I took the blame for that fire because I thought I was

219

guilty. I thought I was *protecting* both of you, and that asshole Darcy threw me under the bus?" He glared at James. "Why the hell didn't you say something? Do something? You let me go to prison for a crime that Darcy committed! You let *him* get away with killing Wesley Emerson!"

James swallowed, forcing his Adam's apple up and down, but he kept his seat. "He told me he'd kill me if I said anything. I believed him. I still do—he would have killed me. But after the other night I knew I had to tell you about it. A lot of bad things have been done just because Earl got dumped by an old girlfriend, a really stupid reason." He shook his head. "It's too much. Too damned much. I wanted to tell you here, in a public place, in case you blew up." He leaned closer. "Darcy is dangerous, Mitch. He's crazy. I think he's going to kill someone else, and I'd bet he doesn't care who."

A quick hodgepodge of images and old memories flew through Mitchell's memory. Cell doors, a burned man in his arms, loneliness, a courtroom, a young widow's bitter wrath, metal bars, Darcy's hard-lined face with a cigarette sticking out of it. One thought rose to the surface of the morass, struggling past fury and resentment and pain: he was innocent. He hadn't killed Wes. He hadn't even started the fire that claimed him.

Mitchell couldn't sit here another second. If he did, he'd punch James himself. This news was too much to absorb while knocking back a beer as if it were any old day in the world. "I have to get out of here."

"What are you going to do?" Now his brother looked just plain scared and younger than twenty-four. "God, don't tell Darcy about this yet, okay? I found a place of my own, and Earl and Darcy don't know about it yet. Just give me a chance to get out of that trailer before you say anything."

"I'll give you twenty-four hours." He jabbed a finger at James. "But you're going to tell the cops about this. If you don't, and right away, I will. You might find yourself in a load of trouble, James. With them and with me, and I'll make the threat of Darcy look like a playground fight."

Mitchell strode out of Lupe's and headed for the Buick, his head buzzing. He couldn't talk to anyone right now, not even Julianne.

He turned west and headed out to the open range.

Three nights later Mitchell stood over the bathroom sink at the Satellite Motel and peered through a clear spot on the steamy mirror. The shower had made him feel half human again, and now he was trying for 100 percent by shaving.

After leaving James, he'd driven all the way to Brackettville for no good reason, other than to keep from strangling someone with his bare hands. He'd tried to visit Alamo Village, the movie set that was constructed for the movie *The Alamo* with John Wayne. In its better days it had been used as backdrop in the filming of a couple of hundred other westerns. But the place had closed in 2010 after the owners died, and only grazing cattle now shared the acreage with the crumbling buildings.

While Mitchell was out on the highway, he seriously entertained the idea to just keep driving. But the thought of Julianne pulled at him and wouldn't let him go. So he drove four hours back to Gila Rock. There was nothing like a five-hundred-mile road trip to vent the steam from a boiling kettle. He was still pissed off about Darcy, but on the bright side at least he knew he hadn't taken Wesley Emerson's life. He'd probably been the only innocent man in the state's custody who sincerely believed he was guilty.

Now he paused, dripping shave cream and water on the counter while he examined his dinged-up face. The swelling had improved, but his eyes were beginning that interesting color-change from dark purple to green and yellow. People still gave him a double-take in public if he went without his sunglasses, although he probably didn't scare kids and dogs anymore. And Darcy's big, ugly Masonic ring had done considerable damage. His brother had found that ring—he *said*—in one of those old cars he'd dragged home, but Mitchell wouldn't be surprised if he'd stolen it. He tried to maneuver the disposable razor around the healing gouge on his left cheek. It was still too tender to tolerate much fussing.

He made a disgusted sound and tossed the razor on the counter, then wiped his face with one of the thin hand towels the maid had left. The injuries would heal in time. On the other hand, any feeling he might have had for Darcy was dead and gone, brother or not.

Whether James had told the cops about Wesley's true killer, Mitchell didn't know. But he was going to find out. The information had to come from James—he was the only other witness.

He put on a clean shirt, then sat on the bed and grabbed his cell phone from the nightstand. Before things had gotten tense at Lupe's, he and James had exchanged numbers. He scrolled through his few contacts. Cherry had put her number on the list herself that night he'd met her for a drink. He'd never used it and didn't plan to. And the number for the Tucker estate was still there. Then he saw Julianne's name, and his fingers on the phone tightened.

She said she didn't need him or anyone else. He'd supposed she was just whistling past the graveyard, but now he thought maybe it was true. She'd gotten so used to making her own way, alone . . .

No, he rejected that notion. He didn't believe she wanted to take on the world by herself. And as soon as all these critical details were nailed down, like Darcy's guilt and getting his own name cleared, there would be no reason for either of them to leave Gila Rock. They had some making up to do. He couldn't bear the idea of living without her any longer. But those details—

Just as his gaze landed on James's cell number, his own phone began buzzing in his grip. Well, what a coincidence—

"Yeah, James, what's up? Did you get moved out of Rancho DeLuxe?"

"Mitch, I've got to talk to you right away!" He was almost yelling, Mitchell supposed, to be heard over the roar of that highway noise behind him. But he also sounded winded, as if he was just one step ahead of a bone-chomping monster from a Stephen King novel.

"What's the matter?"

"I'll meet you at the high school parking lot in ten minutes. You *gotta* be there!" The call ended with three beeps that signaled a disconnect.

An electric sizzle of foreboding shot up his spine and spread to his heart and limbs. Who was in danger? James? Him? Again he wondered whether he was being lured to a trap—he couldn't help it, given the series of events that had occurred since he'd come back to town. Despite that, he lurched to his feet and headed out the door to the Buick.

Moths bumped around him and the exterior lights along the walkway as he ran to the parking lot. There were only a couple of cars besides his own, and the neon **VACANCY** sign buzzed off and on, off and on, in front of the motel office window.

It was hot and stuffy inside the car, and it still reeked of old cat litter. But the tired engine turned over after a couple of preliminary coughs and a soft fart of blue smoke. On the dark road, more night-flying insects whizzed past his headlights, and his mind hummed with a dozen possible scenarios. He didn't know whether any of them were close to correct. He felt certain of one thing, though.

Something bad was going to happen.

Julianne had fallen into a fitful doze with Jack beside her. She was jolted from her sleep by the sound of shattering plate glass. Instantly alert, the dog began barking. She pulled on a T-shirt over her short pajamas and hurried down the stairs. Behind her, Jack's wet nose bumped her calves as she went.

Horrified, she saw flames climbing the edges of the window and catching on merchandise near the front. Cellophane-wrapped cocktail napkins burned exceptionally well, she noticed in a disjointed, irrational thought. Blue tendrils of fire crept across the old floor, turning yellow, then white as they gained energy and heat. The fire alarm, part of her security package, sounded and added to the din and confusion as smoke began to fill the space. The smell of gasoline was strong, and the memory of the barn fire all those years ago came back to her with vivid clarity.

She grabbed a decorative throw that was draped over a white wicker display chair, hoping to beat out the flames, but smoke choked and blinded her. She felt as if she were trying to breathe in hot powder. Flames were gobbling up merchandise like a monster furnace with an insatiable appetite.

Only one coherent thought came to her: that feud would kill *her* this time. She dropped to her knees and tried to crawl toward the door, completely disoriented and light-headed. The dog barked somewhere, maybe even trying to guide her to safety, but she couldn't tell which direction the sound came from. The old building was as dry as straw and catching fast. Heat blasted her, and she thought she smelled burning hair as it flew around her head in the fire's wind.

Which way to go? Which way? Between Jack's barking, the shrieking smoke alarm, and the fast-moving fire, she tried to keep her head and her bearings, but she was losing both. Would she die the same way Wes had? Terrified, coughing, and lost, she thought she might, no matter how strong her will to survive. Her pulse pounded in her head. Her fright, as consuming as the flames, was so powerful the ghastly scene around her seemed to fade in and out of her sight. She tried to hold her breath, but it was impossible.

Bright, dimmer. Bright, dimmer. Sometimes red, sometimes blue.

She glanced down and for an instant recognized the new hardwood flooring near her shattered window. She scrambled around on hands and knees, broken glass cutting both, but for the moment she couldn't feel it. She saw the blood, but it didn't matter. Getting out, that was what mattered.

Jack was still barking, but he sounded farther away now.

"Julianne!"

She knew that voice. It belonged to her other half, the source of her joy and the one who shared her heartache. Was that real, or did she imagine it? She wasn't sure.

The whole world seemed to be burning. And it was screaming, a faraway, urgent sound. It flashed blue and red—Maybe that was the fire department. Maybe.

The smell of it, like gasoline, like burning hair, awful toxic smells . . .

"Juli! Where are you?"

"Here!" she called, her throat dry and hot. She didn't know if the voice was real, but she had to answer. "I'm here!"

Out of nowhere, strong arms pulled her away from the fire and dragged her past broken glass and floating scarves of flame to the sidewalk. She took a deeper breath, coughed, and breathed again. What a relief it was to pull clean air into her lungs. And although chaos filled the street with sirens and the loud, scratchy chatter of radio voices, she knew she wouldn't burn to death. Some spots on her arms and legs stung, but in the terror of the moment, they seemed minor.

A fire truck came roaring down the street, sirens screeching and lights throbbing. Looking up, she saw Mitchell, his face a portrait of fear. His face—it was just like that night—his face was smudged black, and his shirt was singed. Beside him she saw his brother James. That couldn't be right. Maybe she was already dead.

Mitchell held her in his arms and anxiously pushed her hair away from her face.

"Julianne! Oh God, are you okay? Are you?"

"I-I think so," she croaked. "Mitchell?"

"It's me. You're safe."

"Jack—where's Jack?"

"Let him through," Mitchell said over his shoulder, and she felt a wet tongue on her face. "Here—he's here."

225

She reached out a feeble hand, and the dog slipped his head under it. "There's my boy." She looked up again. "James—what are you doing here?"

"Saving your life," he said simply.

Firefighters connected the hose and opened the hydrant on the corner. An ambulance pulled up across the street, and EMTs surrounded Julianne. An oxygen mask was clapped on her face. When someone threw a blanket over her shoulders, she remembered that she was barefoot and dressed only in short pajamas.

Mitchell didn't want to let her go.

"Please stand back, sir," one of the EMTs directed. "We'll take care of her."

He was jostled out of the way, and he watched while the medics looked after her. She looked so small and vulnerable there with the plastic mask strapped over her nose and her clothing scorched. His heart thumped heavily in his ribcage and seemed to climb into his throat. God, she had to be all right. She *had* to.

Nearby, James talked to the officers who'd arrived in patrol cars. They were close enough for Mitchell to hear them.

"—and so your brother Darcy planned this?" Sheriff Dale Gunter asked.

"Yeah, he started boiling when my brother Mitch told him about Earl's old girlfriend. Then after your boys showed up the other night about the broken window, he almost went berserk." James looked at Mitchell. "He was determined to get the last word, no matter how or what that amounted to. Earlier this evening, I saw him make a firebomb out of an old wine bottle, so as soon as he left, I chased down Mitch. I knew we had to do something. We weren't fast enough to stop him, but I'm glad we got here in time to save Julianne. Darcy can't have gotten far. This just happened a few minutes ago." There was some discussion about which junker he might be driving tonight, but James was pretty sure it was the Escort with multicolored quarter panels.

Mitchell joined the conversation, adding, "Buddy Lee Crawford might be mixed up in all this, too. I think I saw him driving a dark-silver Yukon, the same one that tried to run us off the road near Marfa. He's friendly with Cherry."

"Lots of guys are 'friendly' with Cherry," Gunter replied drily, taking it all down. It was the first bit of energy Mitchell has seen him display that didn't involve harassing *him*.

"Hey," he added, "what's happening with Cade Lindgren? He tried to kidnap Julianne, you know."

"Yeah, we're working on that," the sheriff said. "He won't get far. We've got an APB going for him. Right now I really want to know where Darcy Tucker is."

Darcy was just nuts, mean and nuts, Mitchell thought. Why had he started this thing again, long after it was over? What was his complaint? He'd seen guys in prison just like him—aimless men, filled with hate, guilty of crimes like domestic abuse or drug dealing. They were as unpredictable as nitroglycerine: friendly one minute; vicious, snapping, wild dogs the next. He'd never understood that kind of man. But he knew enough to stay as far away from them as possible. The experts called them sociopaths.

"There's something else, something important you need to know about the Emerson barn fire that . . . ," James began, but Mitchell's attention shifted.

He looked back toward Julianne and saw that they had her in the back of the ambulance, and he walked over to see what was up. Under the glare of the lights in the truck, her face was smudged black, and some of the ends of her blonde hair looked as if they might have been singed. But she was sitting up just inside the truck, so that was a good sign, he thought.

"Are you going to take her to the hospital?" he asked.

A female EMT with her hair twisted into a bun said, "I don't think so. She doesn't want to go, anyway. She has a couple of small second-degree burns, but we patched her up. Except for being a little shaken up, she seems to be in pretty good shape, thanks to whoever pulled her out. If they hadn't been so quick, we might have had a different story here."

"Mitchell," Juli called. She held out her hand.

The EMT motioned him forward.

He grabbed her hand and wrapped it in his. "Hey, honey. You scared the daylights out of me."

"You stayed here—I'm so glad you stayed here." Her voice muffled by the oxygen mask, she sounded so much like a frightened girl, his heart wrenched. He felt a serious twinge of guilt for his thoughts about leaving town without her. She had no one in the world except that twenty-seven-year-old juvenile delinquent, Lindgren, and he was worse than having no one. "I was scared, too. What happened?"

"Darcy made a firebomb and threw it into your front window."

"God . . . why? What did I ever do to him?" she asked, steaming up the oxygen mask. "What did I do to make him want to kill me?"

That was the gist of it, boiled down to its basic black heart, he realized. Darcy wanted to kill people. Mitchell had no idea why, but the realization stunned him, despite what he thought he knew about his brother. He'd killed Wes Emerson, and now he was trying to kill Julianne. If he wasn't stopped, he'd get both of them, or someone else. "I think Darcy's true colors are finally on full display. He's always been a mean bastard, even as a kid. His excuses for his actions are never any good. This time, he'll have to explain himself to the law. Anyway, James figured out what he was doing and came to find me."

James trotted up to the ambulance. "They found Darcy. He was with a woman."

"A woman—who?"

"Cherry Claxton."

"Perfect," Mitchell replied, shaking his head. "Just perfect. Well, maybe they'll both do some time if she's an accessory."

He turned to his brother and pulled him aside.

Mitchell gave him a slow smile. "I owe you one for tonight."

James gave him an embarrassed glance. "Naw. I think this is a little payback for everything you did. We would have gone into foster homes after Mom left if not for you."

Mitchell gazed at the fire burning up Julianne's building. "Sometimes I wonder if I did the right thing. Everyone might have been better off if we'd gotten away sooner."

James shrugged. "Who's to say? Anyway, I told Gunter about the barn fire. I'll have to go to the office with them."

"All right. Thanks, James." Mitchell turned back to Julianne.

"Where am I going to stay?" she asked. "I can't sleep here tonight and there's no furniture in the house at the farm."

"You're coming with me," he said.

"I don't have my clothes. I don't have my purse, or my shoes." She was beginning to sound like a fretful child, and she had every good reason.

Mitchell took her in his arms, so damned grateful to be able to do that. And grateful for James, who'd had the conscience and presence of mind to speak up after all these years, and to come find him tonight. "Don't worry, the Satellite Motel isn't fussy. And tomorrow, we'll sort out all of this. I'll bring you back into town, and you can pick up what you need."

"They'll let me bring the dog, won't they? I'm not going if I can't."

"They'll let us bring him."

After more questions from the fire officials and the sheriff's department, Mitchell and Julianne were allowed to leave. This part of the street had been closed to spectators and traffic, but people gathered on the fringes, watching. He left his car where he'd parked it, and they took off in her truck with him driving.

Julianne twisted in the seat to get a last glimpse of Bickham's and wondered whether she'd ever do business from there again. She thought of all the backbreaking work she'd put into reviving the store, and all the times someone had tried to take it away from her. It had looked so nice when it was finished, with the redecorating and her careful planning. But it hadn't lasted more than four months. Now it was a heap of smoking embers, water-soaked, ruined. All the tears she'd choked back so many times began flowing in earnest.

"Juli, what's wrong?" Mitchell asked, a shadow of panic in his voice. He pulled over to a curb and put his arm around her shoulders. "Honey, are you all right? Are you hurt?"

"No, but look at what those people did to my little store." She sobbed. She'd never felt so alone in her life or that she had so many enemies. "Why, Mitchell?" she asked. "Why do they hate me?"

He clutched her to him in a fierce embrace and pressed her forehead against the crook of his neck. He smelled of smoke, just like that other night so long ago, but now it didn't bother her in the same way.

He breathed a shaky sigh. "They don't hate you. They hate me."

Julianne came out of the bathroom in the motel room, a towel turbaned around her wet hair, feeling scrubbed and clean. Jack lifted his head briefly from the floor, glanced at her, and went back to sleep. She envied him—it was almost 2:30 a.m., but she was wide awake.

All she had to put on besides her smoky clothes was one of Mitchell's athletic shirts. Fortunately, it was so long it fell to midthigh on her, but she was still conscious of its scanty coverage.

This was a bare-bones room with nothing that even remotely approached basic hotel standards. The drapes and bedspread had a drab look of the 1990s, and the towels were thin. The carpet had seen the traffic of countless footsteps, stains, spills, and vacuum cleaners, and the orange ceramic bedside lamp had a plastic-and-paper shade. But it was tidy in here, and the paint was fairly new. And as a compensating bonus, the shower didn't skimp on water or pressure.

"Feel better?" Mitchell was propped up against the pillows on the queen-size bed, waiting for his turn in the shower. They had both been tense and quiet since arriving here, while everything that had happened soaked in.

"A little," she said. Despite the dreary surroundings and the horror of the night's events, she realized she felt safe here with Mitchell. But there was a hollow ache in her that throbbed whenever she pictured Bickham's standing helpless while flames licked its beams and poured out of the dark, eyeless windows on the second floor, dragging it toward an unexpected death. She couldn't get the image out of her head. It was as if the building had possessed a thriving spirit of its own. "It hurts. A lot."

"The damage to your store?"

She nodded, feeling her chin starting to tremble again. "I was so proud of how it turned out after we fixed it up. It looked so sweet, and I was doing good business, too. But from the beginning, I had nothing but trouble." She snagged a tissue from the dispenser mounted on the bathroom wall.

"Darcy's in custody," he said.

"Really? Did you call the police?"

"Yep. Jimmy Ortiz, their detective, told me they caught him practically red-handed. No pun intended. He smelled like gasoline and had two more firebombs in the Escort. He was with Cherry at her apartment, but I don't think they've charged her." He tossed aside the newspaper he'd been reading. "Ortiz sounded pumped to capture another Tucker, even if it wasn't me."

She froze in the bathroom doorway. "Two more firebombs. What if his next stop was going to be the farm?"

He hitched his brows, and his expression grew pensive. "I thought of that. It sounds like he was on a rampage. If he hadn't stopped at Cherry's, or the cops hadn't found him when they did, he might have done just that." He slanted her an appreciative look. "I like your nightie. But after we find something for you to wear tomorrow, we'll have to go by the station to give them a statement. I put your pj's in the washer outside in the breezeway, but there are burn holes in them. You'll definitely need something else." He patted the mattress, inviting her over. "Come on, Juli, rest your weary self."

She came to the edge of the bed and sat down next to him. "Thank you, Mitchell—for everything." She glanced down at his hands and arms, at the old burn scars from what seemed like a lifetime ago, and traced light, gentle fingers over them. She also noticed a couple of new burns on one arm. "Oh God, no. I hope you didn't get hurt tonight, sweetie."

He looked up at her, seeming surprised by her endearment, and his furrowed expression softened, like a clenched fist opening into a welcoming hand. For an instant he closed his eyes; then he drew in a deep breath. "No. I'm good."

She leaned closer and took him into her arms, pressing his forehead to her collarbone. "When we had dinner at Paisano's, I said that I appreciated the gesture of your apology. Forgiveness, though—I just wasn't ready for that." She rested her chin against his temple. "You have that from me now. I owe you that, and more. You've been a good friend to me, probably the best I ever had."

He lifted her hand and brought it to his lips. "Julianne"—his throat sounded constricted and he cleared it—"you don't know how much that means to me. Even when I was royally pissed off at you all those years ago, it was because I loved you so much and I knew I had let you down. Well, and I hated losing you to any man." He looked her straight on. "I learned something a couple of days ago that I want to tell you about. It has to do with the night the barn burned down."

232

Julianne smiled, but she felt her stomach flip again. "But we've decided that we're starting over. No looking back anymore—right?"

"Yeah, but this is important. And it changes a lot of things."

Would this night never end? They'd had more than enough to deal with in the past twenty-four hours. "Mitchell, I can't take more bad news."

"This is *great* news."

Still apprehensive, she agreed. "Well, okay."

He kept her hand in his. "James told me that Darcy set the barn fire. Not me."

She stared at him. "You—he—Darcy killed Wes? James said that?"

"Yes, he said it, and yes, Darcy really did kill him, with willful intent. He knew Wes was in there before he lit it."

She tried to pull her hand away. It was almost like hearing it again for the first time. "Why?" she mourned, horrified. "It's so brutal! So—so heartless! What grudge did he have against Wes? I don't understand."

"I'm going to try to explain it." He sighed. "It's hard to think this about a family member, but I think he just wanted to kill someone. It's as if he has no soul. Wes was a ready-made opportunity."

Over the next few minutes, Julianne sat transfixed, both appalled and relieved to hear his story.

"You're sure James is telling you the truth?" she asked.

"Yeah. I am." His voice dropped, and his eyes reflected his own sense of betrayal and loss at the discovery. "I can't think of one reason why he'd lie. He doesn't have the same evil heart that Darcy and Earl do. Besides, it took a lot of courage for him to tell me to my face that I went to prison for nothing."

"Oh God." She looked at their joined hands. "How could Darcy be so cruel? He let Wes burn to death in there, then stood back and let you take the blame when he knew you were innocent." She paused, then added, "So you didn't really need my forgiveness."

"Of course I did. It was my bad idea to come to your place to begin with. If I hadn't thought of it, maybe Wes would still be around and all our lives would have turned out differently." He thought about it for a moment and frowned slightly. "But then—you'd still be married to him."

Her brows knitted, too.

"Anyway I'm grateful to have it because you gave it to me even when you thought I was guilty. I didn't tell you until now because I wasn't fit company for anyone for a couple of days after I found out."

Her shoulders drooped. "Mitchell, I'm so sorry. For everything. For the seven years you lost, for being stubborn and not listening to you—"

"Juli, honey, don't. This is all Darcy's doing. I'm just glad that James decided to speak up. And that he told me what he thought Darcy was planning to do tonight."

She pulled the towel off her hair and lay down beside him on the ugly bedspread. "You're my true hero, you know?"

He made some self-deprecating noise. "I don't know . . . I just did what anyone . . . I had to . . . um . . ."

She laughed a little, amused by his embarrassment. "I don't think you can deny that you saved my life. There's no getting around it."

He hauled her into his arms. "I don't know what I would have done if things had gone differently. I saw that fire explode from down the street and I just started running." Rolling her over on her back, he covered her with his body, solid and warm, and rained soft kisses over her face. "I'm glad I was there. I'm on my knees, thanking God that I was there." His kiss traveled to her mouth. "If I'd lost you . . . if I'd lost you . . . ," he murmured against her lips, then took them. The kiss deepened, and the scent of hospitality shampoo gave way to the smell of charred wood. The fundamental instinct to survive and fierce urgency drove their actions. Julianne tugged at Mitchell's belt buckle and almost succeeded in getting it open when his hand swept up the inside of her thigh and reached for the slick tenderness beneath her shirt. For an instant, the surprise, the thrill, stilled her hands, and she lay on the mattress with one knee drawn up, unable to do more than surrender to his ministrations.

She wiggled around in the long shirt, and its neckline pulled lower, releasing one breast. He captured the nipple in his mouth and tugged slightly, sending a current pulsing low and hot through her belly.

"No one will ever take you from me again," he promised, ripping open his fly buttons and stripping off his jeans. "Not in this life. You're mine." He pushed up the hem of the shirt and plunged himself into her. "And I'm yours."

The sensation of being filled, completed, made her gasp, and she arched her back to press closer to him. Clinging to him desperately, she wound her fingers in his hair. "Always," she swore. They moved in perfect sync, and she felt pulled closer and closer to a knife-edge of the night, where only lovers went and time stopped.

She knew he forced himself to delay his own release while she tumbled over waves of intense spasms. He whispered to her with his voice and his body, urging her on while she moaned his name.

"Mitchell," she begged, "please—come to me. I'm ready for you— give yourself to me, *now*."

"You can have it all. My soul and my love," he muttered. "They already belong to you." He wrapped one arm under her and plunged home to her again and yet again, surrendering his whole self. They were one now, as they'd never been before.

They lay locked together and silent for a few moments, waiting for their hearts to slow.

Julianne grew groggy with the sleep that was about to claim her, and she heard Mitchell's breathing smooth out and deepen. Shifting a bit, she stirred the bedding when she moved, and a whiff of campfire blew back on them.

"Okay, let me up," he said, awake now. He disentangled himself from her embrace. "I'd better get that shower. I don't want to fall asleep with that burned smell on me." He stood, showing her a fascinating rear view of a man, naked except for the white T-shirt he wore.

She lay back against her pillow, admiring his long-muscled legs and backside.

"Oh, and tomorrow while you're buying stuff to get you through the next few days, you might want to think about something to wear to the courthouse when we get married."

Married! Wide awake again, Julianne sat up and pulled him down to the bed again by the back of his shirt. He landed with a screeching bounce forced out of the tired mattress. "Oh *really*. Did I miss it the first time you asked, or is this a backhanded proposal?"

His face flushed. "Sorry. That was pretty clumsy."

"Did you have something you wanted to say?"

He took her hand. "You deserve so much more than I can give you right now. But if you're my wife, I'll make sure that you're never short of my love, respect, or honor. I'll keep you safe and defend you against anyone." He glanced around the room. "We are not going to live like *this*, I hope you know. This is just for a few nights. But no matter where we are, if we're together, we'll be home."

Swamped with emotion, she caught her lower lip between her teeth.

"Mitchell . . . I love you so much," she whispered.

"What do you say, Julianne? Will you marry me?"

She stared at him. She'd never heard him, or anyone else for that matter, tell her something so heartfelt. A year ago, she couldn't have imagined she would be at this point and with this man. She had rejoiced when he was sent to prison. Now, knowing the whole truth and remembering how she had treated him when they first met again, she felt a wave of remorse. "Yes, I will. Mitchell—I'm so glad you came back to Gila Rock." She sighed. "I wish things had been different from the start, all those years ago."

"No looking back, remember?" he said, and kissed her.

She nodded and kissed him again.

CHAPTER FOURTEEN

Detective Jimmy Ortiz stared at Julianne and Mitchell across his desk in the tiny, cramped office at county sheriff headquarters. Mostly he bore down on Mitchell, like a pit viper trying to outstare its prey. Mitchell was determined to remain unruffled by the scrutiny—he knew his healing face still looked as if he'd been in a bar fight—but he sensed Julianne becoming annoyed. She wasn't accustomed to treatment like this.

He was.

The smell of hours-old, burned coffee, microwaved frozen entrees, cologne, and painted cinder block created a familiar but depressing atmosphere. The one bright spot was a dusty green plant in the corner, which he realized was artificial.

"You keep turning up as my special guest, Tucker."

"The party isn't for me this time, Detective."

The short, stocky man frowned at him. Mitchell stayed cool.

"I didn't hear about a scuffle at Lupe's, so I assume you got those panda eyes from somewhere else."

"*Excuse me*, Detective Ortiz," Julianne cut in, "I'd appreciate your help. We've both given our statements. Do you have any information to offer about this whole thing?"

He dragged his gaze away from Mitchell and focused on her. His manners improved. "Ma'am, we know who set fire to your establishment."

"Yes, I know that, too. Has Darcy told you anything, such as a reason for his actions?"

"No. So far, he says he's innocent. GRFD is still investigating the exact cause—after all, we want to make sure we've got every *t* crossed and *i* dotted for a solid lock on the case. I think we recovered enough evidence to go on last night, but we're also holding him on an outstanding assault warrant from Culberson County."

Brows rose. Mitchell didn't know about that one, although it was no surprise.

"He claims someone else is responsible for the fire." Ortiz pushed his chair back, flipped through his notes. "Someone named Cade Lindgren, and he says Lindgren conspired with Cherry Claxton. I think you filed a complaint about him recently?"

"Cade? And—and *Cherry*?" Julianne looked poleaxed. Mitchell was not as shocked, not about Lindgren at any rate. But Cherry, wow. He knew she could be a bitch, but he hadn't realized the depth of her vindictive scheming. Anyway, they didn't even know if it was true. Yet.

"Obviously, we're going to question her to find out just how much she knows."

"You said last night that they found my brother at her place with firebombs in his car, that he smelled like gasoline," Mitchell reminded him.

Ortiz lightened up a bit with the attitude. "Yeah, it's strong evidence. Plus, we have James Tucker's statement."

"You haven't found Lindgren?" Mitchell asked. They should have, he thought. From what he could tell about the man, Cade Lindgren was probably sitting at home with his mom and dad, watching old reruns of *Matlock* and waiting for the police to show up. Then again, he might be hiding out somewhere.

"No. His parents swear up and down they don't know where he is, and we sent a car by the Boyce place two or three times to see if he was staying there."

"Nothing?" Juli asked, a nervous little catch in her voice. "I haven't had a chance to get the locks changed. He told me he parks behind a bunch of creosote bushes down the road from my driveway."

"Don't worry. We'll get him. We put out a BOLO on him."

Juli sent a quizzical glance at Mitchell.

"Be on the lookout," he translated.

"Did my brother James give you a statement?" Mitchell asked.

"Yeah, we're following up on that, too." Ortiz looked vaguely disappointed. He probably couldn't bear the idea the Mitchell was innocent.

Julianne tightened her grip on the tissue wadded up in her hand and tried to keep from losing her temper. She just wanted to get out of here. She pushed back her chair and stood up. "Then I'll wait to hear from you, Detective. If you'll excuse me, there are a lot of problems that need my attention."

"We'll be in touch," Ortiz confirmed, then cast a final, sour look at Mitchell.

Mitchell flashed her a concerned look and stood, too. He put a hand under her elbow and guided her back to the main door.

"Are you all right?" he asked, casually subtle as she paced around the institution-green hallway.

"I'm so angry I was afraid I might slap that man. If someone in this building had taken me seriously from the beginning, I might not be in this position." Her thongs clapped against the linoleum tile floor, emphasizing her indignation. "*Now* he's telling me they'll get it all sorted out. I don't know if I believe it. And they should have been able to find Cade. That shouldn't be hard. He's probably in Cuervo Blanco, running the counter at the family store." She adjusted her purse strap on her shoulder. "Let's just go. I have to buy more clothes and I don't know what-all."

Mitchell had gone out this morning to get her a T-shirt, a pair of shorts, and flip-flops at Dot's Fashion Corral so she could leave the motel room. Otherwise, she felt like someone with no history, no home, no anything.

When they'd stopped to look at Bickham's in the daylight, the sight was so devastating she'd had to bite her lip, hard, to keep from dissolving into hysterical sobbing. Initial figures from Gila Rock Fire Department estimated the damage to the structure at about 35 percent. Not a complete disaster—mostly the front of the building—but bad enough. A fire investigator had still been poking around in the ruins. He'd allowed her to get her purse from the back office, but for the time being, that was all. There was no way to tell how much smoke and water damage had been done to the rest of the building and its contents.

She'd called her insurance rep again. There had been an awkward moment of silence before he responded to her latest news to tell her that she was probably covered for this with money to spare. But it wouldn't surprise her at all to receive a cancellation in the mail. The insurance company must see her as a dismal liability.

"All right," Mitchell said, bringing her out of her thoughts. "Let's do your shopping. It might make you feel a little better to have something else to wear and to talk to a few friends around town. Janey Starr at the Fashion Corral said a lot of people are buzzing about what happened last night. And they're angry, Juli. They're supporting you." He pushed open the main door and held it for her.

She glanced up at him. "Really?" In all these months no one had said much about the trouble she'd been having, even though at least some had known it had been happening. "I didn't think anyone paid much attention."

He shrugged and rooted around in his pocket for the truck key. "They probably didn't take much notice of the smaller stuff, like dog-shit torches or what they might have seen as graffiti." His expression turned wry. "Hell, they probably thought I was responsible for those. At the time, anyway. But breaking display windows and starting fires—man, that's a whole different story."

Mitchell escorted her to several shops along Rosalita Street and Alamo Drive. Although he received some suspicious, even hostile looks when they first walked in, once people saw her with him, most were polite enough to hide their disapproval. Everyone Julianne talked to was sympathetic and supportive, as Mitchell had told her, and some of the places offered her credit for her purchases. At Diller's Pharmacy, Mary Diller came out from her post behind the counter to throw her arms around Juli.

"My God, I'm so glad you're not hurt," she said. She gave Mitchell a quick, baffled glance, but she was polite, which Julianne appreciated. The older woman's reaction was understandable. Most people around town knew only that the Tucker brothers had burned down her barn. Mitchell and Julianne had worked hard to keep their early relationship a secret.

"Thank you, Mary," Julianne responded, heartened by the encouragement she'd received from everyone, just at Mitchell had predicted. "I'll get back on my feet."

"Of course you will, honey, and Gila Rock will help. You have a lot of friends in town."

"I didn't think so sometimes," Julianne admitted, putting her toiletries on the counter. All those years alone, trying to make the hog farm succeed—she'd yearned for the friendships she'd had as a married woman. They'd seemed to dry up after Wes died.

"You've just had your hands full. We're here." Mary rang up the toothpaste, deodorant, and the other items, and bagged them. Julianne handed her a twenty-dollar bill, but Mary wouldn't take it.

"I can pay you."

"Nope. Just think of this as an early Christmas present."

Julianne gaped at her. "You can't stay in business if you give away your stock!"

"We wouldn't stay in business if we didn't think about the people we serve."

Julianne stumbled all over her own words. She couldn't come up with a way to argue with such thoughtful courtesy. "I d-don't know what to say, except thank you."

Mary turned a level, steady gaze at Mitchell. "I'll count on you to be her friend, Mitchell Tucker."

Julianne saw color rise in his neck. "Yes, ma'am. I'm counting on that, too. More than anything."

Mary smiled at them.

"I've got a kitchen table and chairs, a bed, and some other odds and ends," Julianne said, sighing. Under any other circumstances, she might find the situation discouraging. But things were looking up. She sat across from Mitchell in one of the two plastic patio chairs the Satellite Motel called "guest seating" outside the office. They were under a short overhang that offered a bit of shade next to the ice machine. The late summer sun still glared at West Texas, but at least the blacktopped front parking lot didn't shimmer with heat waves. Beyond, traffic on the highway flew past, kicking up dust with tires that whined on the hot pavement. "But I don't want to go back to the farm. It seems so far from help now. Cade is still out there somewhere."

"It's the best choice for the time being," he replied, poking around in a bag of potato chips. "You don't want to stay here, and I'm not crazy about it myself." He tossed a chip to Jack, who pounced on it like a starving street dog.

"I guess."

"I have just one condition."

She turned in her chair. "Oh *really*. And what would that be, Mr. Tucker?"

"You have to marry me before I come out there. Otherwise, what will people think? I have my reputation to consider after all." He lifted his chin and gave her a look of haughty primness.

Julianne couldn't help but laugh. His expression made her think of a huffy spinster. Life had taken the strangest and yet most satisfying turn. Never in her most outlandish daydreams would she have imagined Mitchell Tucker proposing to her at this point in her life. "You look like you've been sucking a lemon." Her laughter trailed off, and she gazed at him with a full heart. "I accept your condition, Mitchell."

He held her gaze for a moment; then he took her hand and lifted it to his lips. "This is our time now, Juli. Everyone else has taken a shot at us. From here on, it's us two, and *our* happiness."

She studied the distant hills that made up this part of the Texas Hill Country. Somewhere out there, an out-of-place saguaro cactus grew in that desert. It was an unlikely little miracle that they had discovered.

Another unlikely miracle had brought Mitchell to her again, so they could start over. They were wiser now, and more careful with each other's tender hearts.

She nodded and squeezed his hand. "We'll take life head-on together."

He smiled back at her. "That was always my plan, Juli. You and me, together."

EPILOGUE

"The defendant will rise."

The defendant pushed back his chair and stood, wearing a black-and-white striped jailhouse jumpsuit. His court-appointed lawyer stood with him, wearing a rumpled suit and a fatalistic expression.

The Honorable Matthew Webber sat on the bench, and stared at the subject over the tops of his rimless reading glasses. "Darcy Lynn Tucker, a jury of your peers has found you guilty of attempted murder, arson with the intention to commit murder, and"—he scanned the page in his hand—"a number of other charges. Ordinarily, these charges alone would be enough to compel me to sentence you to a minimum of fifteen years in a Texas state prison. However, during these proceedings, a witness testified to seeing you commit the very same crime nine years ago. You took the life of Wesley Emerson and let Mitchell Tucker believe that he was guilty. Mitchell Tucker—your *brother*—served seven years for a crime he did not commit, and you will be tried for that crime separately. But in consideration of that additional, selfish act, I hereby sentence you to a term of not less than forty years, with no possibility of parole. Mr. Tucker, please keep your dirty looks and mumbled threats to yourself, or I will add another five years to your sentence. Bailiff?"

Julianne sat next to Mitchell in the front of the courtroom, watching the proceedings. Her heart pounded so hard, she was certain that her necklace was bouncing off her chest. For both of them, it was like reliving a nightmare that ended differently the second time. Darcy was led away, hostile and arrogant, but shuffling along in full manacles, under appropriate guard.

"Mr. Mitchell Brett Tucker, are you present in the courtroom, sir?"

Mitch jumped, obviously not expecting to hear the judge call his name. He stood. "Yes—yes, Your Honor."

"Mr. Tucker, please approach the bench."

"W-what—? Why—?" Julianne stumbled, a rush of fear flooding her. She rose halfway out of her seat.

"Mrs. Tucker, please remain seated," the judge instructed.

She sat again, feeling as if she were being pulled down by the weight of a rock in her stomach. Mitchell walked up to stand in the area in front of the judge, but he didn't get too close.

"You, sir, confessed to a crime you did not commit, but believed that you did. I understand from your testimony that you were trying to protect your brothers, Darcy, and"—he consulted his notes—"one James Nelson Tucker."

"Yes, sir."

The judge removed his readers and gestured at Mitchell with them. "That was a foolish thing you did."

Julianne swallowed hard, trying to shift the knot that had formed in her throat. Her hands had suddenly turned icy.

"I've reviewed that case and find that although you were present, you did not start the fire that took the life of Wesley Emerson. Witnesses stated that you were intoxicated and had passed out when the fire was set."

Mitchell briefly closed his eyes. "Yes, sir."

"I am officially expunging your prison record, Mr. Tucker. As I said, your actions were foolish, but your motive to protect your minor brothers was understandable. Questions?"

"Sir, does this mean that no one can refuse me employment because of my sentence?"

"Your sentence will be a bad memory only to you. It won't exist in the records of the Texas Department of Criminal Justice."

Even from where she sat, Julianne heard him exhale a deep breath. "Thank you, Your Honor."

Judge Webber banged his gavel. "Court adjourned."

"All rise," the bailiff called out.

When the judge had exited the courtroom, Mitchell turned and opened his arms to Julianne. She rushed into them, weak with relief. Around them, attorneys and their assistants gathered papers into folders and briefcases, and people got to their feet. A low drone of conversation buzzed through the room. "Can you believe it? It's *finally* over. Finally over." She gripped her husband in a tight hug.

"Yeah," he whispered. "Thank God." He rested his head against her shoulder for an instant. "Now no one will be able to object to me taking that coaching job at the school. I'm just Mitchell Tucker, ordinary citizen."

"Mitchell Tucker, my husband," she added. "And I can sure use your help now that this is all behind us. I wish we didn't have to come back here for Cherry's trial, but the district attorney said we have to testify."

"Darcy wasn't as nice to her as I was to him. He offered her up and told the police everything they'd done. I guess he was hoping to cut a deal." He tucked her hand into the crook of his arm. "It didn't work."

"I don't feel sorry for her," Julianne retorted. "She and Darcy could have killed us that night they tried to run us off the road." She gripped the reassuring muscle under her hand. "And every time I think of *Cade* in cahoots with her—it just boggles my mind. Those two planned at least a third of the things done to us."

Cade had disappeared three months earlier. Just last week Julianne had received an e-mail from him. In it he had told her that he'd finally seen a copy of his birth certificate at the Jeff Davis County records office in Fort Davis. Everything Julianne had told him was true. His mother's name was Tamara April Lindgren. His father's name was listed as Paul Boyce. Yes, the people who had raised him were his grandparents. His message had included a stilted apology that lacked sincerity, in Julianne's estimation. But Cade was gone. He'd sent the e-mail from a library in Del Rio, a border town about three hours east of Gila Rock. She'd passed on the information to Detective Ortiz, but she wouldn't be surprised if Cade disappeared into Mexico, despite the BOLO alert, and never came back.

Careful scrutiny of her surveillance video by the sheriff's office had put him at the scene of some of the crimes, including when the gallon can of paint had been thrown through the window.

"Would you press charges if he came back to town?" Mitchell asked now.

Would she, despite their history? No question. "Of course. I don't know which man was the real Cade Lindgren, the one who worked for me, or the one who showed himself after you got home. Just the idea of him living at the farm and planning to stay there with me gives me the creeps. It was just so . . . weird. And the property destruction—wow."

"I'd feel better if the law had caught up with him. Especially considering how he lured you back to the farm with that oil-filter setup."

She stood straight and put out her chin. "Hah! I fixed him!" She dropped her brave face. "I was so scared, though. After I caught him trespassing, and with the other stuff, I guess he figured he'd better be gone."

"He figured right."

Julianne had her hands full these days. She had repaired the store, this time hiring professional contractors with the insurance coverage she had. She'd hired a manager and a full-time counter person to help run Bickham's, and good money was coming in. Her attention was currently focused on the new bed-and-breakfast she'd opened at the farm. In honor of the five generations of Boyces who had held that land, she'd named it Boyce's Country Inn. It hadn't been finished in time for the spring break crowd, but she was booked for the fall, and she and Mitchell had moved in last month.

Mitchell had talked again with Ray Schroder, the high school principal, about a coaching job. Now there was no conviction or record standing in the way. If that didn't pan out, they were considering opening a baseball camp on the farmland.

"Let's go home, Citizen Tucker," she said, pulling on his hand to file out with the rest of the spectators. From the moment she'd passed him on the sidewalk last year, he'd been around, watching out for her, loving her. But he'd also respected her as a person and a woman, and he'd never tried to dominate her. Mitchell was her partner.

"I don't know. After all this, I think we deserve a little vacation."

"A vacation—where? Not to the Satellite Motel."

He laughed as he followed her. "What, you didn't appreciate my humble lodgings?"

"I guess compared to sleeping in a burned out building or in the truck, it was okay." They stepped out into the glaring West Texas sun.

He laughed. "I was thinking about a week in San Antonio at the Menger Hotel."

"Isn't that place haunted?" she asked as they walked to the sleek, new silver truck they'd bought.

"Only if you believe that stuff. Anyway, I'll protect you," he said, thumping his chest. She laughed, too. "We can go anywhere you want. After all, we're free."

Julianne leaned against him as they walked, and she knew now that no matter what, he'd always be there for her.

This was real happiness. This was theirs forever.

ABOUT THE AUTHOR

Photo © 2011 Elena Rose

Alexis Harrington is the award-winning author of more than a dozen novels, including the international bestseller *The Irish Bride*. She spent twelve years working in civil engineering before she became a full-time novelist. When she isn't writing, she enjoys jewelry making, needlework, embroidery, cooking, and entertaining friends. Harrington lives in her native Pacific Northwest, near the Columbia River, with a variety of pets who do their best to distract her while she's working.